The Shadow of the Grail

The Lost Journal of Christopher Columbus

by

MARTIN TASCHDJIAN

PINECONE BOOK COMPANY

ISBN 978-1-949053-04-3

Pinecone Book Company
P.O. Box 65 | Evergreen, Colorado 80437

PineconeBookCo@gmail.com

Dedicated to my wife, Carolyn,
who seemed to enjoy our research trips
and encouraged me to finally finish.

Let him who seeks continue seeking until he finds.
When he finds, he will become troubled.
When he becomes troubled, he will be astonished,
and he will rule over the All.

Gospel of Thomas
Nag Hamadi Library
http://gnosis.org/naghamm/gthlamb.html

Table of Contents

Preface

It is well known that in February, 1493, on the return leg of Christopher Columbus' first voyage to the New World, the two remaining ships of his little fleet encountered a fearsome storm of the type that is frequent during winter in the North Atlantic. The *Niña* and the *Pinta* were separated. (Columbus' flagship, the *Santa María*, had struck a reef and sunk in the Caribbean on Christmas Day, 1492.)

Fearing the *Niña* would sink under him, Columbus hurriedly completed a manuscript describing his voyage and the events in his life that led up to it. The document is a combination of his autobiography, his last will and testament, and his final confession. He apparently hoped that, were he to perish, his discovery would be recognized and the members of the crew left behind in the New World would be rescued. Columbus wrapped the manuscript in oilskin, stuffed it into a barrel, and cast it into the sea.

The *Niña* and the *Pinta* survived the storm, and Columbus lived to tell the tale of his exciting quest, with results well known to history.

Now the lost manuscript has been found. Written mostly in the Italian dialect familiar to Genoa, and sprinkled with Greek, it reveals that Columbus feared his imminent death in the storm. Either because he lacked a priest—the Franciscan friar assigned to his voyage had remained in the New World—or because he knew that given the nature of his revelations he might not receive absolution for his sins, he committed what he thought was his last confession to paper.

This is the astounding personal journal of Cristóbal Colón. I have interpreted (not translated) it into English, though I confess I am no scholar of medieval Italian. The reader may discover anachronisms that I have allowed to creep in.

Part I
Christopher Columbus

February 12, 1493

*H*eavenly Father! Forgive me, for I have sinned. Let this be my last and true confession, for I am certain the good ship Niña will not survive this fearful storm, and I would not go unshriven to a watery grave in the Ocean Sea.

In seeking the merciful forgiveness of Our Lord Jesus Christ, I must also reveal the true facts and secret knowledge which have motivated all the actions of my life. I would not have this knowledge die with me, nor would I reveal these secrets were I not certain that I will not survive this storm.[1] As He did to Moses, our merciful Father has allowed me to see the goal toward which He has led me, but I fear He will not allow me to cross the threshold to the Promised Land.

It is my fervent prayer that the finder of this manuscript will carry it to a merciful monarch who might launch an expedition to rescue those brave souls whom we were forced to leave behind. Perhaps they are the fortunate ones, who may survive there while we perish beneath the waves of the Ocean Sea. I pray also that the same monarch will assure the care of my two children and my dear Beatriz who, though she is not my wife, is their guardian and mother.

I have never revealed my true origins, or those of my ancestors, beyond the least which I could not conceal or which were of no consequence. To reveal my true family history would have exposed me to great danger and made it impossible for me to pursue my quest.

---

[1] The *Niña* and the *Pinta* did survive the storm, which lasted from February 12 to February 14, 1493, but the two ships were separated and landed in different places.

The source of my quest lies in the mission begun by an ancestor and handed down through my family. This forefather was a Frenchman named Gerard de Villiers, though that was a great family secret, never to be revealed to others. I never knew him, of course, but his stories and lessons were part of the lore that permeates all families, and were repeated over and over in mine. To me, they were a mix of bedtime stories, anecdotes told at the holiday table, stories and family traditions repeated so often that, as adults, we are able to pass them on to our own children with the same intonations, inflections, and language that they were told to us. Even so, it was the case that certain elements were held back—certain secrets that were deemed too dangerous to share at weddings and funerals, perhaps to be overheard by in-laws and guests.

And with the passage of time, some things were forgotten.

Part II
Gerard de Villiers

October 13, 1307 – Paris, France

In the manner of inquisitors before and since, they burst open the door at three o'clock in the morning and hauled the disoriented nobleman from his deepest slumber. The acolyte who slept outside the bedchamber was bypassed unnoticed in the deep shadows cast by the flickering torches but, wakened by the intrusion, he noted the royal insignia on the cloaks of the intruders. An intelligent man, he immediately understood that there would be no intervention from papal protectors. Indeed, this outrageous treatment of the Grand Master could not have been contemplated, much less executed, without the complicity—or at least the assent—of Pope Clement. The acolyte's conclusion was affirmed when he heard the charges being read out.

William Imbert, the Chief Papal Inquisitor of France, addressed the nobleman who had been forced painfully onto his knees, though the softness of the thick ornate red-and-gold Anatolian carpet spared him the worst the stone-tiled floor had to offer. "A vehement suspicion has arisen," Imbert intoned, "of heresy; a bitter thing, a lamentable thing, a thing which is horrible to contemplate, terrible to hear of, a detestable disgrace, a thing almost inhuman, indeed, set apart from all humanity.

"Therefore, Philip, King of France by the grace of God, has decreed that every member of the Order of the Knights of the Temple be held in captivity for ecclesiastical judgment, and that all goods, both movable and immovable, be seized and kept in royal custody."

The Inquisitor's voice rang with righteousness as he lifted his eyes from the warrant and intoned the charges as though he were chanting the Kyrie at a solemn high mass.

"You are wolves appearing as lambs, and you defile the land with your filth.

"You are charged with defiling the Holy Cross. Confess!

"Your novices spit on the cross of Christ and trample on it. Confess!

"They deny Christ and are obliged to indulge in carnal relations with other members of the Order. Confess!"

Imbert leaned forward and breathed menacingly into his prisoner's ear. "For if you do not, I promise you will suffer Christ's pains."

Jacques de Molay, Grand Master of the Knights Templar, raised his head so that his shoulder-length brown hair fell away from his face. He met the Inquisitor's eyes and spoke quietly. "I know you, William Imbert. You dress as a priest, and you are confessor to the king. You claim to serve the Lord, but all know you are a tool of King Philip. He uses you to cloak his greed and lawlessness. Now you serve his impiety as well."

Molay's voice fell, as if in prayer. "I will answer only to the Lord God and to His Holiness Pope Clement V." Despite his courage, he swallowed hard. "I know that through torture you can make me confess to these false charges, but the confession will mean nothing, and the Order of the Knights of the Temple and I will be exonerated."

Then, more strongly, so he could be heard clearly outside his bedroom: "The king may seize our knights and our lands and our wealth, but know this, Imbert! The king will *never* obtain that Holy Cup of Our Lord Jesus Christ, for the Lord God will only allow it to be held by the worthiest and the purest. In the eyes of God and man, King Philip is not the Grail Knight!"

Cloaked by the dark, the companion sentry understood the orders he had just been given. Hugging the darkest shadows, he made his way undetected out of the chateau. But as he passed under the window of Jacques de Molay's bedroom, he was halted in his tracks. A seasoned veteran of the horrors of hand-to-hand battle throughout the Crusades, Gerard de Villiers was chilled by the screams that all but drowned out the sound of nails being driven by a heavy hammer. The flickering candlelight from within cast the shadow of the last Grand Master of the Knights Templar through the window onto the cobblestones. The shadow uncannily resembled the ancient symbol of the swastika, as Jacques de Molay hung crucified in the doorway of his bedchamber.

One week earlier: October 6, 1307 – La Rochelle, France

On his way to La Rochelle, Gerard de Villiers followed the roads westward that paralleled the rivers. He made good time over the relatively flat plains outside Paris, but was forced to slow his pace as he came to Poitiers. Riding through the steep-walled canyons and cliffs, the soldier almost unconsciously evaluated the military advantages and disadvantages of this ground. As he approached La Rochelle, his way was slowed by the miles of marshes extending from far inland all the way to the sea. His horse had to pick its way through the winding paths and over the small wooden bridges. As he rode, he again reflected on the defense this difficult ground would pose to an invading army. Knowing what was coming, the thought pleased him. La Rochelle would be defended on land by its English soldiers and the difficult terrain.

It was early autumn, and de Villiers was bundled against the chilly morning fog that rose from the rivers and the fields. By midday, he shed his scarves and overcoat but kept his hat against the still-warm sun that might burn through his hair to redden his scalp.

It was a lovely time of year; the trees had not yet shed their leaves but were beginning to show bits of color here and there. Where the marshes had been reclaimed by laboriously building canals to drain the water, rich fields were evident. There, the harvests were mostly over. The more prosperous farmers guided their plows behind horses or oxen, while their less fortunate compatriots swung picks and hoes to turn over the rich soil, exposing it to winter rains and occasional heavy wet snows. While it all looked peaceful and prosperous, de Villiers knew that under the serene scenery and agricultural routine, the reach of King Philip's forces would burden these people with taxes, and would soon take their men away to die in his wars, just as had happened around the world for centuries.

In time, de Villiers came in sight of the limestone walls and crenellated battlements surrounding the city of La Rochelle. The sea air brought a freshening chill. In the distance over the trees he could see the towers that guarded the entry to the sheltered harbor. The channel between the towers was narrow—only wide enough to allow one ship to pass at a time. The gray stones of the towers formed a rounded tube; any missiles launched at them by an attacker from the sea would be deflected into the water. Between the towers was strung a heavy chain to prevent unwanted entry, and when the tide flowed out, the current made it impossible to enter the harbor without assistance. De Villiers passed through the gate in the protective city walls and made his way through the winding streets to the harbor. To his right, the tower of the stone lighthouse pierced the sky. Bobbing in the water by the quay that ran along the outer harbor were the ships that were his destination.

The naval fleet of the Knights Templar lay at anchor in the harbor of La Rochelle, rising and falling gently to the breezes and swells off the Bay of Biscay. The Templar ships lay together outside the narrow entrance, separated from the cogs and hulks that were the most common vessels in the waters of northern Europe and the Baltic Sea. Those single-masted, open ships had a deep draft that gave them a clumsy appearance, but they were well-designed for their mission as capacious, coast-hugging cargo vessels, carrying wine from Bordeaux to the Hanseatic northern cities like Lübeck. With their square sails, they looked very like their ancestors, the agile warships that had carried the Norsemen into battle.

The two-masted vessels of the Templar fleet were markedly dissimilar and drew the curiosity of sailors and shipwrights walking on the quay of La Rochelle. These ships were the result of a different tradition of builders, the ultimate evolution of the Mediterranean round ships, built with all the skills developed in Marseilles, Genoa, and Venice.

As well as being much larger than their Baltic and North Sea counterparts—the greater size needed to accommodate the twin masts—the ships of the Templar fleet were enclosed and covered with two or three decks. Some had additional half decks or gangways known as *corridoria* on the main deck along the bulwarks on either side. Their sails were huge, hanging from yards even longer than the overall length of the ship. A typical 800-ton vessel carried eighty officers and sailors, as well as servants and ship's boys. In addition to the sails, they had massive steering oars, and carried up to twenty-five anchors. Astern, they towed another boat, and they carried up to three more boats aboard. Their cargo capacity was enormous, with room for about 560 passengers and crew, and up to a hundred horses.

Despite their size, these ships were more maneuverable than their northern-European counterparts. Their huge triangular sails, lateen-rigged in the Mediterranean style, unlike the square sails of the northern cogs, improved their ability to beat to windward.

It was clear to the experienced sailors idling on the dock, and to the stevedores loading cargoes along the quay, that these were not coast-huggers designed to run before the wind, but open-sea vessels adaptable to long voyages under variable conditions. Unknown to the onlookers, it was to the open sea that these ships were soon to be bound.

In the flagship's forecastle, Theobald Gaudin, commander of the Templar fleet, led a file of men into the cramped cabin. The senior officers, looking grimly serious, were followed by a few younger aides and specialists, an air of eagerness about them. Brief scuffling sounds echoed around the room as the sailors found spaces and looked curiously at the man standing before them. To all but the commander, Gerard de Villiers was a stranger, for these were navy men, not soldiers.

De Villiers, in his early thirties, was a seasoned soldier. Like the naval officers in the cabin, he had the perpetual tan of one who has spent long hours in the hot sun of the eastern Mediterranean. But he was no seafarer; his body was hardened from a life of riding and soldiering. He was a veteran of many battles for the Holy Land, battles that of late had so reversed the fortunes of the Crusaders that they had been expelled by the Mamluks from the Kingdom of Jerusalem.

He took off the dark felt hat with the elongated, pointed brim that shadowed his eyes. A simple hood covered his head and neck, concealing most of his dark hair, which was cut in short bangs that hung down with a slight curl over his forehead. Like his naval counterparts, his eyes had the slight squint of one used to scanning out far distances to the horizon; but unlike them, his gaze was accustomed to searching for horsemen through the heat haze of a desert landscape, not for distant sails on the sea.

A sky-blue shirt covered woolen bias-cut hose. His short *bliaut*, a tunic of rich silk decorated with embroidery, peeked out from the neck and the large armholes of the heavy woolen jacket known as a *gamache*, for early October on the Bay of Biscay was already blustery and chill. Over all came a white knee-length tunic, emblazoned with the simplest red cross, with cross-beam centered and as wide as the upright was tall. Over the last two hundred years, the Templar warrior-priests had become so identified with the fight for the Holy Land that their cross had come to be the generic symbol of a Crusader.

Gerard de Villiers first greeted the commander of the Templar fleet. "I am glad to see you well, Theobald."

"The Lord be with you, Gerard. When last we met, things were not so peaceful."

"Indeed not. We lost many comrades when Acre fell. Without your brave seamanship and escape the night before the fall of the city, the Temple's most treasured relics would certainly have fallen into the hands of the Saracens."

Both men remembered that fateful night in Acre in the early summer of 1291. The Saracen army had laid siege to the city for several weeks. On June 17, they breached the walls. Prisoners were mercilessly beheaded; in the light of the burning buildings, women could be seen running and weeping through the streets. The Grand Master of the Temple, William de Beaujeu, and a large number of his knights were killed. During a truce, some Saracens rounded up a group of women and slaughtered them like vermin. It was an echo of the roundup and slaughter of 2,700 men, women, and children that England's King Richard the Lionheart had ordered when he in his turn had first captured Acre almost exactly one hundred years before.

While these memories coursed through his mind, Gerard de Villiers had been frankly examining the other men in the cabin. Now he greeted them. "The Lord be with you, my dear brothers in Christ."

The men automatically responded, "And with your spirit."

"You are all priests of the Knights Templar. You have sworn to uphold and defend the Faith." From his tone, the listening officers knew that their courage was about to be tested once again. "You have proven yourselves worthy of that vow in countless battles and voyages throughout the Crusades."

De Villiers continued. "Now a new enemy is upon us. The Order of the Temple is in mortal danger. But this new enemy is no fanatic believer in Islam, no defiler of the holy places of Israel." He paused, lending weight to his words. Above, a seagull cried shrilly.

"We have learned that our liege lord, Philip, King of France, is planning to attack and destroy us." He raised his hand to still the exclamations of disbelief and the questions. "Our intelligence is without error."

De Villiers spoke softly. The words were an effort, for he was road-weary and sore from the three-day ride from Paris. But the Crusader was accustomed to such demands, even after days in the field.

"You must understand the king's plans in order to appreciate our countermoves." The ship swayed softly, and the rigging creaked as the incoming tide lifted it slightly.

"You know that our King Philip was only three years old when Saint Louis died. So while he never really knew his sainted grandfather, he grew up in the shadow of his ancestor's pious achievements as King of France. But piety often interferes with judgment. The pious too often place their trust in God and the righteousness of their cause, and cast prudence aside. So it came about with King Louis. Philip has always remembered with bitterness how, after the loss of Jerusalem to the Saracens in 1244, King Louis was captured. Our brother Templar, Stephen of Otricourt, who had warned against the folly of the king's strategy, was a bit slow to lend the necessary ransom money. Though Philip was only three years old, that bitter memory was passed to the old king, Louis' son, and now to Philip, the grandson."

De Villiers paused, pushed knuckles against his red eyes, poured some wine from a flask, added the customary water, and sipped. "Many men nurse resentments and long for vengeance for the real or perceived wrongs done to their families and countrymen. That alone is rarely enough to make enemies of their contemporaries. For King Philip, the opportunity for revenge on the Knights of the Temple merely adds spice to his feast, for, as the saying goes, revenge is a dish best served cold.

"When he became king in 1285, the seventeen-year-old Philip came to the Temple for a reckoning of the accounts of the kingdom. It is too little to say that he was displeased with the result. To repay the debts incurred by his father would take over three hundred years— even if he used all his disposable income, and even without interest payments. Philip was not about to accept a lifetime of penury.

"Moreover, by the age of twenty-six," de Villiers continued, "Philip was at war with Edward I of England. The costs of this war came on top of the inherited debts. Today, his expenses are running at about four thousand pounds per day. He has been forced to devalue and debase the coinage. And just last year, you know that he seized all Jewish property in France and deported the entire Jewish community.

"King Philip's father and sainted grandfather relied on the financial services of the Knights Templar in Paris to carry out the monetary obligations of the kingdom. We were the trusted servants. But when our brother John of Tours, Treasurer of the Temple in Paris, protested against the way Philip was beggaring the kingdom, Philip replaced the Knights and installed his own treasury at the Louvre. Still, much of the kingdom's debt remains owed to the Temple.

"Even the King's new advisors in the Louvre have come to recognize the ruin that is coming on the kingdom from these policies. They have convinced the king that he must find a new source of precious metals suitable for coining. The Temple treasury is just such a source. King Philip will visit on us the same treatment that he accorded the Jews of France.

"By attacking the Temple, the king will revenge himself for the slowness to ransom his grandfather from the results of his own folly. He will replenish his treasury, repudiate his debt, and strengthen his coinage. His circumstances leave him no recourse but to destroy us and confiscate the wealth of the Order."

His listeners began to understand the enormity of the stakes at play. The more intelligent among them realized that the forces at work were irresistible.

One young officer protested. "Monseigneur de Villiers, does the Order of the Temple not remain under the protection of the pope? Surely the king will not risk incurring excommunication and the loss of his immortal soul by attacking us. Rome must protect us. Otherwise the pope and Holy Mother Church herself will be the next to suffer from this man."

The young man knew, as did all those assembled, that the Order had historically been exempt from both secular and canon law. Since the time of Pope Innocent III, the Templars had been granted a stunning list of privileges. Their churches were places of sanctuary from civil authority; they were exempt from tithes and taxes; and they were completely independent of the authority of local bishops, mostly appointed by royal rulers. Those who attacked a Templar were excommunicated, and regardless of the crime, Templars could not be legally tried by any court, civil or religious, other than the pope himself.

De Villiers shook his head and smiled wanly at the young man. "It is true that our Order is sanctioned and protected by the Vatican. But this king does not fear the wrath of Rome. You cannot know of the letter that he wrote in response to Pope Boniface after His Holiness decreed in a bull that all princes are subject to papal authority in both temporal and spiritual matters. The words are etched in my brain:

"Philip, by grace of God, king of France, to Boniface, acting as supreme pontiff, little or no health. Let your extreme folly know, that in temporals we are not subject to anyone.

"You are too young to recall how King Philip publicly burned the papal bull to the accompaniment of a mighty fanfare of trumpets. And even were you older, you would not know of the letter of excommunication that was sent by Pope Boniface, only to have it intercepted by the king before delivery and destroyed. Nor could you be aware of how King Philip sent William de Nogaret, whose parents had been burned at the stake during the Cathar Crusade in Languedoc and therefore harbored a mighty resentment against Rome, to break into the pope's palace in 1303. There His Holiness was kept prisoner and abused for three days before the local people could rescue him. Boniface died within a few weeks.

"Pope Benedict IX succeeded Boniface, and in fear of a similar fate, removed the sentence of excommunication against Philip. But he then showed some signs of courage and began attempting to uphold the power of the papacy. Benedict was quickly killed by poison, and the Throne of Peter was again vacant."

The assembled sailors were numbed by the news. Nothing in their ken or experience had prepared them for such an outright attack on the order of things—the pope as the Vicar of Christ on earth, the kings chosen and consecrated by popes ever since the crowning of Charlemagne on Christmas Day in the year 800. Their world was truly ending.

"The King will soon move against us, bringing charges of heresy. His informant, Esquin de Floyran, has already denounced us to the King of Aragon, who, to his credit, was skeptical. We know that King

Philip already met with Pope Clement in May of this year. We know this because we intercepted a letter from His Holiness, written on the twenty-fourth of August, that discusses the accusations to be brought against our Order. In that letter, the pope proposes to initiate an investigation of those accusations after the fourteenth of October. Philip therefore must act before the Holy See asserts jurisdiction. We believe the move will come next Friday, the thirteenth of October .

"Therefore, the Grand Master has imposed on you a heavy mission, from which you will not return. Your success or failure will determine the direction of history for the next thousand years."

De Villiers turned to Commander Gaudin. "Are your ships prepared and loaded as we have ordered?"

Gaudin nodded. "Yes, my lord. All eighteen ships are loaded to the maximum for an open-sea voyage. The fifty Knights of the Order are aboard. All we lack is our destination."

"That you shall now have, Commander. But it must remain secret, so that in the event of betrayal or capture, none can reveal it even under the severest torture." He turned to the others crowded in the cabin. "For your own protection and safety, I must ask your trust. Now, go and make your ships ready. You will sail with the morning tide. But first, pray with me."

Making the sign of the cross, de Villiers touched his forehead, his breast, and each side of his chest as he intoned the opening words of the prayer, "*In nomine Patris et Filio et Spirito Sancto*. God be with you."

Once the cabin had been cleared, de Villiers turned to Gaudin. Stiffly, he rose from his seat. His voice, quiet from weariness before, had been barely audible above the creaking of the ship as it swayed in the harbor. Now it rose and took on a new intensity. "My friend, you should not believe for a moment that King Philip is attacking the Order of the Temple merely out of revenge for old slights on his family. Nor does he seek purely our worldly wealth for his treasury to fight the war against England. Important as these are, they are as nothing to his true objective."

His voice rose. "This man . . . this . . . king . . . seeks to destroy the authority of Holy Mother Church itself. He has learned that the Knights of the Temple hold the greatest of all holy relics—the cup used by Our Lord Jesus at the Last Supper."

Gaudin felt his knees grow weak, as though the ship had suddenly encountered a great wave at sea. He grasped the edge of the table for support. "How . . . ?" De Villiers smiled at the look on Gaudin's face, for he had felt the same when the secret had been first revealed to him. "What I am about to tell you is the greatest secret in Christendom and the world," he said. "Prior to Christmas Day, 1119, when the Order was officially founded under the charter of Pope Honorius II, a small group of French knights who had participated in the liberation of Jerusalem in 1099 quartered themselves on the Temple Mount. These included our founder, Hugue de Payens. Over the course of the next weeks and months, this band secretly explored the caverns under the Temple Mount, caverns that may have been the fabled Stables of Solomon.[2] Our founders came upon a grotto that had been concealed for a thousand years behind a rock door which had been rolled in front of the opening, just as the Bible describes the Tomb of Jesus. Upon entering, they found the preserved body of the holy Lazarus, and many holy relics. They found a manuscript clearly written by Lazarus himself, for it lay under the bones of his hands and described the provenance of the relics, including the cups and plates that had been used by Our Lord Himself at the Last Supper."

De Villiers continued. "This is the source of the power of our Order, Theobald. This is the Holy Cup that was held in the hand of Jesus of Nazareth and in which he performed the transformation of wine into His own blood. It is the possession of this holiest of relics that led the supreme pontiffs then and since to grant the Knights Templar the

---

[2]These large caverns under the Temple Mount (now occupied by the Al Aqsa Mosque) were actually cisterns. The Mount is honeycombed with tunnels that can be readily traversed and explored and some of them have become modern tourist attractions.

---

authority they needed to protect themselves. Knowledge that the Grail was under the protection of the papacy and the Order was kept secret, for once its whereabouts were known, it would be sought out by those hoping to reflect in its power and glory.

"Despite all our efforts, however, it was impossible to keep the Grail's existence a total secret. Therefore, the Grand Master instructed one of our Order, a monk named Chretien de Troyes, to build a mythical poem around the Holy Grail that could be used to conceal its reality. This he did, in 1188. Subsequently, the Order encouraged others to embellish the stories and encircle them with fabulous magical events so the reality was totally submerged. But the reality nevertheless persists, and the Grail is the object of desire for the most powerful of heaven and earth.

"Philip knows that if he obtains the Grail, he can challenge the very legitimacy of the papacy itself. With the Grail in his possession, he can claim that he is king directly by divine right. He can claim to be the Grail Knight, with no need to seek the approval for his reign from the Vicar of Christ in Rome. This is his ultimate goal. We have sworn to protect Holy Mother Church from its enemies, and King Philip, by attacking our Order, is attacking the very succession of the Holy Father from Our Lord Jesus.

"Few sanctuaries remain. We have lost our last refuges in Outremer[3] to the Saracens. If you try for the safety of our fortress in Cyprus, there is no certainty that you would reach the destination; you would have to sail around Spain and Portugal, through the Pillars of Hercules, and pass once again close to Philip's ships in the Mediterranean Sea."

Gaudin nodded. "Could we not take refuge in Spain, out of reach of King Philip?" He quickly answered his own question. "But no, of course not. For it is not just King Philip who will be seeking us, but the whole might of Christendom and the forces of the pope. Knowing

---

[3]"Outremer" was the term used by Crusaders to refer to Palestine.

---

that we have the Holy Grail, the Church must have it under its control to support the pope's power to speak as God's earthly representative." His eyes widened as the realization hit him. "The Grail will not be safe anywhere in Europe!"

Reaching under his cloak, de Villiers pulled out a rolled-up parchment scroll, which he smoothed out on the table. "This map has come to us from an ancient source. It was originally in the library of Alexandria, but when that was destroyed, it was carried to safety in Jerusalem. When Jerusalem, in its turn, was destroyed by the Romans in the year 67, the map was almost lost—but copies had been made, and one was kept in the library in Constantinople. When Constantinople was sacked by Frankish Crusaders, the map was brought to the Order."

Gaudin's practiced eye ran over the map. He looked up in disbelief. "My lord, this is not possible." He was stunned. "This map shows impossible things. We know from the Holy Book that there is but one mass of land surrounded by the waters of the Ocean Sea. Yet this map shows another great land to the west!"

De Villiers nodded. "Indeed, it does. And it shows, as well, that there is charted land below the Antipodes."

"Your great adventure, my dear Theobald, will be to sail for that land that lies beyond the reach of pope and king, using this map. If it is genuine, and truly based on ancient knowledge from Egypt and before, then, God willing, you can establish yourselves far from the conflicts of kings and popes. If it is not genuine, and there is nothing beyond the Pillars of Hercules, then I send you to your death. But I assure you, death at sea will be quicker and more honorable than you will receive at the hands of the Holy Inquisition if you stay."

Commander Gaudin nodded slowly. "We measure the chance against the certainty. And if we fail and are lost at sea, the Holy Cup will sink with us and be beyond the reach of these evil men who would pervert its possession into power."

De Villiers put his hand on Gaudin's shoulder. "God is truly watching over the Order of the Poor Knights of the Temple of Solomon, to send us such brave, holy, and dedicated men as yourself, Theobald. I know you will embrace this bitter cup."

De Villiers opened the cabin door and peered into the passageway. Certain they were alone, he nevertheless spoke softly. "I have kept hidden one copy of this portolan map, Theobald. Knowledge of its existence has been kept even from the Grand Master, for he will be the first to undergo arrest and torture. As long as King Philip does not know of its existence, he will not search for it, or for you. I am the only person who knows of its existence and location. With it, we can someday search for you and for the Holy Cup. But you must not rely on seeing us soon, or even during your lifetime.

"To assist you, I have one other small thing to guide you." From his pocket he drew out a small metal needle and a piece of paper. "The Order received this from a trader who says he got it from sailors trading with ships from Cathay. It has a miraculous property; if it is suspended so that it is allowed to swing freely, it will always point to the north. On the map I have given you, there are drawn points where you can see the changes in course that are needed to reach your destination and find a landing in a place where you can be found when we come for you. This paper has been marked out with the true angles of the circle, so you can easily trace out the direction you must deviate from your previous course. With this needle, you can be sure that the course change is accurate and can be reproduced."

Gaudin looked into de Villiers' eyes, then down at his own feet. "You will not be sailing with us, then."

"No, my friend. I return to Paris. I must stay at the side of the Grand Master, for he will suffer greatly at the king's hand. And if I disappear now, suspicions will rise and the king may move more quickly. You and your fleet need time to get clear, for it is with you and your companions that our future rests.

"I have one more matter to conclude with you before you sail. It is unlikely that you will ever return to these shores. You are leaving behind your families and friends as well as your Templar brothers in Christ. You will never see them again. If the map is true, you will find yourself on a foreign shore, perhaps among strange people who have not been exposed to the Word of Christ. You will be isolated and separated from all that you believe. So you must become a monastery among yourselves to retain and keep true to the rules of the Order.

"You have no women aboard your ships. To be sure that the Word of Christ is retained and the Holy Grail and the rest of the Order's treasure are safeguarded, you will need to have families that can continue your mission through the generations. For this to happen, you are hereby released from your holy vows of chastity. Have children, and teach them about this day. Educate them in the teachings of Jesus. Your vow of obedience remains in place in this matter. Thus I charge you."

The comrades in arms embraced. Both knew they would never meet again.

As King Philip unleashed his full fury on the Knights Templar, few escaped his net. The Holy Inquisition was perverted to the power of the king, and the use of torture was permitted and, indeed, encouraged. Many brethren had their teeth torn out with pliers one by one while being questioned. Others had their nails ripped out or had wedges hammered beneath them. The *strappado*, whereby the victim's arms are bound behind his back and he is lifted off the ground, sometimes with weights attached to his feet or private parts, caused excruciating agony.

In the face of these tortures, which were still widely used by the Dominican Inquisitors of Spain in Christopher Columbus' lifetime, the strongest of men would confess to anything. The confessions thus wrung from the arrested Knights strengthened the case being made by King Philip that the Order was a proven source of heresy, and that Philip was therefore acting on behalf of the Church in his pursuit of the Knights. During the rooting out of heresy, the Knights were also pressed to reveal the location of the Templar treasure. Yet none spoke, because none knew—except Columbus' forefather, Gerard de Villiers.

De Villiers made his escape through the areas of France most sympathetic to the fugitive Templars. He disguised himself as a pilgrim returning along the route from Compostella in Spain through Toulouse and along the southern route to Lombardy. In the Languedoc, where the people had suffered the violent pleasures of the French crusade against the Cathars, there were still those who remembered that the Knights Templar had refused to take part in those horrors and were willing to give de Villiers assistance. Through Provence, he made his way eastward until he left France and could feel a bit safer. Yet the Inquisition continued to seek out Templars everywhere, and the pope could or would offer no succor to survivors of the Order.

Finally, in Moconesi, a small Italian village in the mountains of Liguria, safe from the French Inquisition, Gerard de Villiers disappeared and a new name emerged. The Temple of Solomon in Jerusalem had been built on four pillars. These columns were of great symbolic significance to the Templars. In order to both conceal his past and at the same time remember it, Gerard de Villiers took the name Colomne.

Over the years of the great wars between France and England and the time of the great plague that took so many lives, Moconesi was a quiet sanctuary. News came of the trial and conviction of Grand Master Jacques de Molay in 1309 after two years of imprisonment and torture. This was followed, after years of wrangling between the French king and the pope, by the news that de Molay had been burned at the stake in the courtyard of Notre Dame Cathedral in 1314. Along with that news came the whispered information that, at his execution, he had uttered a curse on both the king and the pope, who had betrayed the Knights Templar, stripped the Order of its wealth, lands, and property, and hounded the remaining members of the Order into exile, prison, or death. Some claimed that the great plague was sent in fulfillment of that curse.

Colomne lived quietly and modestly, marrying a girl from the village. In due time he had children, and his offspring had children, until, one day, Giovanni Colon left Moconesi and settled in Quinto, a village near Genoa. There, the half-literate local priest entered his name on the parish rolls as Colombo, and thus, in 1451, a descendent of Gerard de Villiers, grandson of Giovanni, was born and baptized Cristoforo Colombo, son of Domenico Colombo.

Part III

Christopher Columbus

February 12, 1493 – Aboard the Niña

*W*e *have run today some eleven or twelve leagues, but the high seas and stormy weather put the fleet in much trouble and danger. The Pinta is no longer visible across the tops of the waves that toss us, and I fear she and her crew may be lost. This gives urgency to my writing, for were this little caravel not so stout and well prepared, we would already be lost. We are, at the moment, in a relative calm, but this will not last, and the storm will soon resume.*

A name is a clue to the parents' hopes and desires for their new child. In the significance of our name lies the answer to the riddle of our existence. Named for an ancestor, the child is a living monument. Bestowing a parent's name is a bid for reincarnation. Choosing a saint's name is a dedication. The parent asks the saint to be the personal link between the child and God. It is also a sacrifice. The child is offered to the saint, and the saint is offered to the child. The bond is vague but strong. There is a contract—emulate the saint, and the saint will protect you in this life, and the next. But there is also a cruel catch. The parent makes the contract, but must rely on the child to conform to its earthly performance. Beyond providing food, clothing, and shelter, raising a child is a process of molding it into the character that fits the model of the saint, at least in the eyes of the parent.

In choosing to call me "Christopher," my parents must have been conscious of the implied expectations they were imposing on me. According to the legend, due to his size and strength, Saint Christopher chose to serve Christ by assisting people to cross a dangerous river, where they were perishing in the attempt. After Christopher had performed this service for some time, a little child asked to be taken across the river. During the crossing, the river became swollen and the child seemed as heavy as lead so much that Christopher could scarcely carry him and found himself in great difficulty.

When they finally reached the other side, Christopher said to the child, "You have put me in the greatest danger. I do not think the whole world could have been as heavy on my shoulders as you were."

The child replied, "You had on your shoulders not only the whole world, but He who made it. I am Christ your King, whom you are serving by this work." The child then vanished.

Children know nothing of these things, and I was no exception. These secrets lie coiled in the hearts of parents, showing themselves only in things unsaid, stories half-told, swallowed disappointments. But from my earliest days, I felt that great things would be required of me. By invoking Saint Christopher with my first name, and the columns of the Temple with my last, I believed myself to be called upon by God to devote my life to a mission to uphold His Church. But that sentiment and sense of mission were still to come.

The life of a five-year-old boy growing up in Genoa in the mid-fourteen hundreds was much like today, near the turn of the century. My personal needs and my family defined my horizons. My world was the street outside my house. For me, history was yesterday, and tomorrow was a time beyond the next meal. My daily life was regulated by the tolling of church bells, the needs of my stomach, and the rise and fall of the sun. Intrusions from beyond came in the form of conversations at table that were beyond my understanding.

Genoa in the 1450s was reeling from a disaster that had occurred shortly after my birth: the capture by the Ottomans of Constantinople, the ancient capital of Byzantium. It is said that God abandoned the city, plunging the moon into eclipse on May 22, 1453, as a prophetic signal that His favor had been withdrawn. Four days later, the whole city was blotted out by a thick fog, a condition unknown in that part of the world in May. The lifting of the fog allowed observers to see a strange light flickering from the dome of the Hagia Sophia, and from the city walls lights were seen in the countryside to the west, far behind the Turkish camp. Many felt that the light around the dome signaled the departure of the Holy Spirit. Whether the fault lay with God or man, it came about that on Tuesday, May 29, 1453, the soldiers of Sultan Mehmet the Second breached the walls of Constantinople. Later that same day, the sultan accepted the surrender of the Genoese colony of Galata on the western shore of the Golden Horn. During the fighting, the Byzantine commander, who was Genoese, was fatally wounded and retreated with his men to his ships, where he succumbed to his injuries.

This defeat by the Ottomans was a tragedy for Genoans, but the longer-term impact was even worse. Much of the trade between Europe and Golden Cathay to the east, begun three hundred years before by Marco Polo, was routed through the hands and banks of Genoese merchants and sailors. Their colonies at the Golden Horn and along the Silk Road past the Black Sea suffered as the sultan imposed high taxes and restricted passage of goods. Making matters worse, at about the same time, Cathay came under a new dynasty of emperors called the Ming. Given the need to consolidate his rule, the new emperor of Cathay focused inward and closed much of the frontier. The result was that, over time, the previous flood of Genoese trade was reduced to a trickle, and the fortunes of my home city fell disastrously.

This was the slow-moving catastrophe affecting the Genoa into which I was born. The city's role as a great center of trade and power, where banking was virtually invented and from which legendary voyages had sprung, was now becoming the story of our history. Over the years of my growing up, the population declined, and the few remaining merchants were forced to seek new markets and trade routes.

But these trends and tendencies occurred far above the head of a young boy. The struggles of my father to adjust to the loss of demand from the east caused him to shift his focus to markets in Portugal and England. While this shift was the eventual consequence of the titanic struggle between east and west, no connection was made in our minds to the clash of civilizations in which Genoa had been on the losing side. Instead, it was the natural search for the next deal, the next voyage, and the next meal that drove our focus westward. Our fortunes were more pinned to the ebb and flow of our local political struggles, and it was these that led me to a life of the sea.

In that time, Genoa went through paroxysms of political conflict that affected the course of my life. My father had long been committed to supporting the powerful Fregoso family and their allies, the Fieschis and the Spinolas, united in their support of France's Anjou dynasty in opposing the claims to Genoa by Spanish Aragon, which hoped to extend its control northward from Sicily to Naples and Genoa with the help of the pope. The Fregoso forces took control of the city on Christmas Day in 1446, five years before my birth, with my father fighting among their ranks. His reward was appointment as Keeper of the Olivella gate—an appointment made personally by the Doge, Giano Fregoso, in 1447. The Colombo family's fortune bloomed like the roses that grew outside our front door.

The losers in this political fray retreated to the sea and became pirates. The ejected Adorno family and their followers joined with Catalonian seafarers in raiding the coastal areas, coming ashore largely unmolested—sacking, pillaging, and burning, and leaving with arms full of booty. Eventually, with the support of Aragon and Catalonia, the Adornos came back into power in Genoa. Now it was the turn of the expelled Fregosos and Fieschis to take on the role of pirates and raiders. It was the ebb and flow of these political tides that swept me from the shore to a life at sea.

I was eight years old in 1459, had the previous year taken my First Communion, and I had reached the age when boys ceased play and were expected to begin a trade, perhaps as an apprentice or working within the family business. My father probably expected that I would work with him trading wool. My childhood time spent running about on the steep slopes of the Ravecca indeed came to an end, but not as expected.

The Fregoso and Fieschi families had been run out of Genoa, and for years, like the Adornos before them, had become corsairs and sea raiders. In 1459, they made a move to retake their former possessions. In September, supported by Alfonso, King of Naples, their forces attacked the city. My father, who hoped that the success of the Fregosos would return our family fortunes to their former luster, joined the invading forces, while my mother and we children sheltered in our house with barred doors and closed shutters.

In the event, the battle went badly for the attackers. Pietro Fregoso suffered a grievous wound from a mace blow to his head. Half-conscious and reeling, his horse clattering wildly through the narrow cobblestone streets of the city, Pietro tried to shelter with his lieutenants and some followers beneath the walls of the Sant'Andrea gate. Here Domenico Colombo found him, surrounded for protection by his brothers and a few loyal guards. My father promised to guide Pietro and his protectors away from their enemies, who were hunting him like a beast. But Pietro's injuries so weakened him that he insisted on being left behind. The Adorno forces came upon him lying on the cobblestones, blood streaming from his head. His capture gave the remaining Fregosos an opportunity to escape while Pietro was bound by his pursuers. He later died at the doors of the ducal palace where he was taken as a prisoner.

My father was able to lead the other survivors of the attack through back streets to our house. From there, he directed me to guide them to the harbor by the back ways that all children learn, where they could escape to their ships. I was too young to feel fear, only the excitement of sneaking through alleys and back lanes in a game of high-stakes hide and seek.

By the time we gained the quay, our pursuers were close behind, and Pietro's brother Tommasino, who was now commanding the surviving Fregosos, realized that the way off the quay was cut off. He knew better than an eight-year-old boy how hard it would go with my family if I were captured and identified. Seizing me by my jacket, he hauled me across the gangplank and aboard the ship, though I struggled and cried like a sheep being trussed for shearing while the crew cast off the moorings.

Thus began my life at sea.

The waters of the Mediterranean Sea are rarely calm. Whipped by winds from Africa, the waves rush hither and thither in currents and counter-currents, recoiling from the cliffs of Europe to dash against the deserts of Africa, mixed by the swirling currents that run from east to west and west to east. Storms arise on the Turkish coast, and their waves sink ships in the seas of Sicily. The voyages and vicissitudes of Odysseus document the vagaries of being seaborne on the Middle Sea.

Once on a ship, there is no escaping the pitching and yawing in these vicious conditions, and I spent the next days longing for and then being indifferent to death as I hung over the side or lay on the deck, exhausted from retching. I was vaguely aware of the activities around me, and barely felt it when a gruff sailor tied a rope around my thin waist to save me from slipping over the side. So my first days aboard passed in a miserable daze. Gradually, though, I got my sea legs, and over time came to adjust so comfortably to the pitching of the deck in even the highest seas, that when I went ashore, walking on solid land caused me to struggle for balance. Thus I evolved from being "at sea" to being a seaman.

For the next two years, I served as cabin boy under the watchful eye and tutelage of both Tommasino Fregoso and his other brother, Paolo, who was the exiled Archbishop of Genoa. Between them, my soul was instructed in the ways of God while I learned at the same time the ways of the sea. Archbishop Paolo did not neglect the catechism and the rituals and rites of our Catholic faith, but he was also very learned about the politics of the tensions between Church and State. As an exiled archbishop, he was acutely aware of the struggle between the temporal powers that the Church had long practiced over civil rulers, and the kings' counter-assertions that they ruled by the grace of God. Not many eight-year-olds had the benefit of personal schooling at the hands of such a distinguished churchman and political leader.

Many of the archbishop's lessons took the form of homilies, dwelling on passages from Scripture and the lives of the saints. I suppose his own situation of exile from Genoa also made Paolo Fregoso dwell within himself on the relationship between temporal and spiritual authority and the nature of God's interventions into the affairs of man. Sometimes he seemed to forget that I was with him in the small cabin or on the deck under the stars. Looking back, I think he used my lessons as an opportunity to ruminate out loud before an uncritical audience, probably not realizing the effect that his (perhaps unformed) ideas might have on an impressionable boy.

I particularly remember his explanation for the great plague that had swept through the world in the previous century. In his view, it stemmed from the curse that Jacques de Molay had placed on King Philip and Pope Clement when, after more than three years of torture and abuse, he was finally burned at the stake before Notre Dame Cathedral in Paris. From his execution pyre, he predicted that God would strike them both down within a year and a day. In months both king and pope were dead, and their deaths were followed within a few years by the Black Death that swept across Europe, killing hundreds of thousands. To Archbishop Paolo, these events were evidence of the wrath of God and a sign that His supremacy over the temporal affairs of kings was not to be challenged. I had no reason to dispute that view.

The life of a cabin boy on board a seafaring ship is not given to long bouts of study and contemplative thought, and most of my time was spent on my duties. A boy between eight and eleven soaks up knowledge through his skin, and I was no exception. On my first days aboard, the officers and crew were generous in sharing their skills, and I quickly learned (for if I did not, they were equally generous in their criticism, often with a rope's end or a backhand) to judge currents, winds, and seas, navigate by the stars, judge our latitude by the noon-day sun, and, most important, plot a course that would bring us to a destination over open seas. I became able to differentiate from a distance in the haze a Portuguese *barinel* from a *carrack;* I learned the different types of sails and their uses under varying wind conditions; and I grew to understand the interactions between wind and currents. Under Tommasino Fregoso's watchful eye and sharp instruction, I studied how geometry and trigonometry were applied to navigation, and eventually I was able to pass the stiff tests that were put on me. I learned to read and write, and I began to keep a detailed sketchbook of shorelines, reef locations, and harbor moorings. Over the course of the seasons, I noted the shifting patterns of prevailing winds and currents, the temperature and color of the water, the migration patterns of birds and fish. The stars wheeled through the heavens, and they rose and dipped on the horizon as the seasons turned. Just as today, as a grown man, I can still recall perfectly the words to songs I learned in those days, so those elements of nature and the sea became seared into my brain, never to be forgotten in this life.

Besides my schooling in matters that were over the ship's rails, I learned the techniques of handling a large sailing vessel. Ours was a Catalan-built *não*, which combined the balance and upwind maneuverability of the lateen sail derived from our Genoese sailing tradition with the ability to run before the wind afforded by a northern square mainsail and foresail. As a young boy I was of course not part of the sailing crew, but I watched closely and pestered the sailors with questions about wind and sail, reefing and steering. Over the two years I shipped with the Fregosos, I learned all there was to know about sailing these vessels.

The Fregosos were not at sea for pleasure. Their voyages were a form of exile from Genoa, and their livelihood consisted of the booty gained from raiding the shipping and property of their Genoese antagonists. Nor were the Fregosos alone in these ventures. Corsairs sailing from city-states across Italy, up from the coast of North Africa, and from as far away as the Black Sea also plied these waters. Sometimes these corsairs came together in short-term alliances to attack a shore that was heavily defended. Alliances were tactical, not strategic, and dissolved as quickly as they formed. An ally on one venture could become a target just days later.

Battles on land and sea were similar, with the crew of the ship swarming over the side to attack the crew of its opponent, and the swinging of swords and pikes was much the same whether the battle was on land or sea. A few caravels began to arm with small swivel guns and a few cannon, but these rarely made any difference to the outcome of the conflict. Ships were not sufficiently maneuverable to bring these weapons to bear with any effect.

At my age, I did not directly participate in any of these events. My role was to assist in bandaging the wounded and hauling water to sluice the blood from the decks after the battle. The most profound lessons I gained from my observations were those derived from avoiding a sea battle—how sails, winds, and maneuvers gave one ship an advantage over another, either as pursuer or pursued. I learned that a ship could cut off the wind to a pursuer by crossing in front of it, gaining the margin that could mean escape. I learned how a crew that was trained and practiced to undertake a sharp and rapid tack could pull away from—or closer to—its adversary. Success or survival often depended on the ability of a ship to beat closer into the wind using lateen sails, or run faster before the wind using a square rig. And, more than anything, it depended on the ability of a crew to be more rapid than that of the other ship to raise and lower sails on command. The years of my childhood spent on board the Fregosos' ship formed me as a seafarer. But my true destiny still lay ahead.

Two years after our escape from Genoa, on my eleventh birthday, I knelt on the deck while Archbishop Paolo Fregoso anointed my forehead with holy chrism in the sacrament of Confirmation that affirmed me in the One True Faith, and heard my oath accepting the authority of God and the pope. From that day, my allegiance to the Holy Roman Catholic Church has been complete and unequivocal.

The tumultuous politics of Genoa had not ceased during my sojourn at sea with the Fregosos. The conflict between the Adornos, who were supported by the French Anjou dynasty, and the Fregosos, who were loyal to the pope, was a source of unrest and instability that interfered with the true goal of the people of Genoa: commerce. Unhappy with French rule as administered by the Doge Adorno, the people revolted and drove the French out. In this vacuum, the Fregosos and Adornos negotiated a *modus vivendi* under which the Fregosos would return to Genoa, and Paolo Fregoso would resume his role as archbishop while an Adorno would hold the office of Doge. This arrangement paved the way for my return to Genoa. I was finally able to go home.

While I had changed a great deal over the past couple of years, my father had changed only slightly. I was of course taller and stronger, but most of my changes were inside; my experiences at sea and the tutoring I had received gave me a wide perspective on the world. My father, on the other hand, had not changed his views of the forces at work in his life. He was a little bit grayer, a little bit thinner, and substantially more embittered at his fall from grace and prosperity.

The celebrations surrounding my return to the home of Domenico Columbo were somewhat muted, to say the least. Like much of Genoa, our household had not prospered. My father's identification with the Fregosos and his loyalty to papal power worked heavily against him during the time when the Adorno family, supported by the French, had control of the city. While his politics hurt his standing, the more important factor was the slow decline of Genoa that followed the fall of Constantinople and the loss of prosperity that resulted. The tragedy of Genoa was gradual. The decline in our fortunes was slow, and at that time had evidenced itself in scarcer and less-rewarding trade with our traditional markets in the east.

Despite the fall of Constantinople, trading expeditions from Genoa continued. My father continued to load cargoes laden with our wool, destined for such of our colonies in the Bosporus that still operated under the watchful eyes of the sultan's tax collectors. Based on the skills I had garnered with the Fregosos, my father allowed me, after considerable argument and pleading, to accompany these shipments and act as his agent on board ship. While I served as his shipping agent, my older brothers took on the role of merchant, negotiating the sale of wool, bartering for cargo on the return voyage. I saw with wonder the dome of the Hagia Sophia, and also the rise of the minaret towers built by the Ottomans as the cathedral was transformed into a mosque.

The sultan had allowed much of the city to remain undamaged, but in truth, it was not an exciting place anymore. Between the sacking by the Franks in the Fourth Crusade, the depredations and mass deaths of the great plague, and the overall decline under the last of the Byzantines, the great city had sunk into something more resembling a cluster of villages separated by open fields by the time I was visiting it. Sailors could still find the usual entertainments around the port and harbor, but these were not yet appealing to a young boy.

From the Bosporus, our return trade routes took us often to Alexandria. There we would lie over while my brothers dickered and haggled in their trade with the canny Egyptian merchants, and I had time to explore the mysteries of that ancient land.

On our voyages, I was expanding my familiarity with the ways of the sea by observing and incessantly badgering with questions the captains with whom we sailed. It was in Egypt that I learned the most important sailing lesson of my life. I quickly came to understand the wondrous nature of traveling by boat on the Nile River, where the river water flowed northward to the sea, while the wind blew steadily southward. Thus could the wind push our sails upstream against the current to Cairo, where I could see the great mysterious pyramids and the form of the Sphinx staring impassively across the river to the rising sun. I would then float northward, sails furled, using the river's current to rejoin my brothers in Alexandria for the trip to Genoa and home.

Imagine! One could use wind to sail in one direction and ride the current to travel in the reverse. It is this lesson that I carried in my heart and that underlies my present voyage.

My experiences on these voyages sharpened my skills, and I labored hard to understand the whims of wind, water, and tide. As my experience grew, so did my reputation for skillful navigation, and the captains of our merchant ships came to rely on my ability to steer their vessels accurately from port to port, even across open seas. My growing confidence in these skills led to some adventures, and, as a result, my voyages were not exclusively mercantile.

The continued commercial and political competition and strife between Genoa and the Aragons and Catalans of Spain that had led to my early years at sea with the Fregosos did not cease upon my return to my father's house. In the fall of 1472, when I was twenty-one years old, the raiding forces of René, Duke of Anjou, were under siege near Barcelona. The encircling forces were to be reinforced and resupplied by an Aragonese galleass called the *Ferrandina*. To prevent this, I was chosen to lead a voyage to capture the Spanish ship before it could achieve its mission. Spies had identified the *Ferrandina* anchored in the harbor at Tunis.

We set out from Genoa and, sailing due south, reached the island of Sardinia, where we dropped anchor in the harbor of San Pietro Island and sought additional intelligence in the town. Here, to our shock and the captain's dismay, we learned that the *Ferrandina* was not alone, but was accompanied by two other ships and a galleon. My captain and crew became frightened and sought to turn back, but I was determined to sail on, confident of success. I was averse to being branded a coward or overly cautious, which would certainly have been the result of slinking back without accomplishing the mission. I was adamant—especially as this was my first real command—that I would be seen as courageous and steadfast.

Still, I could not physically force the captain and crew to sail on, so I resorted to subterfuge to achieve my goal. The crew desired to sail back with the prevailing winds to Marseille, and I pretended to surrender to their demands. Secretly, however, I spun the ship's compass around so that while it appeared that we were sailing north, we were in reality continuing southward. As the evening approached, I ordered the unfurling of the sails, and we made such speed before the wind that by sunrise we were passing the headlands of Carthage, though the crew was convinced that we were approaching Marseille.

Arriving in the harbor of Tunis, it soon became apparent that the *Ferrandina* was not there, alone or accompanied, and that the crew's fears had been groundless. Though not a shot had been fired, I was surprised and shocked to find that there was a single casualty to be counted—me! What I had considered courage and cleverness was taken amiss by the captain of our vessel, who accused me on our return of mutiny and piracy by having taken command of the ship against the will of captain and crew. He darkly suggested that my goal was to deliver the ship to the enemy, and only bad luck and his resistance to my command had prevented such an outcome. Badly embarrassed by the ease with which they had been deceived by someone they considered a young upstart, this view was pressed and supported by the crew. With so many accusers ranged against me, my chances of defending myself successfully before a magistrate were slim, especially as I had been serving on behalf of the French who, though currently in alliance with the Fregosos, remained the enemies of Genoa in the popular mind.

The result of these intrigues was a determination on my part to leave before some travesty of justice could be played out to my sorrow. With help from my father and the Spinola family, I was able to secretly book passage on a merchant vessel sailing to the island of Chios, the large Genoese trading colony in the Aegean Sea near the coast of Turkey. The Spinolas dominated trade with the Levant after the Ottomans conquered Constantinople, and the furthest point in their trading empire was Chios, so it was naturally to that most distant port that I fled in 1473.

Ah! Chios! When the Lord takes me, I hope that heaven will be like Chios. Gentle breezes off the blue-green sea caress the skin, carrying the scent of the mastic trees from the southern part of the island. Waking to the crying sea birds and the sunshine reflecting from the white stone of the mountain peaks, shooting its rays across the narrow strait that separates Chios from the mainland of Turkey, warming the morning and absorbing the night mists from the sea. The cooling that comes in the afternoon, as the sun moves behind the island's high central massif whose shadow creeps down to the coast.

Each day I swam in the sea and built up my endurance and strength in the water. My strokes became fluid and easy, and I imagined that I was becoming a fish, one with the ocean. After my swim I would take a breakfast of olives, white cheese, and flat bread, and then turn my attention to the business of buying and selling the mastic gum that came from the trees on the south of the island. I earned a good living, for it is only on Chios that these trees exist, exuding drips of the stuff. There was a ready market for the gum among the women of the sultan's *hareem*, just across the strait in Turkey, so I was able to apply my knowledge of commerce and shipping that I had gathered in the wool trade.

I spent the afternoons studying Greek—and although I never became fluent, my vocabulary was enhanced by many Greek words. In the evenings, I took supper in a tavern by the harbor and conversed with sailors about their voyages, drinking the local red wine. I remember with aching nostalgia sitting on the shore, and I can still hear in my head the musicians playing their island songs on the *tsampouna* bagpipe and the *toumbaki* drum while the men danced slowly with exaggerated steps, arms upraised. I could imagine the same scene thousands of years earlier, my place taken by the young and perhaps not yet blind poet Homer, who was said to have been born on this island.

Aware of my precarious position in the eyes of the law in Genoa, and conscious that Chios remained a Genoese colony, I was careful to protect myself. I took discreet quarters in a house partway up the hill from the port, where I could monitor traffic in the harbor and oversee anyone coming up the hill toward me. The house had a ready back door, and with a few steps to a turn in the path, I could disappear into the mountains and canyons of Chios.

My precautions turned out to be for naught, as ultimately, it was not from the village that I was accosted, but from the back door, by a man who came down from the hills.

While I was becoming prosperous—if not rich—in the mastic markets of Chios, my father's fortunes in Genoa continued to decline. As a consequence, he found it necessary to shift his household to smaller quarters, and in the process reduced the scope of his belongings. The man who appeared unannounced at my back door was a monk from the monastery of Nea Moni. This ancient holy site sits on the mountain Provateio Oros in the island's interior, about three leagues from the harbor. The monk told me he was called Father Pantaleon. He had recently returned from Genoa, where he had been in contact with my father. Hearing that the priest was returning to his monastery on Chios, my father entrusted to him two things to deliver to me: a letter, and a small locked chest.

The letter reported that my risk of being prosecuted for piracy in association with the *Ferrandina* affair had been eliminated by the intercession of the Spinola family. I was free to return from my exile, and it was his wish that I do so. I received this news with distinctly mixed emotions, as I found my life on Chios exceedingly pleasant.

Ah! But the chest! Its contents proved to be the turning point of my life, which was henceforward ever divided between "before the chest" and "after the chest." Its significance was not revealed upon first inspection. The ancient lock looked like it had not been opened for decades, perhaps generations. A quick blow with a hammer parted it and revealed its secrets: a folded tunic emblazoned with a simple red cross, some old French coins, and the baptismal certificate of someone who had been christened with the name of Gerard de Villiers. This surprised me, but ultimately not as much as the remaining item. At the bottom of the box lay a thick package wrapped in what was clearly ancient oilskin.

Carefully I unwrapped the package and discovered that it was an ancient manuscript. The characters of the writing were Greek, but the language was not that of the people surrounding me on the island of Chios. The pages were made of vellum that had been scraped thin and preserved. It was impossible for me to determine the age of this document, but it was clearly ancient.

When I showed the package to Father Pantaleon, he confirmed the letters to be Greek, and identified the language of the writing as Aramaic. He suggested I take the manuscript to another monk in the monastery who was a scholar of Aramaic and could provide a translation. I was a bit reluctant to disclose the document to someone else, since I did not know its content, but in the end I was unable to find an alternative.

The monk was very old, and his mind and memory were almost gone. Because he lacked the strength to write, I sat with him as his scribe, and he laboriously read each sentence to me in Greek while I penned his words. The effort stimulated him to press to its completion, for the content of the manuscript entranced him and seemed to give him the energy he needed to see the job through. The work was exhausting, and the content of the completed translation, while a great shock to me, was plainly an even greater one to him, as he died almost immediately after we finished. His return to Our Lord was truly a blessing—both for him, suffering the infirmities of old age, and for me, as his passing ensured that the content of the document would remain my secret.

Here is the text of the manuscript. I have organized it into chapters and given them titles, although these were not evident in the original.

Part IV
The Gospel of Lazarus

Soon the lamp will gutter out. In the light that remains, I shall finish my account of the events that have led me from my first tomb to my second. Perhaps one day someone will roll away the stone covering the opening of this small cave, deep under Jerusalem's Temple Mount, and find some interest in these words.

Chapter 1: My Resurrection

I awoke slowly from the dead. My name and my soul and my body found each other and came together, groping through the dark. "Lazarus. Come forth!" I heard it as from under the ocean, but the words moved distantly across the face of the deep. Silence followed, and for several moments I thought myself still dead. What an absurd thought.

My nose tickled; I sneezed. A momentary buzzing filled my ears, and then gradually died away. The sharp stink of dusty decay stung my nostrils and I sneezed twice, more quickly. Once again the buzzing sound welled up and subsided. I ran a quick check list: I am breathing and my ears are working. Sneezing is not common among the dead. I am thinking; my senses are working. Hmmmm. I must be alive.

As feeling returned, I became aware of a slight weight over my face. I realized that the total darkness in which I lay was because something covered my eyes. My fingers crawled across my chest, searching blindly for my face like worms on the surface of the soil after rain. The buzzing resumed. It dawned on me that I was hearing the sound of thousands of flies. They rose resentfully into the air when I moved, then gradually settled back to reclaim their reservations at the feast.

Each of us knows the feeling of waking—that time when we lie with closed eyes, appearing to others to be asleep but conscious of sound and thought and feeling. Or, maybe not? Sometimes we dream we are awake, so that only when we really awaken do we realize that we were actually sleeping, and for a few moments before we get busy, we wonder about the line between dreams and reality. I lay in that in-between state.

The linens that covered my face and crisscrossed over my torso were not tightly bound. The women who applied these burial cloths after washing my body could not have expected that hands would remove them. My hand slid limply back to my side, dragging the covering from my eyes. I examined it as best I could and saw in the dim light that it was my death mask, apparently painted hurriedly, for it resembled my true features only slightly. The large dark eyes were an accurate depiction, though not the arching eyebrows. My skin was not that white, and the lips of the mask were as full as those of a young woman. Nor was my face that round; mine was narrower with prominent cheekbones tapering down to a pointed chin. I am sure the mask's creator had not expected its wearer to examine his work. Everyone is a critic.

So now I was conscious of sight, sound, thought, and feeling. Especially feeling, as the stone pillow that supported my head dug its sharp corner into my neck. And scent—in my case the scent of putrescence captured in the burial linens wrapping my limbs. The smell alone would have prompted me into motion, but with my face now exposed, the flies directly crawling on my flesh became unbearable and goaded me into movement.

"Lazarus! Come forth!" The voice was insistent and could not be ignored. I peered through almost closed eyelids and detected toward my feet a source of light. This was not the bright light of morning, filling the eyes of the newly awake and causing a blinking, squinting blindness. This light was soft, indirect, and gentle, slanting away from the opening of the shallow cave in which I was interred, into the faces of those whose shapes I could see outside. The glow illuminated them and, in its quality, seemed to emanate from them. Their robes were suffused with the light, and their eyes reflected the glow of the sun as they peered into the dark hole of my tomb. I managed to sit up and swing my legs around so I could slide off the narrow stone ledge on which I lay.

Lightheadedness overcame me, my vision clouded, and I thought for a moment that I was about to die again, but I was able to steady myself on the bench, and my head gradually cleared. I slowly emerged, ducking though the low doorway cut into the stone cliff wall, and lurched out clumsily on half-bound feet, plucking weakly at the winding cloths that hindered my pace.

Before me was a tableau. The small group surrounding Rabbi Jesus of Nazareth stood frozen, their eyes fixed on my emergence. Their silence was accentuated by the slight shuffle of my feet and the afternoon breeze that sighed through the gray-green leaves of the nearby olive trees. Above us, the last flock of swallows was giving way to the first few evening bats, darting through the purpling sky, seeking the sunset hatch of insects.

The living have no fear in the presence of the dead. The women converse with one another as they prepare the body for burial, as if preparing meat for dinner. The dead are not a threat. Rather, it is in the presence of the dying that solemnity prevails. Here are the hushed conversations and downcast eyes. The witnesses to the event know that one day they will be the main attraction, and each wonders what form death will take. Each prays for a quick, painless, dignified end. Children, not understanding the transition underway, are sent from the room so their cheerful liveliness and noisy, insistent demands for attention do not distract their elders or, by disturbing the dying one, unduly hurry him along. It is the transitions that are the solemn times—and mine, from death to life, was received solemnly. At first.

It is normally the newborn baby who makes the emergence into life a noisy occasion. In this case, I was not able to perform that role, as the dryness of death in my throat made sound impossible. Instead, it was my sister Mary who adopted the role of noisemaker. Mary fell to her knees with a cry, like a bullock stunned by the butcher before slaughter. The tableau dissolved into a maelstrom of motion. Led by my eldest sister Martha and our Uncle Joseph, they ran to me, their long cloaks flapping back comically from their legs, stopping abruptly as they reached me. Their sandals stirred up the dust so it shone golden, hanging in the slanting afternoon light.

Several beats passed, and we eyed each other until Uncle Joseph stepped forward. Removing his red woolen cloak, he draped it gently around my shoulders, then stepped back. His eyes traveled over my body and dropped to my unshod feet. I could see him thinking to remove his own sandals to give to me. To ease his embarrassment, I began to walk, my bare feet shuffling on the ground. I could feel the earth's dusty warmth absorbed from the afternoon sun that shone down from the late spring sky. Sudden laughter burst from my throat like the cawing of a raven as we approached Jesus. Turning to my eldest sister, who was clinging to my arm, I croaked my first words. "Martha, the next time you visit the dead, bring along some extra clothing. And don't forget the sandals."

The frozen moment of my emergence from the tomb had yielded to this sudden burst of activity, but now that I appeared before them fully resurrected, their initial amazement gave way to an embarrassed uncertainty. What do the living say to the recently dead? Should one tell of the interesting things that had happened during the sojourn in the tomb? The results of that weekend's sports matches? It might be rude to suggest a nice refreshing bath, since that would indelicately draw attention to the appalling smell wafting from my burial cloths under the robe. Maybe some small talk . . . "So, Lazarus! How was it? How do you feel? Are you hungry?" And left hanging in the air the most important question of them all: "Is there life after death?" At least in my case, I could answer that question affirmatively.

The awkward moment was relieved by my sister Mary. Raised to her feet by Jesus' hand, she came in a belated rush to me, and the group parted to let her through. With no regard to my recent condition or the stink that emerged from the folds of Uncle Joseph's robe, she kissed me and ran her hands over my face and through my hair. She kissed my fingers and my palms, and wiped her tears on the stained linen rags that still clung to my frame. She repeated my name again and again—"Lazarus! Lazarus!"—as though the naming would somehow stop me if I took it into my head to turn around and return to the tomb.

Rabbi Jesus stood motionless. In the early twilight over Mary's shoulder, I looked into his face, which was becoming indistinct under the shadow of the shawl that covered his long hair. Somehow, using powers that I could not comprehend derived from sources that I dared not contemplate, Jesus was the instrument of my resurrection. I did not know the purpose of this act, but in that moment, suspended between death and life, I thought I could see many things in his dark eyes.

Weariness was certainly there, as though he had just completed long hours of toil in the heat of the day. A welcoming pleasure was also evident in the faint smile that curved the lips under his dark beard. Jesus and I had become close over the past year, though I sometimes suspected that his personal affection for me was coincident with my status as younger brother to Mary, who was the closest person to his heart, and whom he often called his Beloved Disciple.

Wariness was also visible—a sense that Jesus was poised to endure a blow from a strong fist or cudgel. Thinking back now, it was evident that he could foresee the consequences of my resurrection. As the word spread , he would be unable to avoid the attention of the Temple authorities. No longer a mere itinerant preacher, his reputation would now become that of miracle worker. The inevitable accompanying notoriety would be seen as a threat to their power, and their reaction would not be to extend a welcome befitting the Messiah. The afternoon breeze blew a strand of his long brown hair from under his shawl, and he reached up to tuck it back.

The sun was lowering in the sky. With Uncle Joseph's robe wrapped around my shoulders to fend off the rapid cooling of the March late afternoon, we turned away from this place of interment and climbed with the sun behind us until we reached the top of the hill to make our way to our home.

Our house stood high on the east side of the Mount of Olives, with a view of Bethany and the land beyond to the east—the mountains opposite that formed the hazy horizon of Judea. In the morning, the spring sun pleasantly warmed our courtyard, but as the heat of the day rose, the oxen ceased grazing on the prickly pear and mustard plants and sought shelter under the large fig tree that had been pruned to provide shade around the house. This thick, cooling canopy gave a sense of solitude, and its peaceful embrace was conducive to meditation and prayer.

The sun was setting as we reached the house, and we all turned to watch its last moments as it slid rapidly into the horizon. Its rays cast golden beams into the sky. My father had once written how he missed that sight, for the sunsets of Israel demonstrated the special relationship between God and the Jewish people in a way that did not occur in the dank climate of Britannia, far to the north. These sunsets took away the breath and suffused us with the power of the glorious city fifteen furlongs away to the west, glowing in the fading twilight—the city of Solomon and David, Jerusalem.

The sense of power that emanated from the city came not only from its fortifications, although these were impressive enough. From the Mount of Olives, one walked down into the deep ravine of Kidron where the cemetery of Jehosophat lay, and from which the prophet Joel believed that the souls and bodies of men would be gathered together on the Day of Judgment. This valley was shaded in the morning by the Mount to the east and in the afternoon by the immense wall of the city that loomed over it. From these dark depths one looked up as far as the neck could crane, the wall soaring into the sky, to the height of nearly twenty-five men standing on each other's shoulders. Towers a spear's throw apart marched at intervals along the top of the wall, which was built of enormous blocks of stone. The tower that stood on the corner to our left, where the wall turned west, climbed another distance into the sky equal to the height of the wall—so high that from the bottom of the valley the eye could barely see the top. From that tower, watchers could monitor the land far into the eastern and southern distances. And in the event of danger, soldiers could be mustered out of the Antonia Fortress at the corner of the Temple Mount. But most of the time the Temple guards' attention was focused inward, devoted to watching the activities below them inside the city, for that was where the primary danger lay.

Resting in the center of this massive masonry was the Temple itself, with its squat rectangular structure in the middle of a solid floor of golden tiles that reflected the bright sun back into the blue sky. The shadowy door into the Holy of Holies symbolizes the separation of the human from the divine, and at the same time offers a portal through which the people of Israel could delegate a representative to bind them to God and God to them: the High Priest.

This edifice is the real source of the power of Jerusalem, for it is through the Temple that the Jewish people derive our special and personal covenant with the power of the divine—the covenant that makes us the Chosen People. The power of God protecting the children of Abraham renders these walls impregnable. The power of the Temple depends on the strength of the people of Israel, and it was the people of Israel who would weaken and undermine these walls.

Chapter 2: My Life Resumes

We reached our house just after nightfall. The swallows that swooped after the evening hatch of insects were replaced by the darting bats pursuing the survivors of the earlier onslaught. I was taken in hand by servants who led me to the familiar tiled bath, filled with pitchers of warm water and scented oils. The discolored winding burial cloths were borne away on the end of a stick with a look of distaste and consigned to the fire. The cloak with which Uncle Joseph had covered me was taken away to be washed and returned to him, but I never saw him wear it again. The stench of the grave was scrubbed away to be replaced by the scent of perfume, and I was dried off and wrapped in a freshly laundered toga.

Slipping my feet into new sandals, I examined my reflection in the polished silver mirror. There appeared no trace of a golem-like creature—I was formed from flesh and blood, not clay. I was capable of speech, though I decided firmly that I should be a little less inclined in the future to let every thought in my mind come out of my mouth. In appearance I was unchanged; my wavy hair remained dark brown to my shoulders, my eyes a similar color. The skin that covered my tall, thin frame was perhaps a bit paler than the olive hue that had suffused it before, but that could be credited to my extended stay indoors—both on my death bed and in my tomb. I felt no twinge in my back where the sicarrius dagger had penetrated me and let my life blood spill onto the floor of the Temple.

When I returned from the baths to the common area of our house, I saw that Martha had arranged for our supper to be served outside in the mild spring evening. Divans had been set around the courtyard and a fire burned brightly, occasionally sending crackling sparks into the darkening sky. The flames in the oil lamps flickered a bit in the light breeze, casting moving shadows against the frescoes on the courtyard walls. The whole scene was bright and cheerful to celebrate the return of Lazarus to his house, alive and well.

Jesus reclined on a divan in the Greek style that had become fashionable among Romans. He appeared uncomfortable, first supporting himself on his elbow, then lying awkwardly back. Quickly tiring of craning his neck, he finally sat up, hunched with his forearms on his thighs and his feet on the ground. His followers arranged themselves around the fire on stools and couches. I was led to a divan on the other side of the fire from Jesus, and a plate of tangy olives and creamy goat's cheese was placed before me, along with freshly made flat bread that warmed my hands as I tore it into strips. Another plate stood by with chopped parsley, sliced cucumbers, and cracked wheat, all drenched in olive oil and vinegar. A cup of wine stood on the small table along with a flask of water to dilute it in the Roman style. I recognized the table as a gift from Jesus, who had planed the planks and joined the legs with his own hands, then presented it to Martha and Mary as a gift.

With a smile, I thanked the servant girl who waited on my table, but she looked quickly away and departed rapidly. I saw her make a gesture behind a fold of her cloak to ward off evil. Maybe I did not feel like a golem, but that feeling apparently was not universally shared. This was the first time I noticed the widespread view that I was an object of fear and superstition. For many, I remained dead, not to be spoken to, not to be looked upon, an omen of death and darkness.

The sounds of food being served and consumed, the clatter of plates, and the idle chatter suddenly died away. From beyond the flickering firelight, Mary appeared. Silently, she dropped to her knees in the dust of our forecourt. Digging with her fingers into the ground, she took handfuls of dust into her hands and slowly poured them over her long red hair, which she had loosened so that it hung down, concealing her face. On her knees across the dirt and stones, she made her way toward Jesus, who sat quietly on his divan. The fire popped and shot sparks into the air. Unconsciously we all held our breath.

Still on her knees at the foot of the divan, Mary removed Jesus' sandals. Using a wet cloth, she washed and perfumed each foot, then kissed and pressed each to the top of her bowed head. Small streams of powdery dust cascaded from her head and shoulders as tremors shook her. Her tears glistened on his feet. This seemed to distress Mary, as though she had somehow defiled him. She wiped his feet dry with her flowing red hair.

I watched with a sense of wonder, for I knew that Mary's abjection was her thanks to Jesus for my living presence in this house. I looked around at the faces of the others in the dancing firelight. Most were simply astounded, silently watching to see what would happen next. Some eyed me with sidelong glances, looking away quickly when our eyes met.

Mary left Jesus' feet and, still on her knees, moved behind him to the other end of the divan. From her robe, she drew a small alabaster bottle worked around with silver wires and studded with precious blue gems. Removing the stopper, she poured the contents into her hands and worked it into the hair of the man who reclined before her. The rich scent of the oil carried across the courtyard. This container and its contents were a luxury that even King Herod Antipas rarely enjoyed, for the quantity of silver required for its purchase could maintain a peasant family for a year.

I knew that these happenings were a reflection of Mary's feelings for me. But more important, they revealed the feelings she had for Jesus. And he for her.

It was the one they called Judas whose face reflected shock. His lips were tight and his jaw clenched so that a small muscle in his forehead bulged and pulsed under the skin. He leaned forward as if barely restraining himself from some outburst. In the cool evening air, his face had the sheen of sweaty shock, like someone who has just been badly injured but does not yet feel the pain. His eyes were not on the drama being played out before him by my sister and Jesus. Instead, they were fixed on me. Judas Iscariot did not look pleased.

I smiled placidly at Judas. I had been anticipating this confrontation. Since my resurrection that morning, I had looked forward to seeing the consternation on his face when Judas saw me—alive.

I rose and strolled over to him. In the leaping light of the fire, I must have appeared ghostly as the flickering flames behind me cast a shifting shadow over my face. Judas shrank back and his fingers mimicked those of the serving girl who sought to ward off evil.

"Surprised to see me, Judas? I guess no one bothered to inform you of the reason for this little celebration?" Judas stared, speechless. "You thought that by killing me you could protect your scheme to blame Jesus for the attack on the Temple." I spoke softly, so those nearby could not hear me. "Do you fear that I will reveal your perfidy to the Rabbi Jesus? You *should* fear that, for without a doubt, I will. And then your scheme will fail."

Judas' eyes darted about. "If you betray us you will betray yourself as well, Lazarus." He could barely bring himself to speak my name. "You were there, too! You cannot reveal the identities of the Zealots without also incriminating yourself. No one will believe that you were killed to silence you, for here you stand. And even if they believed that you were dead and resurrected, your testimony would be that of a golem, to be feared and distrusted."

I had not thought of that. "Even if you are right, Judas, I can still testify that Jesus was not there. Witnesses can be called to testify that he was in Galilee. The three days that I lay in the tomb was the time it took him to make the journey to Jerusalem. I can testify that it was you and Bar Abbas who led the attack and occupied the Temple. The high priest will send out the Temple guards and arrest both of you. He will convince the Romans of your guilt, and they will hang you both on a cross for the crows to pick your eyes out."

Judas suddenly recovered his aplomb. "Go ahead, Lazarus. For I can tell you that the high priest needs a sacrificial lamb, and he has already determined that it will be Jesus, not me or Bar Abbas. Israel needs a lamb to satisfy the Roman wolf's hunger so the rest of the flock can survive. The wheels are in motion, dear Lazarus, and you will not stop them with your wild tales of murder and resurrection."

"You know I was dead, for you saw my blood spilled onto the courtyard of the Temple." I leaned over him and dropped my voice into a sing-song, like that used by the rabbis when they intone prayers during the Sabbath.

"Now I have been reincarnated as your conscience, Judas. Many saw my corpse carried away, and the tale has spread so that even servant girls fear me. You should fear me as well, Judas, for I will haunt you to your death. Even if you escape punishment for the Temple attack and are able to pin the blame on Jesus, I will know your guilt. I will spread the tale of your betrayal across the whole world. It would be better for you to kill yourself now than to hear the name 'Judas!' spoken as a curse throughout the ages. My curse is on you, Judas Iscariot, and I will never lift it. The Followers will know, and they will chronicle your perfidy."

I turned on my heel and returned to my place. Shortly thereafter, I saw Judas scramble to his feet and disappear into the darkness.

The fire in the brazier was dimming, and the shadows around our evening meal were growing deeper. Although I had gone unfed in the tomb, my appetite for food was minimal, and I only picked at the plate of white cheese and black olives that had been put in front of me. Something about being dead must have affected my thirst, however, and I drank steadily so that the cup Martha brought to me was refilled many times from the water skins. Reclining there, I thought back to the events that had led me to this juncture and pondered my next move.

Chapter 3: Mary, Martha, and Me

If Mary and Martha had hoped that my resurrection would return to their house the younger brother they had known, I'm afraid I must have disappointed them. I had been a cheerful and energetic person by all accounts, but now I found it hard to generate the impetus to action. Mostly I sat in the shade; my one-word responses to conversational gambits soon caused the well-intentioned attempts to evaporate. The household became a quiet place, where speech was confined to necessary interactions, and inhabitants went about their business as though still in mourning.

As a boy, I viewed it as my responsibility to bring some excitement into our household. But the home that others saw as orderly and serene, I saw as constricting and boring. The composition of our household was very different from that of our neighbors. This difference had profound consequences for the life we lived. My parents and my father's brother Joseph were engaged in an enterprise to mine tin in the faraway mountains of West Britannia. My father and mother spent long periods there, managing and overseeing the extraction and refining of the tin ore and its shipment to Rome and Jerusalem.

This meant that, unlike our neighbors, there was no strong patriarch to rule over the miniature tribe that constitutes a family in Israel. The fact that I, as the only male, was also the youngest child meant that my older sisters dominated our daily household life in ways that were unknown, indeed forbidden, in other homes. The role of high priest that would have been filled by our father was adopted by my Uncle Joseph, who was my father's brother and business partner.

After their boyhood in Arimathea, the two brothers had worked for a time in mining, finding and exploiting the deposits of salt around the Dead Sea. Through this experience they established commercial relationships with the court of the emperor in Rome. They parlayed these contacts into a concession to mine and smelt tin ore in the western mountains of Britannia, where the island country sticks out into the great ocean to the west. From the south coast there, the metal was shipped to Gaul and thence to the larger cities of the Empire, where it was fashioned into swords and spears, armor and dishes.

This link through my absent parents to the wild lands at the fringes of the Empire had filled my young head with visions of barbarian warriors of the frozen north, of savage Picts, attacking in hordes Rome's legions on the border, fighting to the death in highly romanticized circumstances of heroism and martial exploits. Handsome and muscular Roman soldiers stood their ground with spears bristling out like hedgehogs in ten-by-ten ranks under the command of their centurions against the berserk charges of the blue-painted Pict barbarians. My heroes swung their short swords under the blood-soaked legion standards of my daydreams. As a young boy, I repeated those strokes with swords and spears carved from the wood of Israel. These vigorous activities invariably were accompanied by appropriate martial sounds of clashing metal and shouting battlers, as well as the inevitable screams and groans of the wounded and dying.

My childish fantasies contrasted sharply with the realities of Roman legion life that intruded each day into the lives of the Jews of

Israel. These legions were not Rome's finest heroes out to conquer new lands, but were an occupying force whose mission was to subjugate and enforce the control of Rome over the people of Israel.

No heroism is needed for the task of occupation. The required skills are brutishness, a bent to cruelty, and a low regard for the dignity, religion, customs, and lives of the indigenous people. Vitellius commanded four legions, but only the senior officers were Roman, and not even all of those. The common troops were Idumaeans, Samarians, and Syrians, many from Caesarea itself, where they sometimes amused themselves by insulting the local Jews and throwing stones at them. They were so ill-behaved that the previous Governor of Syria, Varus, had disbanded similar units because, according to his proclamation, they "behaved in a most disorderly manner, disobeying my wishes and being intent only on the profits they could make from their misbehavior."

The legionnaires in Jerusalem of my time were cut from the same cloth, and emphatically unromantic. The life of our occupying soldiers consisted of tedious guard duty in the hot sun, interspersed with fits of drunkenness and whoring. The soldiers lived in barracks outside the city and were largely isolated from the population. Most of their contact with the Jewish people came as a result of limited financial transactions, primarily with wine merchants and prostitutes. These engagements were not of a type that inspired respect or trust between the buyer and seller, nor did they undermine the sense of superiority that each side felt over the other. The certainty of each that they were being cheated by the other alienated both, and created a level of resentment and contempt that stayed at a constant low boil.

The intermittent demonstrations of resistance by the Jews to the rules imposed by Rome and enforced by the king and the high priests often caused the steady simmer to bubble up. Conflicts tended to coincide with religious festivals, especially Passover, which brought thousands of Jews from the countryside into Jerusalem. The combination of religious fervor, crowded streets, and separation from the routine of domestic daily life added the salt to the water that could make the kettle more easily boil over. It was at these times of strife that the soldiers, supposedly there to maintain order, could get back at the greedy shopkeepers and grasping whores who represented the bulk of their contact with us, and they fell to with gusto. A few seasons of these types of exchanges created an atmosphere of resentment, mistrust, and underlying fear on both sides.

As I grew older, the identity of my heroes changed, as did that of my villains. The Romans now fulfilled the latter role. The hero's mantle was donned by the Maccabee Jewish fighters against Rome's occupying tyranny. But the loud commotion of battle that filled our house and garden remained pretty much the same.

Older sisters take it upon themselves to act motherly to a younger brother, even when the mother is present. In our mother's long absence, Mary and Martha took to their self-appointed role with relish. They dispensed criticism and correction freely, practicing on me for the day when they might have their own husbands and children. Perhaps it is in their early experiences, playing house with dolls, that women form a picture of their perfect mate, setting a standard that no real husband will ever embody, and laying the groundwork for later bitterness and frustration. Girls play the mother role with dolls when younger brothers are not available, and it is perhaps easier for them to bend to their will an inanimate bundle of straw and cloth than a jumping, shouting, highly mobile, exasperatingly disrespectful male sibling.

Uncle Joseph was scrupulous in looking to our economic well-being and care, but most of his energy was devoted to managing and protecting his relationship with the Romans, the palace, and his own household. As the youngest of his brother's children, it was natural that I would be largely under the control of my older sisters. Martha took on the management of our household as she came of age, directing the activities of the servants, the preparation of meals, and other matters that were of little interest to me. She was very competent, and the house ran smoothly. It's a good thing, too, because Mary had no interest in domestic affairs and the minutiae of cooking, cleaning, and managing servants. Had it been left to her, we would have all wound up starving ragamuffins.

Trapped between a confident and competent sister and a younger brother worthy only of disdain, Mary grew up in a difficult position. With my birth, she lost her role as the family baby and with it the center of attention. I remember once when our house slave was working with Martha, teaching her to sew, and the nurse was busy with me, Mary burst into the room like a desert whirlwind, trailing a red scarf behind her as she ran in circles, laughing uncontrollably until she collapsed into the pile of sitting cushions. She deferred—mostly—to Martha as her older sister. She picked on—mostly—her younger brother Lazarus. And she developed an entire repertoire of tricks (some good, some less so) to draw attention her way. Often she would hide something from me—a toy sword, a shoe, a bite of dinner—and then ask me where it went, taunting me and driving me into an angry fit of shouting and ineffectual threats. That drew attention, too, but far fewer laughs.

In contrast, Martha was always correct in her behavior and clothing. She never went out alone, and she was never seen without her head modestly covered. Mary often paraded around with her head uncovered, and with her long red hair streaming down her back. She called it her "bad boy" routine. It was always good for attention, though not of a positive sort. When she was a little girl, such behavior could be overlooked, especially in the absence of our parents. As she transformed into a young woman whose growing beauty was becoming apparent even to a little brother, the men of Bethany were increasingly lectured by their women about the young slut who tempted their eyes.

But Mary was no slut. The rebellious and outrageous were only two manifestations of her complicated personality. She could be contemplative and thoughtful, caring for the feelings and needs of others. Her intelligence was superior. It led her to question things that were regarded by the Jewish society of Jerusalem as beyond question. The blind acceptance of the Law as prescribed by the Pharisees and the Temple priests was not for Mary. The frequency of her questions was poorly matched by satisfactory answers, but generally exceeded by the frustration and annoyance of those whom she interrogated.

As Mary got older, the sophistication and difficulty of her questions grew accordingly, and it was only a matter of time before she developed a reputation as "difficult." Unable to provide satisfactory answers, the Pharisees and priests used their position of authority to halt the questions. Mary's position as the daughter of a wealthy merchant and supplier of tin to the Roman legions prevented them from bringing the formal charges that could have resulted in her being stoned to death as a heretic. Instead, the priests used her refusal to cover herself in public and her questioning ways to spread the story that she was possessed by devils. Since she could not therefore be responsible for her actions, neither could they be held responsible to attempt to answer her questions. As Mary's questions became more difficult, the answers became more inadequate. The lack of satisfactory answers undermined the authority and position of the priests, who found it therefore necessary to dismiss the questions as the provocations of demons speaking through Mary's mouth.

As she became more mature and thoughtful, Mary's relationship with me changed. Or maybe it was I that grew more mature and thoughtful. In any case, we grew quite close. Mary's questions got her into trouble in ways that only my intervention as the responsible male in her life could alleviate. But for me, her deep spirituality combined with her questioning habits brought me to a sense of respect and protectiveness that bound us ever more tightly together as we grew up.

It eventually came to pass that Mary stepped over the line with the Pharisees once too often. The threat of formal charges followed by a death sentence loomed. Uncle Joseph and I agreed that she had to be sent away until things cooled down so she would not bring harm on herself or the household by her rebelliousness. At first, she went to Uncle Joseph's house in Arimathea. Joseph could not keep the kind of close watch on her that was needed to avoid stirring up the locals of that area, especially since Mary's reputation preceded her and the village was hyper-watchful for real or imagined transgressions the instant Mary arrived.

One person who was not wary of Mary was an older woman named Miriam who lived near Uncle Joseph's house. She and Mary became fast friends, and Mary spent a good deal of time with her. Miriam came from a wealthy family which had arranged for her marriage to a rabbi in Arimathea. By all accounts, this rabbi was no man of god. Avaricious and grasping, he bent his efforts to extract the maximum amount of wealth from his flock.

His father-in-law, seeing the nature of the man who had married his daughter, put the most barriers possible in the way of the rabbi's getting his hands on Miriam's wealth, but that effort could not extend beyond the grave. When her father died, he had no siblings or male children to inherit, so all his wealth went to Miriam. Of course, that meant it went to her husband.

The now-wealthy rabbi's eyes began to wander, and it did not take long for them to alight on my sister Mary, who was often present in his house. With her wanton reputation, it is not hard to imagine that he thought her an easy conquest. As she told me the story, the rabbi approached her one day and offered her money to lie down with him, fully expecting that this whore would jump at the chance.

Mary responded in the worst way possible—she laughed at him. In his anger and hurt pride, he accused her of being possessed by devils and threatened to denounce her to the village elders. The rabbi was, of course, one of the elders himself, so he was sure of a conviction and a sentence of death by stoning.

Mary turned the tables on him. She threatened to accuse him of adultery, and informed Miriam of the events that had transpired. Miriam confronted her husband, who was now in a tenuous position, for such an accusation, if proven, carried in its turn a sentence of death by stoning.

To protect himself, the rabbi pre-emptively accused Miriam of adultery. And not just adultery, for the accusation was one of committing unnatural acts with another woman—namely, Mary. By doing so, he could be rid of her, take full control over her wealth, and revenge himself on Mary. He invented a liaison between Miriam and Mary, and brought his charges before the elders of Arimathea.

Hearing of these events, I hurried to Arimathea. The elders duly formed a tribunal, and on the appointed day the called for testimony. The rabbi stood before them as the accuser and aggrieved husband and spun his tales. I suppose he must have assumed his status in the community should make the simple accusation sufficient for a finding of guilt. But when I rose as Mary's brother and began to question him on the details, his confidence faltered. When I asked him about the date of his discovery of the two women, he clearly made one up on the spot, and this proved his undoing.

Miriam had been seen in the village of Arimathea on that day, while Mary had been seen with me, attending the preaching of one of the many wandering rabbis. Caught in the lie, the husband tried to bluster his way through by declaiming that the date did not matter, and that the truth of the accusation was dependent not on evidence but on his stature as a rabbi who was entitled by his position to a presumption of truthfulness.

While the evidence for Mary's whereabouts was sufficient for her exoneration, the village elders accepted the bluster of the rabbi and found Miriam guilty of the accusation against her. Accordingly, they sentenced her to death by stoning, and she was dragged to the execution place outside the village. There she was stripped and thrown into a shallow pit. Her executioners stood around its rim, looking down at her. A few picked up stones, urged on by the prisoner's husband.

Mary suddenly stepped to the edge of the pit and picked up a stone. Holding it out, she offered it around, saying, "Here, take this stone and be the first to cast it at this innocent woman. Who among you is so certain of her guilt, so pure in your own heart, that you can cast the stone with a clear conscience? Come! You have found her guilty under the law! Can you not bring yourself to cast the first stone?"

One by one, the villagers dropped their stones and quietly turned away. The rabbi was nearly apoplectic as the last of the executioners disappeared into their homes, leaving him standing alone. Mary stepped down into the pit and covered Miriam with her cloak, whispering softly words that I could not hear. The three of us walked back to the house of Uncle Joseph. Miriam filed for divorce against the venal rabbi and was able to separate with her inheritance intact.

After these events, it was impossible for Mary to stay in Arimathea. She had publicly shamed the elders of the village, shattered the reputation of one of its leading citizens, and demonstrated a strength of will and justice that was unthinkable for a young woman.

So, in her fifteenth year, we sent her up to stay with friends in Magdala in Galilee. There she was joined by Miriam. Somehow during her stay there she matured to a point where she understood the danger she was bringing on herself and her family. She never lost her rebelliousness or her passion for the defense of the poor and outcast, but she learned a bit of discretion and polity. It was in Magdala that she picked up the sobriquet that followed her throughout her life: the Magdalene.

Galilee also transformed her in another way. Bethany was a place embedded within the flesh of Roman and Greek influences. King Herod Antipas was the son of the self-styled King Herod "the Great," and, like his father, a Jew by birth. As one of the sons of the elder King Herod, upon the old man's death Herod Antipas was given rule over the northern portion of his father's kingdom. To his frustration, the Roman emperor gave him the lesser title of "Tetrarch," and he was not allowed by the Romans to claim the title of "King." He sought constantly to attain the more exalted title by slavish adherence to Roman wishes, both real and imagined.

Herod Antipas was scrupulous in observing the more visible and public elements of Jewish law, but his ambitions for his office required that he make every effort to maintain good relations with Rome. His constant interactions with his Roman masters made it important that he appear sophisticated and at ease with them. Clothing, hair, language, and music of the court conformed to the latest fashions of Rome, and there were frequent trips to ensure that styles did not become dated. Ambassadors and visitors of all stripes were grilled intensely on such matters. Travelers were summoned to the palace and questioned not only on the purpose of their mission, but on their clothing and customs, as though they were arbiters of fashion. The conduct of court affairs was also according to Roman and Greek style, as were the structure of the buildings and living arrangements.

I heard a story that one winter during the reign of old King Herod, three Nabataean travelers came out of the desert beyond the Jordan River to Judea to bring gifts of tribute on the occasion of the birth of a child that was somehow significant to them. No one telling the story seemed quite sure how the travelers knew about this birth, nor why they found it important. In any event, they came—but they were unsure how to find the child. They asked around, being certain the child's birth was so significant that it would have somehow been marked. Eventually, word came to the palace of old King Herod, who had them summoned.

And here is the point of my anecdote—Herod was not the type of ruler who liked having strange potentates from other nations wandering around his kingdom, so he questioned them closely about their purpose in Israel. But they were interrogated not only about their mission, but also about their clothing, the nature of their gifts, and their customs and fashions of clothing and court behavior, all to keep Herod's court current on styles and fashions of other countries. That focus brought sullen contempt and resentment from the Jews of Israel, who felt that a Jewish king should be more focused on the defense of the Jewish people and the Jewish religion than on foreign fashions.

The resentment against the king waxed under the rule of his son Herod Antipas as a result of the frequent frictions created with the Jewish people by the young ruler's actions. Take, for example, the Tetrarch's disastrous marriages—disastrous not for him, of course, but for the Israelites that he ruled. He was long married to the Arab princess Phasaelis, a daughter of King Aretas IV of Petra, whose kingdom was strategically located on the east-west caravan route just beyond the Dead Sea. This was an important diplomatic relationship, as Petra sat astride a critical trade route from the east. Nevertheless, during a visit to Rome, Herod Antipas met one of his brother's wives, who was also his brother's daughter, named Herodias, and became bewitched by her beauty. His brother agreed to divorce Herodias so that Herod Antipas could marry her, but Herodias first made Herod agree to divorce his current wife, Phasaelis.

In the house of Herod, such divorces typically came about as a result of a mysterious fatality, but Phasaelis got wind of the plan to replace her and escaped across the Jordan River to the city of Machaerus, by the Dead Sea, to join her father. From there they moved to the safety of the king's fief in Petra. King Aretas was infuriated and scandalized, for not only was Herodias the ex-wife of Herod Antipas' half-brother; she was also Herod's own niece, making the marriage incestuous.

King Aretas' fury was fed further by disputes over territorial boundaries. In the ensuing war, Herod Antipas' army was completely destroyed—some said through divine punishment, others cited the treachery of Antipas' key soldiers, who went over to the enemy. It was only when Antipas appealed to Rome that legions were sent down from Syria and defeated Aretas.

From all this lust, jealousy, and conspiracy came a more personal disaster that indirectly touched us through our later relationship with Jesus. Jesus had a cousin named John, called the Baptist. Among other things, John preached publicly against Herod Antipas, citing his marriage to Herodias as a sign of his immorality and corruption. Stung by this criticism, especially in light of his military defeats, Antipas had John arrested and brought for trial to Machaerus. John was beheaded at the urging of Salome, who was Herodias' daughter by Herod's brother. So Antipas' wife and stepdaughter were also his nieces. You can imagine how well *that* went over with the stern interpreters of Jewish law.

Herod Antipas' alienation from the Jewish population increased even further when he decided to found his new capital city in the north, to replace Jerusalem. He called the new city Tiberias, intending by this flattery to curry favor with the Roman emperor, Tiberius. Evidently he hoped this might convince the emperor to promote him from Tetrarch of Galilee and Peraea and grant him the title of King, like his father. Unfortunately for Antipas' ambitions, it was quickly discovered that he was building this city on top of an old Jewish graveyard. As a result, no pious Jew would enter Tiberias, which consequently was populated solely by Greeks and Romans. So even though Antipas celebrated Passover and Sukkoth in Jerusalem, his Jewishness not only failed to endear him to his subjects, but made them even more critical, since they expected a far higher standard of behavior than he evidenced.

Despite the antipathy of the common people, the style of the court set the tone for the rest of the population. Antipas frequently visited Rome to maintain his political links and test the winds to see which way they were blowing. These visits became more frequent as the fractious Jewish people came to be viewed by the emperor as increasingly difficult. But the visits also brought to Jerusalem and Judea the latest styles, recipes, jokes, fads, and gossip that stimulated imitation and spread through the population.

That was the world and times in which we grew up. Herod Antipas focused on maintaining relations with Rome and on his own aggrandizement. The Temple priests and rituals were tools for keeping the Jewish people in line to smooth Antipas' relations with Rome. The population's resentment and occasional resistance kept the atmosphere in Judea at a low boil.

All this provided a stark contrast for Mary when she was sent to Magdala. Coming from the urbane and sophisticated surroundings of Jerusalem, Mary found the bucolic atmosphere of Galilee a dramatic change. In these northern hills and along the shores of the Sea of Galilee, there was virtually no contact with the Hellenistic influences that suffused the atmosphere of Judea. The people of this country practiced their religion and led their lives in ways that would have looked very familiar to the Jews who had accompanied Moses to this Promised Land many hundreds of years before. Their ways had not been tainted by generations of outside contacts with traders and soldiers, and the ways of travelers and traders, soldiers and sailors traversed neither their lands nor their minds.

Mary was exposed to this simplicity and purity during her time in Magdala, and it touched her deeply. She found a version of Judaism that differed markedly from that practiced around the Temple. Along the shores of the Sea of Galilee, she found a set of beliefs and practices that made sense and came naturally to a people who were herders, fishermen, and farmers. The tribes of Israel had followed their flocks in the desert, heard the word of God in the wind and the bushes. Their last sight before closing their eyes in sleep or death was the vast heaven full of stars. Theirs was a god who did not need legions of priests to develop and explain intricate rituals needed to satisfy His desires. This god did not strike bargains and grant favors that could be bought and sold; He could not be made to dance to the rattle of shekels. Theirs was not a god who resided in isolation like the king or the emperor in an elaborate and expensive building, but one who was beside them in every moment of every day, and who spoke personally and directly to His people.

While in Galilee, Mary became increasingly convinced that the hordes of priests, with their demands for ever-greater payments and their intricate rules derived from obscure logic and obscure texts, stood in the way of achieving that personal covenant. This conviction led her to question the sources, the validity, and the motivations of the Temple priests. Mary's questioning of the priests in Jerusalem and Bethany was not motivated by any desire to embarrass or undermine them, although she delighted in pricking the bubbles of the pompous and the self-righteous, and she had plenty of targets in Jerusalem. Her pressing came rather from a desire to understand the personal relationship with God that is the essence of being a Jew.

With her return to Bethany, Mary's frustration turned to anger at the duplicity and hypocrisy, until she came eventually to an actual loathing for the institution of the Temple and its priests. She recognized it as a machine designed and maintained for the purpose of extracting money by exploiting the faith of worshippers and pilgrims. The machine cranked in piety and churned out wealth and comfort for the priests. Mary's loathing for this exploitation was not a rejection of her faith, but an outcome of it.

"The priests cannot tell us God's will," she explained. "Instead, they demand that we perform sacrifices at the Temple for which we must pay them. All that noise and smoke and bustle only interferes with God's messages. We must look within our hearts in a quiet place to hear the word of God." Rejecting and rejected by the pious institutional orthodoxy of Jerusalem, Mary searched elsewhere for spiritual revelation.

Perhaps it was the absence of our parents that influenced her to her search for meaning and belonging. She and I spoke about this once in one of our more sibling moments, and I remember vividly her words. She said she wanted to understand her purpose. "Each of us is here to do God's work. The hard part is discovering what that work is." That is our responsibility as Jews, she said—the effort of discovery.

Chapter 4: Judas Iscariot, Right-Hand Man

Mary's search for spiritual meaning after her return to Bethany from Magdala attracted her to many of the preachers and rabbis who wandered Judea in increasing numbers. She was constantly hearing about this or that preacher. Claims by believers were extravagant, and each was presented as a miracle worker and the Messiah. In their desperation, Israelites sought a hero sent by God who would free them from the shackles of Rome. For most of us, this meant relief from the enormous tax burden. On top of the levies from the growing number of priests and high priests came the continuing debt that remained from the reign of old King Herod, who began the rebuilding of the current Temple to replace the Temple of Solomon.

The extravagant building process had gone on for years and showed no sign of coming to an end. On top of those taxes, Herod Antipas' construction of the city of Tiberias, not to mention his profligate court expenses and the taxes demanded by Rome, added a crushing burden so that more and more people were being forced off their lands due to unpaid taxes. There was a desperate army of the displaced wandering the land seeking some form of livelihood and sustenance. People became bandits by night and beggars by day. The beggars adopted ever more horribly disfiguring diseases in order to arouse sympathy and evoke contributions.

A new disease emerged that had not existed in my childhood. The resulting epidemic of beggars displaying rotting limbs and missing parts, often enhanced by stained bandages and crutches, became a public nuisance, and all decent people strove to avoid them, though usually in vain. Finally, to impose some order, the priests required that these beggars identify themselves by ringing a bell as they moved through inhabited places, so as to warn shoppers and pedestrians that one of them was at hand. Those "lepers," as they came to be known, who were discovered not complying with the rules, were forced out of the towns and congregated in little colonies, evolving quickly into banditry for survival.

Those not genuinely ill became adept at displaying exaggerated wounds, disfigurements, and suppurating sores, and those lacking the courage or physical skills to be successful bandits often turned to preaching. Mary dragged me along to hear many of these self-proclaimed messiahs who promised to bring the wrath of God down on the Romans and the oppressors of Israel. It usually took only a few moments to conclude that the preacher of the day was interested solely in the alms he could collect from his listeners. I quickly became adept at identifying the categories. Some appealed to fear and the punishment of an angry God who would revisit the punishments wreaked on the Pharaoh of Egypt. Others evoked the stories of Lot and Noah, appealing to the desire of the gullible to be counted among the righteous who would be saved from the coming destruction of the earth by God.

Many posed a basically secular argument, claiming to have been chosen to lead Israel in an uprising against Rome and its impure lackeys in Jerusalem, and to throw off the shackles of the Romanized Temple and the taxes that supported it. This category attracted much support, but rarely were the preachers of sufficient significance to draw any official attention and response. To be sure, once in a while someone would attract enough of a following to warrant arrest and a quick crucifixion for sedition, but mostly they were left alone and tolerated as a necessary evil to defuse people's emotions. In some ways the Romans could be very tolerant; as long as the taxes were paid, the people of Israel could say pretty much what they liked. It was the responsibility of Herod Antipas, not Rome, to keep the land peaceful and the taxes flowing.

The first time we heard him speak, it was evident that Jesus of Nazareth was different. First of all, he was not a beggar. Indeed, those who came to hear him preach were not asked to provide alms, but on the contrary were given food. This attracted large audiences of the displaced, often still wearing the rags and carrying the crutches of their begging costumes. And word spread rapidly through the countryside, so when Jesus of Nazareth was in the area to preach, the crowds swelled dramatically.

Jesus also differed from his preaching competitors in that he was careful not to preach against Rome and Jerusalem, and this kept him out of trouble with the authorities. Instead, his message encouraged people to help the poor and sick by sharing their wealth and possessions—not very different from his mendicant competitors, but since he was not demanding for himself, far more credible.

Most important, Jesus did not claim to be appointed by God. It was others who called him the Messiah, although he never actively contradicted them. He was just a man from Galilee, moved by the suffering he saw around him. He was a very simple man in many ways, lacking the sophistication and learned veneer of the Pharisees and those steeped in the atmosphere of Jerusalem and the Temple. But that country simplicity and directness of speech concealed clarity of vision and a sensitivity to nuance that often helped him avoid pitfalls and danger.

The race between ever-increasing crowds and the supply of food eventually and inevitably brought a crisis. I was there when it happened, and I can tell you, it was a dangerous moment. For Mary, Martha, and me, it was our first direct exposure to this rabbi, although Mary had heard of him while she was in Magdala, for Nazareth was not so far away on the other side of Mount Tabor.

It was clear to us that Jesus of Nazareth was not the usual mendicant, tax rebel, or liberationist. When we went to hear him, he had recently come down to Judea from Galilee. He preached that day from the top of a small rise on the outskirts of Jerusalem. A substantial crowd had come out from the city and the surrounding towns to hear him speak. Many were there for the free food that rumor had it would be provided. Some had come with inquiring minds, wanting to examine this rabbi of whom their friends had spoken. Many were simply unemployed idlers, having neither field to tend nor employment to occupy their time.

At first I resisted being dragged by my sisters to this event, seeing it as yet another tedious demand that would waste my time listening to some incoherent message of self-serving hypocrisy. Mary and Martha insisted, however. As two single women, without the company of a male relative they would have been unable to attend. They persuaded me to accompany them, assuring me of their unlimited gratitude and love as well as allowing me thereby to avoid the potential risk of a significantly reduced, delayed, or unsavory food supply.

In the event, I was glad I went along. All of us were drawn to the magnetism and appeal of this Galilean man from Nazareth. Jesus' message was electrifyingly simple: the poor, the sick, and the homeless were the blessed of the earth, and those of us who helped them would also be blessed. This was the obligation of each of us. Mary was captivated instantly. I could see it in her eyes. This was a message that resonated in her soul. Dramatically radical in its simplicity, Jesus' message was clearly aligned with Mary's innate spirit of generosity and her rebelliousness against the life of privilege in which she had matured. No special rituals, no expensive sacrifices, no intervening layers of priests and acolytes . . . Jesus' lesson was that each of us should treat people as God would treat them, and that we each knew in our soul how that would be. The spark of divinity in each of us meant that we each had a personal responsibility, and that the commitment to fulfilling that responsibility was the essence of our personal covenant with God. This was a message and a messenger that moved her in a way I had not seen from the ragbag variety of self-proclaimed prophets, revolutionaries, and hucksters to whose speeches I had been tiresomely dragged again and again.

When Jesus fell silent, there was a long pause as the crowd emerged from its reverie. Gradually we all returned to the present. Mary turned to us with sparkling eyes, brushing aside the strands of red hair that had escaped from under her head covering. "We must speak with him, come on!" Martha and I followed as she pushed through the crowd to reach the top of the small mount from which the sermon had been preached. As we approached, we saw that Jesus was surrounded by a small group of men in animated conversation, hands and bodies twisting, fingers raised and pointed as they leaned in to make their emphatic points. They were mostly dressed in the rough garb of working men from Galilee, but we could hear one who by his accent was clearly a local man from Judea.

"Rabbi, we have a problem. This is a larger crowd than I had anticipated. We never got crowds like this in Galilee. These people are hungry, and we do not have nearly enough to feed them." A man with broad shoulders standing next to him nodded as though confirming the report. "It's true," he said, "and there are troublemakers here. Judas is right. We need to get out of here, Jesus. I cannot protect you from a mob."

Judas nodded vigorously. "Simon Peter is right, Lord. We must leave immediately, before things turn ugly." One of the others interjected, "Either that, or we must get our hands on more food, and quickly."

Jesus responded in exasperated tones, "Where will we get more food? Do you think that I am some kind of miracle worker, Judas? I depend on you to handle these kinds of matters. If there is not enough food, then we cannot feed them, it is as simple as that." He turned to Simon Peter and said, "And you must live up to your nickname for all our sakes. You are Peter the Rock. It is on you that we all depend for our safety and protection."

Simon Peter struck a resolute pose that was sufficiently imposing that I decided I would not like to have those thick arms swinging a club at my head. He cast a look at the crowd, searching for the beginnings of trouble. "I will do my best, Lord," he said, "but there are many of them. It would be better for us to leave."

Judas was still stinging from Jesus' rebuke, and his lower lip began to protrude. His voice took on the sing-song quality of a small child making excuses to his mother. "Rabbi Jesus, you ask too much of me. Is it not enough that I find bed and food for the thirteen of us? That I come ahead and spread word so people know you will be speaking at this or that time and place? That I arrange for us to have a place to sleep and a roof over our heads? How do you expect me to feed this crowd with no money? We have had no time to raise the funds to deal with this size of crowd!"

I could see that the less pious members of Jesus' audience were beginning to realize that the food they had expected was not immediately being rolled out, and signs of restlessness moved over the crowd like the rising of wind through the trees. The man called Simon Peter was looking about for an escape route, and his hand crept under his cloak. The sun was well past its peak in the sky, and noticeable shadows were stretching to the west. Whatever breakfast had sustained the crowd to this point was giving way to a stomach-rumbling discontent. I myself was feeling peckish, and I had dined well this morning. For those who had started their day with little, there would be a distinct disappointment at having wasted their time listening to this preacher in expectation of being fed, instead of doing whatever other things might have availed them of their daily bread.

To my horror, Mary suddenly pushed her way into the group. Simon Peter's arm rose to restrain her, but he pulled it back, startled when he saw that he had come close to physically touching a young girl. Ignoring his bulky obstacle, Mary spoke in a low voice to Jesus. "Rabbi, if these people are not fed, there will be trouble. Look, over there some of them are gathering stones. What do you have to give them here?" Jesus looked helplessly about him; it was Judas who responded. "We have some bread and a few fish, but that is only enough for a few dozen people. There are hundreds here."

Thinking quickly, Mary responded, "Begin to distribute what you have. Be very visible. Start with the scattered individuals, and proceed slowly. In the meantime, send people to the shop there in Bethany and get enough for the rest of the crowd. The shopkeepers know me there. Tell them the bill will be paid by the household of Mary of Magdala. Make sure the quality of what you get does not differ from that which you already have. Otherwise you will provoke jealousy among those who think themselves worse provisioned. Go quickly!" Judas looked at Jesus, who just shrugged. His concerns did not include the logistics of food, and concepts of crowd control were far from his attention.

With a quick gesture to several of the others to accompany him, Judas scurried off as directed. But the look he shot over his shoulder at us, and at Mary in particular, gave no indication that he was pleased with her assistance or with his sudden new role as messenger and errand boy.

It was quickly apparent to the entire crowd that the followers of Jesus did not have enough food. The scanty provisions were evident in the small baskets they carried as they fanned out across the hillside.

What the crowd did not see was Judas and his helpers out of sight in the lee of the hill, coming from Bethany laden with bread and dried fish, replenishing the baskets as they were emptied. The supply of food seemed endless. Eventually, the entire crowd had been fed and the people lay back on the hillside, the sun on their faces, content with the warm day and their full stomachs.

Sitting on our blanket in the crowd, eating like the rest, Mary turned to me and Martha and said, loud enough for her voice to carry to others sitting nearby, "How is it that Jesus can turn a few loaves of bread and some fish into enough to feed a multitude like this?" She dropped her voice histrionically, so that those nearby strained to hear.

The evening after the "miracle" of the loaves and fishes, at Mary's insistent invitation, Jesus and his twelve followers accompanied us to our home in Bethany, where they could be fed and find shelter for the next few nights. Martha directed the servants to prepare the evening meal, and we sat outdoors in the darkening courtyard, our ears filled with the shrill twittering of thousands of invisible birds settling into the olive trees for the night. We ate Roman style, reclining on low couches with raised arms at either end for support. A low table made of polished olive wood sat in front of us, and the servants put out the dishes of food, prepared under Martha's watchful eye and demanding rule.

I looked around at our guests. At first glance, they mostly appeared to be a commonplace group of men. One or two stood out, but the rest were just people, ordinary in their appearance and behavior. It was only as one got to know them that their individual characteristics made them in any way memorable.

At the superficial physical level, it was Simon Peter who first drew the eye. Peter had the body of a laborer, a working man's body. He was tall, with thick forearms, and his shoulders stretched from one horizon of his cloak to the other. I later learned that his strong physique was a result of long hours as a fisherman on the Sea of Galilee, pulling the rough oars daily to row out his heavy boat, swinging the heavy paddle in a long arc over his head to slap the water, driving the fish toward his nets, then hauling them in, water-logged and often fish-laden. His skin was dark and leathery from his outdoor life in the hot sun. In contrast to his skin, his lips were pale and thick like those of a Greek statue, and his oyster-colored eyes protruded somewhat from their sockets, giving him the appearance of one of his netted fish that had lain a bit too long in the basket in the market. His forehead sloped slightly back and gave the impression of a prodigious depth of bone, and his jaw was large and rounded. His body was geometric—a tower of stacked rectangles. A smaller rectangle represented his head, decorated with a fringe of sun-bleached reddish hair that surrounded his freckled scalp. It sat solidly atop the larger rectangle of his body, with very little neck to intervene.

Simon Peter was basically friendly and trusting, admired by his companions and looked up to for his strength. His stature, combined with his unquestioning loyalty to Jesus, was the basis for the role he played among the twelve. He provided the muscle, protecting Jesus and all of them from the many bandits who infested the roads of Judea and Galilee. Although the Romans strictly forbade it, and he could have been crucified had it been discovered, Peter habitually carried a short sword which he concealed under his cloak or carried wrapped in a cloth.

While Peter had many virtues, overpowering intelligence was not among them. Part of his charm was that though he was not very smart, he knew it. For thinking power, he relied on others. He trusted others easily, because he projected his own instinctive honesty and loyalty onto his friends and was unwilling to believe they might have other motives.

Like any close-knit group of men working together over a long period of time, the followers of Jesus had developed nicknames for each other. I learned later that Peter's companions had come to call him by the Greek name of Peter, ostensibly to denote the rock-like character of his loyalty and the strength of his body. But outside his hearing, they also jokingly intended the nickname of "rock" to refer to his intelligence, for while the Creator had exaggerated Peter's physical gifts, his intellect was akin to a slab of marble.

At the place next to mine, Judas sat upright, perched at the edge of his couch, leaning forward with his elbows on his knees. He ate quickly, like a bird, the abrupt movements of his hands systematically shifting the olives and bits of meat into his mouth, tearing the soft, flat bread into strips to sop up the yogurt-flavored sauce. Occasionally, he would brush back a lock of hair that fell into his face as he leaned over his dish. His speech singled him out from the others. Unlike them, whose accents revealed origins in Capernaum and Bethsaida on the northern shore of the Sea of Galilee, Judas came from Judea, and his vocabulary carried none of the rough language of fishermen and farmers.

The contrast between Judas and Simon Peter could not have been starker. Where Peter was defined by his physical strength and modest intellect, Judas was just the reverse. His stature was in the normal range, and he only appeared small when standing next to Peter. But it was readily apparent to anyone watching the dynamics of the group for more than a few moments that it was Judas who was in charge. He was always the center of bustling activity, his dark eyes tasting his surroundings like an adder's tongue—assessing, measuring for advantage or threat. His fingers constantly raked though his hair to push it from his face, or stroked his beard distractedly while directing others in the many tasks required to fulfill the needs of such an itinerant group.

It was Judas who directed the movements of the band following Jesus. He organized and dispatched the others to seek food; it fell to him to find lodging for them all in advance of arriving in a town; it was Judas who spread the word that the rabbi would be preaching at some particular time and place. The myriad of organizational details that were necessary to support Jesus and his followers were overseen by Judas with meticulous attention.

Often Judas would send for one or the other of the disciples and, after some private discussion, dispatch him on a mission to investigate their next destination or make arrangements for lodging at an inn or with some friendly contributor. And it was Judas who organized them into the small work groups that were sent out separately to beg for the food and clothing that sustained them and those who came to hear Jesus speak. Without his tireless efforts, this group—essentially homeless, without income except what was donated, and pursuing a mission that drew the attention of both the interested and the suspicious—would have starved, been robbed and murdered, or been arrested long since.

For Judas also kept a wary eye on the authorities, both Roman and Jewish, who in their turn kept a wary eye on mendicant groups like Jesus and his followers. It was a delicate balance between, on the one hand, making Jesus' presence known to the populace and spreading his word among the Jews of Israel, and on the other hand fending off any official concerns that Jesus might be spreading a message of sedition and rebellion against the king, the Temple authorities, or the Romans.

In Judas these organizational skills and energy were combined with another trait that made it all work. He was charming. He always had a ready smile, and an observer would notice that he created a physical bond when speaking with others by putting a hand on their sleeve or an arm around their shoulders. He stood close when he spoke, so that his face filled the view and crowded out distracting surroundings, creating a sense of personal intimacy and trust, bridging the physical gap. The listener, in turn, felt that he was the sole object of flattering attention, and being given access to some secret knowledge. Judas had a way of inspiring trust and dependence by his manner, and it was this key ingredient that made it possible for Jesus to effectively spread his message, and for his followers to stay fed and out of prison.

Judas regarded himself as the essential element that made this little band of men around Jesus work, and, indeed, he was not wrong. But, like many smart men, the charm and energy that made him initially successful became a source of pride. He felt there was no challenge he could not overcome, no person he could not charm into alignment with his wishes. The little scene we had witnessed at what came to be called the Sermon on the Mount, where Jesus had reprimanded him mildly in front of others, and where in Judas's own eyes he had failed, only to be bailed out by this strange young woman, rankled. A proud man, he felt humiliated, and the humiliation had happened in public. Worst of all, he had been bested by a woman—and in Jewish society, a woman was automatically denoted an inferior, regardless of her wealth, beauty, or intelligence. Judas Iscariot would not forget this blow to his ego.

Size and motion were what first drew the eye to these two—Peter and Judas. It was only after the eye tired of the superficial that the natural focus shifted to Rabbi Jesus of Nazareth. Around Jesus was a deep pool of silence and a near-darkness that seemed to absorb the light. Once one's gaze lighted on Jesus, focus seemed to sharpen and narrow, and the surrounding activities and sounds faded into the deep background. The only similar feeling I have experienced is that of seeing a beautiful girl, whose eyes, lips, hair, and smile hold the eye until she looks up and catches you staring. You quickly look away in embarrassment, but then look back again to see if she is still looking.

Stare as I might, I could never look at him enough, though it was not his physical beauty that held the eye. Rather it was the sense that there was more to see, that his physical self almost shimmered, but only when one looked a bit away from him. Sometimes the shimmering quality would almost solidify, when he laughed or when he made a move that was extraordinary in its normality, like rising clumsily from a seat or burping after a drink. He was not particularly muscular, though his forearms were sinewy and the knots of his shoulder muscles stood out, well-developed from his youthful years sliding a saw through hard wood or planing out boards in his father's carpentry shop.

It was when Jesus was challenged that the strength of his spirit and mind became most evident. He was pretty adept at dealing with the many attempts at entrapment that came at him from the Temple authorities. He was often approached in public by Pharisees and engaged in debate—transparent attempts to trap him into advocating positions that were either treasonous or heretical. But Jesus used a wonderful technique to avoid the snares. His favorite tactic was to launch into a story so lengthy that by the time he was finished, the original point of the question had been forgotten. Often the parable was clearly intended to convey a lesson—but it was hard to discern what that lesson might be, so the interrogator needed time to mull it over and decide whether it was seditious or heretical. So Jesus protected himself with a cloak of ambiguity.

I introduced myself to the man leaning on one elbow on the divan next to mine. He told me his name was James, and, smiling, said Jesus was his brother. At first I misunderstood, thinking he meant this figuratively, as someone who shared a common set of beliefs, but he assured me that Joseph and Mary were the common parents of them both, as well as two other brothers and a pair of sisters. I thought nothing about this revelation, as it sounded perfectly natural to my ears, and simply asked, "Well, then, what can you tell me about your brother? What kind of man is he?"

This is the story James recounted to me.

Chapter 5: Joseph was a Carpenter

"As you well know," James began, "the evil of King Herod was great. He served the Romans faithfully, and they in return allowed him full reign to tax the children of Israel into poverty and death. The Romans feared a recurrence of the traumatic decades of rebellions and wars in the Asian provinces. Mithridates, the King of Pontus, had slaughtered without warning eighty thousand Romans and driven Rome out of Anatolia and Asia Minor only twenty years before Herod became king. It took Rome twenty years of war to reestablish control. To ensure no recurrences of rebellions at this scale, the Romans bought Herod's loyalty by giving a free hand to his cruelty and rapaciousness.

"But God was not blind to the suffering that this monster visited on the Chosen People, and, in His wrath, He struck the fat king with a richly deserved horrible death. Perhaps from overuse, his testicles died and turned black. The dying skin of the King sloughed off like a snake shedding its scales, and the intense pain was only alleviated when he became unconscious. His already corpulent body swelled with gas, and the disease quickly spread the terrible pain from his testicles throughout the rest of his body. The gas bubbles in his body would burst with a smell so strong that none could approach him or even enter the room. The physicians had to wrap their noses and mouths with cloths dipped in the strongest perfume before they could approach, and, even so, they had to quickly go out and vomit after only a few moments. I would not wish such a death on my worst enemy, but God's punishment was proportionate to the evil Herod had visited on the Jewish people. The full moon darkened while he was dying, and only when he was actually dead did the light return to the night sky.

"After the death of Herod, his kingdom of Judea was divided among his children. Galilee and the north was part of the territory granted to Herod Antipas. With no capital city of his own, Antipas decided to build his capital at Sapphoris, to be called Tiberias, for he was a toady and a suck-up, forever trying to win favor with the emperor. Ironically, it was the ambition of Herod Antipas that enabled our family to prosper.

"Our father was named Joseph. He was well known throughout Galilee as a carpenter. Our family was quite comfortably off, for Joseph had plenty of work building the new capital city. We benefited from the building of Sapphoris, as did many other artisans and laborers who were hired for the construction and finishing work. Indeed, the city provided a lifetime of work for Joseph, and hence sustained our family until our father's death last year. But to pay for this construction, Herod Antipas levied heavy taxes on the farmers and villagers of Galilee, creating enormous hardships.

"On top of Antipas' levies, the people of Galilee were obliged to continue paying taxes to the priests in Jerusalem to support the Temple, including its large group of high priests and their retinues. And even though a portion of the taxes paid to the civil government in Judea was shifted over to Antipas in Galilee, the burden was increased in order to build the new capital. Not only that, but Antipas insisted on the need to build a system of forts and other cities across his holdings. And, of course, tax payments to Rome continued and increased as Rome extracted the wealth needed to support its adventures elsewhere.

"As a result of these levies, constant hardship was imposed on the people of Galilee. The people rose up often in protest against the burden of multiple taxes, but instead of providing relief, such revolts were quickly and viciously punished. The Romans had only recently finished fighting their twenty-five year war against Mithridates, their greatest foe since Hannibal of Carthage ravaged Italy, so they were not inclined to tolerate even the slightest sign of rebellion.

"So that is the world in which Jesus and I grew up. Our family, living a sheltered life in the small village of Nazareth, saw little of the suffering the people in the countryside experienced. That changed one day when our family went out from our home in Nazareth to travel to the nearby village of Cana, to the wedding of a family friend."

As James recounted his experience at the wedding, it came to life in my head. Jewish weddings are raucous affairs, incorporating rituals that reflect our nomadic roots as shepherds and desert wanderers. Living this nomadic life, the Israelites of old were a people constantly beset by death from hunger, thirst, accident, predation by neighboring tribes, and infant mortality. So weddings are opportunities to not only forget the daily routine, but also to cement family relations and to anticipate a replenishment of the tribal numbers by the potential for new children arising out of the union of the bride and groom.

After the formal marriage ceremony, which is largely a private affair, the celebrations begin in earnest. As James described it, the wedding they attended in Cana was no different. The initial burst of merriment and comment from the assembled guests focused graphically on the sexual capabilities of the groom, with special emphasis on the stamina and equipment he would need to function in the marriage bed with such a lovely and nubile bride. The better bred and more urbane of the group contented themselves with offering toasts to the couple's happiness, the number and health of their potential progeny, and the good fortune of their parents.

Having run the course required by both bad and good manners, and well lubricated with wine and well fed by delicious roast lamb, bread, and roasted vegetables, the conversation eventually turned to other matters. Knots of people gradually grouped themselves in the shady spots according to family, and, in the case of village dwellers, neighborhoods. In the manner of farmers throughout history, the sun-darkened and hard-handed tillers of the land discussed the fine points of raising olives and grain, and the prospects for the coming harvest. Much beard-stroking accompanied intense speculation on the prospects for rain and the level of water in the Jordan River and the Sea of Galilee. There was general agreement that the trend of increasing production that had run for a number of years would continue for another season. Uniformly, the cautious farmers conceded the probability that this year would be one of the most fruitful in recent memory.

As James recounted the events, the conversation evolved naturally to a discussion of prices and markets. Pent-up anger and resentment were fueled by the steady flow of wine provided by the parents of the bride and groom, but bucolic reticence suppressed the flames. That is, until one young guest innocently set the blaze.

"'How is it," the young Jesus asked, "that Galilee is so rich in the production of olives and grain, but at every gathering, the women mutter about their difficulties? My Aunt Elizabeth was telling my mother that no matter how hard they work on their farm, there is barely enough to eat, especially after the tithe is set aside for the priests and a portion is paid for the sacrifices at the Temple's holy feasts."

The explosive reaction was immediate. Clearly, the feelings of anger it expressed were widely shared.

"It is Antipas and his damned taxes to build that city of his. He sends his tax collectors to our mills and olive presses and takes away the best part of our production to pay for his vanity and luxury."

Another chimed in. "And if it weren't enough to build a Galilean capital for the territory he inherited from old King Herod, he tries to outshine the glory of Jerusalem! At least Herod could draw on the wealth and produce of the whole of Israel to raise his nine hundred talents a year. Antipas tries to build Sapphoris with two hundred talents from only a quarter of the territory."

"Yes, and most of what he leaves is taken by Rome. The Emperor Tiberius is a soldier; he knows nothing about farming, and he cares nothing for us. If we have to eat our seeds to stay alive, and cannot replant, he will punish us for not meeting his needs the next season."

"Don't they know that farmers must eat and raise children so the work in the fields can be done? Does he imagine that, even in a land flowing with milk and honey, crops emerge with no tilling, watering, pruning, and weeding? And harvesting?"

"Old King Herod had only one capital city to support. He was a cruel old bastard, but at least he confined his nastiest attacks to his own family. Antipas has been harassing and burning villages in Galilee that protest the confiscations, accusing them of treason."

"He crucifies the head of the village Knesset, jails the village magistrates, and sells the people into slavery."

"Aye, and the ones who escape become bandits and prey on the remaining farmers and on pilgrims and travelers."

"Do you remember how they hunted down King Judas, the son of Hezekiah?" This sounded like a possible adventure story to the younger men there. It might offer a welcome departure from the chorus of complaints that had been going around.

"Yes, but his triumph was short-lived, as was he."

When Jesus and James pressed for details, they were told the well-embellished story of the popular Jewish king Judas, who had cobbled together a large group of brigands and dispossessed men into a small army. When King Herod died, they assaulted the royal palace in Jerusalem. The brigands made off with all the goods that were stored there, while the desperate farmers burned the tax records so they could retain their lands.

"And remember when we threatened to leave our crops unharvested in the fields? The Roman governor Gaius backed down then, didn't he? He was going to put his ugly face on a statue in the Temple. God gave us the strength to come together and resist that sacrilege."

Jesus pursued the point. "Why don't we do that again? If they backed down once, they will again, won't they?"

The storyteller looked pityingly at the naïve young man. "The Romans know that the children of Israel will go to their deaths willingly to preserve the sanctity of our Temple. They would rather have us alive and planting our fields. But they also know that against anything less than blasphemy, we will do what we can to preserve our lives and families, even if it means that we all eventually suffer. So they can divide us into groups, and pit us against one another, keeping us weak.

"And we cannot resist the Roman legions. We have taught them not to trifle with our worship of God, and we have convinced them that we would willingly die. It is to their best interest that we live, for only then can we produce what they need. But we have likewise learned that we cannot long resist the press of taxation, for they will quickly and willingly kill resistors. The Romans know that if they show weakness, and allow tax resistance to succeed in even one place, were that news to spread, it would destroy the Empire from Scythia to Iberia. People would rise up against all taxes. The legions would not be able to stop the rebellions. Remember that they were barely able to defeat Mithridates of Pontus and his son-in-law, King Tigran of Armenia. And that took twenty-five years of war. To prevent that, they now make an example out of the slightest hint of resistance. Nonpayment of taxes and levies is tantamount to rebellion."

There was a pause. The villagers considered what a world without Rome would look like.

One grizzled old farmer said, "Last year, I had to go to the money lenders to borrow to pay the taxes. Now, this year, my repayments have put me further in the hole for next year! I cannot feed five people and replant and pay the offerings to the Temple when they take over a third of my crop for Herod Antipas and for Rome. Next year I will likely lose the land that we have held for so many generations. If I am lucky, I will be able to work as a tenant farmer, but it is more likely that I will have to become a day laborer. When the tax collector takes my bread, he takes my body. He drains my blood when he takes my wine."

His neighbor made an ironic suggestion. "Maybe you would be better off joining a band of brigands. At least that way you will die quickly at the hands of a soldier instead of being worked to death for the benefit of some faraway landlord."

Silence again fell for a time as the group considered the grim prospect of this downward spiral. Finally, in an attempt to lighten the tone somewhat, one farmer, sure that he was among friends, confided that in order to set aside enough for his family, he did his first harvest at night, secreting the best of the fruits of his labor down wells and in hidden caves to keep it from the tax collector. He was not surprised when his listeners expressed no shock, for they all did the same with greater or lesser success. The conversation turned from harvesting and complaining about taxes to stratagems for defeating the tax collectors.

"Did you see how the wedding party served only their poorest food and wine as long as the tax collectors were nosing about? When they finally left, we drew the good wine out of the well, where it had been hidden in water vessels. Remember, Jesus, how your mother made you and James help draw it out." There was general agreement that the new wine had been far superior to the initial servings. "Isn't it a miracle how here in Cana we are able to change water into wine!" James remembered saying with a laugh.

Young Jesus, whose innocent question had set off this seditious spiral, sat in silence, pondering the things he had heard. Joseph was a carpenter, and made a good living creating the cabinets and richly carved tables, chairs, and wooden elements that furnished the cities that were being endlessly built and rebuilt by the new king. The home he kept in the village of Nazareth was comfortable. Jesus had taken all this for granted, had never considered the sources of the payment that Joseph received for his labors.

His story over, James gestured toward Jesus in the glow of the firelight in our courtyard and said to me, "So you see, Lazarus, that day in Cana was a turning point for Jesus. He came to realize at that point that the people of Israel were enslaved by Rome, but he realized also that there could be no successful rebellion. He could see that any attempt to rise up would result in the total destruction of Israel and the Chosen People."

Chapter 6: The Attack on the Temple

In my previous life, just a week before, I had sat around a similar fire and had a similar meal, but with an appetite fresh and hearty as befitted a young rebel against Rome. The group was larger then, comprised of acquaintances of Judas who had been summoned for this meeting. Jesus himself was not there, having returned to Galilee to attend to family matters. Across the circle of diners, a large and fierce-looking ruffian named Bar Abbas maintained a careful focus on the wine skins. For someone his size, he seemed exceptionally vulnerable to the effects of wine, and he was not in the habit of diluting it with water in the Roman way. As the evening wore on, he slumped gradually onto his divan and began snoring heavily. It was fortunate that his response to wine was to fall asleep, for if a man of his bulk and strength were to become aggressive, as some others did under the influence of alcohol, all around him would suffer. As it was, experienced companions stayed at a distance, not when Bar Abbas was drinking, but when he awoke from the succeeding stupor, for it was then that the temper of the bear was short.

The group was quite animated, and their voices swirled like the rising sparks of the fire around which we sat. Bar Abbas' voice initially provided the bass notes of the chorus, although that became slurred and eventually went silent, to be replaced by the sound of his snoring. Judas Iscariot was the conductor, setting the rhythm, orchestrating the discussion, recognizing this speaker for a moment, then by a move of his eyes or a shift of his hand, giving the floor to another. Small groups of men began to drift into the forecourt of our house. By sunset, almost fifty men were gathered around the fire.

I looked around the group; it was clear that these were not men gathered for the purpose of discussing the Kingdom of Heaven. Scholars they were not. I saw large hands wrapped around stout staffs, broad shoulders and thick necks, an occasional scar that did not look like it came from a farming accident. Those who were not as physically formidable made me uneasy, for their eyes when they happened to meet mine had a certain quality that made me look away. The faces of these men reminded me of the faces of the Roman legionnaires—not the cruel occupying Syrian troops that filled Judea, but those true combat veterans who had fought in the forests of Gaul and swung their swords in personal combat against men whose faces had the same look. I felt I was being measured, sized up—my strengths and weaknesses noted, my reliability in a crisis evaluated.

We gathered our robes for sitting down to our meal. On my left, Bar Abbas grunted and shifted his rough brown robe awkwardly before he reclined, making the little adjustments needed to accommodate something concealed in one's clothing. As he did so, I saw outlined the shape of a long dagger. Like Judas, these men were "iscarii," carriers and wielders of the long, sharp daggers called Sicarii, which they concealed in the folds of their garments.

Attacking the Temple would not be blasphemy, reasoned Judas; rather, it would be a cleansing. The venal and corrupt entourage of the high priest who had already blasphemed by implicitly accepting the power of Rome would be driven out. It was the high priest who, by failing to fight the Gentiles, was sinning by omission, by not fighting to free Israel from the foreign yoke, and by not repudiating the power of the emperor. It was the high priest who was at fault.

Judas reasoned rightly that attacking and occupying the Temple would strike at the very heart of the political, financial, and religious cords that had been knotted around the necks of the Jewish people. Moreover, he hoped it would be an act of liberation that would be recognized by the people of Israel as the signal to arise and defend the Temple against the counterattack that was sure to follow.

Judas stood and struck the pose of a Roman senator, gathering his robe around him. "Tomorrow the people of Israel will return to our role as keepers of the Covenant! The corruption of the High Priest Caiaphas' collusion with the idolaters of Rome will be exposed. Our redemption of the Temple will return Israel to favor in the sight of God, and, just as He returned the Jewish people from captivity in Babylon, He will deliver Israel from its occupation by the idolatrous and godless Romans. I am certain that the people of Israel will see our liberation of the Temple as a sign to rise up, destroy the Romans, and cleanse the priesthood from the Temple! We will be God's scourge against the evil that has severed Israel from Him, and we will return Israel to its rightful place in the world as the Chosen People."

Judas gazed around the group of men surrounding him. "We—you all and I—are the Chosen of the Chosen People. We are the Zealots who will return Israel to the natural order desired by God so that his people are free to worship Him as we have been told. God does not wish to see his people under the heel of Rome. He is testing our commitment. He is testing our zeal! Israel will be restored to her promised position of blessing in this world, rather than in the next.

"And so we will be zealous, and remove the blight of Rome first from the Temple and then from this Holy Land. The people of Israel will rise up with us, and the order of heaven will be restored. Israel will be restored to her promised position of blessing. The Kingdom of Heaven will be established, and the Messiah will rule."

We held the Temple for almost three days before the Romans came from their barracks at the request of High Priest Caiaphas to drive us out. During that time, the Jewish people entered the Temple to pray without having to endure the harsh scrutiny of the priests and the scourge of the money changers. They bathed themselves without charge in the *mikvehs*, and the Roman coins offered in ritual payment to enter the Temple to pray were exchanged into Jewish shekels without the exorbitant surcharges imposed by the money changers. The large, jostling crowds that normally were forced to cluster at the approved stalls to purchase the perfect white doves for sacrifice became small and orderly, because for these few days, sacrificial animals could be bought at reasonable prices, and even brought in from outside the Temple walls. The focus of the worshippers was prayer, not commerce, and the whole atmosphere in the Temple forecourt was relaxed, with people's attention focused on their relationship with God.

In the afternoon of each of the three days, Judas stood and preached to the crowd. He became transformed. Unlike the sermons of Jesus around Judea, these were not gentle pleas to love thy neighbor. Instead, Judas turned his voice into a great trumpet, preaching like Joshua, and his trumpet tore down the walls of privilege and exclusivity and self-righteousness that had been the edifice built by the keepers of the Temple. In no uncertain terms, he denounced them, accusing them of hypocrisy and corruption. He attacked the Pharisees and Sadducees for their willing dealings with the Romans, and equated with idolatry their acceptance of Roman coins with the face of Caesar depicted as a god.

Judas attacked the very foundation of the religious institutions of Jerusalem, accusing High Priest Caiaphas and his many lieutenants of heresy and blasphemy for turning the Temple into a place focused not on God, but on money—a den of thieves. His words recalled to the minds of his listeners the wealth that Caiaphas and his family had been able to amass in the eighteen years he had served as high priest. Judas reminded the crowd of the extortion that forced them to pay such high prices to use the *mikvehs*, and how the priests refused to allow the entry of sacrificial animals from outside the Temple grounds, confiscating a perfect animal on the pretext of some unnoticed blemish, forcing the worshipper to replace it with one purchased from the priests, and then turning around and selling the "flawed" creature to the next worshipper.

Judas used his most powerful rhetoric to rain down curses and predictions of woe on the scribes and the Pharisees, the chief priests, the false teachers who spoke of piety and mercy but behaved as predators; who appeared outwardly holy and righteous, but were filled with hypocrisy and iniquity.

By the end of the third day, it became obvious that the people of Israel, though happy to have free run of the Temple, were not buying Judas' fire-and-brimstone rhetoric. Those who were more worldly were too accustomed to obedient acceptance of authority, while those who shut out the world and found solace in their religious studies simply were too removed to bother about this act of insurrection. The vast number of practical folks between these extremes were simply unwilling to bet their lives that there would be enough power in any uprising to sweep away the power of Rome forever. In any case, Judas' call for rebellion against Rome and the high priest went unheeded.

Our occupying force of Zealots began to get visibly nervous about our prospects for escape. The cross loomed over our heads, and we knew we had to find a way out. We gathered in the forecourt of the Temple to work out a plan. Bar Abbas spoke first. "We must fight them! We must make them pay with blood for their sacrileges. In any case, I would rather go down fighting than be captured and crucified. And if I die for the sake of God, I will arise again with the righteous."

Judas sat quietly while the pros and cons of this option swirled around him. He finally spoke. "We can yet win and survive to fight another day. No one knows us; we are grouped in people's minds as the followers of Jesus of Nazareth. We can simply evaporate in small groups."

Bar Abbas said, "But we will be hunted down! The high priest cannot let this go unpunished. We have challenged his authority in the very heart of his domain. He must find someone to punish. And the Romans will support him."

Judas smiled. "You are both right and wrong, Bar Abbas. Yes. Caiaphas must find someone to punish. But you are wrong to think that the Romans will help him. For the Roman procurator Pontius Pilate, this is a religious dispute, not an insurrection. The Temple is not the Romans' jurisdiction; it is the responsibility of the priests and the Temple guards. But there is another option. Here is my plan."

As Judas spoke, it became clear that something was suddenly horribly wrong with the electrifying story that was about to make its way to the people of Israel. Somehow, the instigator and perpetrator of this stunning act of heresy against the high priest and the Temple was not the suddenly diminished Judas Iscariot, but Jesus of Nazareth. The story that would be put out transformed Jesus instantaneously from the gentle preacher known for his Sermon on the Mount into a firebrand revolutionary and prophet. Jesus taught that failure to adopt his teachings would result in the undermining of the covenant between God and the Jewish people, and he had used as symbolism the destruction of Jerusalem.

In the hands of Judas, Jesus' symbolic language was transformed into a call for an armed uprising to purify the land of Israel and to drive out the pagan ways and idolatry of Rome, following the example of the Maccabees, who had fought to the death only decades before. Judas Iscariot said that God must be with him and his Zealots, for otherwise they could not have successfully attacked and occupied the holiest place in Israel—the Temple itself—without divine retribution. But as it now appeared that the divine retribution might come in the form of crucifixion, Judas sought to shift the responsibility.

Jesus was up in Galilee. This gentle man, preaching love and charity, focused on another world, could never have led an assault like this; such actions violated every principle that Jesus stood for and preached. The anger, fury, and violence that accompanied the attack and the occupation of the Temple were not to be found in Jesus' personality, and he had never displayed any hint of those kinds of feelings and emotions.

How could these actions be attributed to Jesus? The lie would put him into mortal danger, for the high priest could never allow the perpetrators to go unpunished. Caiaphas' authority and dignity, as well as the flow of funds into the Temple coffers, would be threatened. Worse, it would weaken Caiaphas' standing with the Roman authorities, who had demonstrated again and again their willingness to brutally dispose of high priests who were unable to use the power of religion to keep the Jewish rabble quiescent and paying their taxes. For Caiaphas and the whole Temple entourage and priesthood, it was imperative that there be a highly public trial, and that punishment be meted out to the ringleader of this blasphemy.

Judas understood this. "We must give Caiaphas someone to pursue . . . someone recognizable who can carry the symbolic guilt of us all, so they will leave off pursuing us and allow us to carry on our struggle." He sought to assuage the fears of those concerned that Jesus might be innocently convicted. "Do not be concerned for Jesus, for he is not here, and so if he is caught, no evidence can be brought against him to convict him. They will have to release him. But by spreading the word that it was he who drove the moneylenders and idolaters from the Temple, the authorities will be distracted from searching for the rest of us."

I protested vociferously. "Judas, you are a fool! It takes only a moment of thought to realize that our conspiracy will be rooted out, and that no steps will be spared in hunting us all down and convicting the leaders. You try to protect yourself with this story that it was Jesus who led the attack, who drove out the moneychangers, who occupied the Temple and sought to return it to a house of God."

I railed on, unconscious of the noose I was placing around my own neck. "If they arrest Jesus on the basis of this story, there is no chance that he will be released for lack of evidence! Caiaphas *must* see him convicted; and Pilate, who seeks only a pacified and compliant Jewish people, will allow it."

"I warn you, Judas, if this comes to pass, I will bear witness to the truth, that Jesus of Nazareth had no hand in this attack, that he was not present, and that his conviction would send an innocent man to Golgotha."

The group of Zealots fell silent, and Judas contemplated me. I suddenly realized that only I stood between all their safety and the executioner's cross. Judas' eyes flickered briefly, shifting to the point just over my shoulder where Bar Abbas stood. The sudden sharp blow near the small of my back was somehow not unexpected, and I felt no pain when the sicarrius dagger pierced deep into my vitals. I fell to the dust of the Temple courtyard, and all went black.

Chapter 7: Judas and Bar Abbas

"Bar Abbas has been captured by the Romans!" cried one of the Zealots.

The color drained from Judas Iscariot's already sallow features. "By the Romans? You are sure? Not by the Temple guards?"

"No, Judas, it was the Romans. They have been hunting him for months because he was already charged with rebellion and sedition against Rome. Someone told Pilate where he was, and Pilate sent soldiers into the tavern where he was drinking. They pretended to be off duty, and they listened to him brag about the attack on the Temple. He was arrested on the spot."

Bar Abbas was well-known around Jerusalem as a rebel, not to mention a thug and a robber. Had he been arrested by the Jewish police from the Temple, he would have stood accused of the religious crime of blasphemy. But with the Romans, the charges were much more serious—rebellion against the emperor, and treason. The charges were well-founded and further supported (as if any more evidence were needed than the multiple identifications of his victims) by the discovery of the sicarrius assassin's blade on Bar Abbas at the time of his arrest. The blade itself was a badge of rebellion, but even without that connotation, it was illegal for non-Romans to carry weapons, and Bar Abbas' possession of the dagger was enough to have him arrested.

That afternoon, Judas slipped a purse of coins soundlessly into the cloak of the centurion in command of the prison guards. Just as soundlessly, Judas slipped through a side gate of the prison and was led down the stone corridor to the cell holding Bar Abbas. The cell was as dark as the inside of a pocket; only the sound of labored breathing revealed that the cage held an occupant.

"Bar Abbas?" Judas breathed. A low growl emerged from the back of the shallow grotto in the rock, tailing off into a whimper as a shadow laboriously detached itself from the dark floor. Judas swallowed the temptation to say something stupidly mundane, like "How are you?" That question was superfluous and likely to invite a catalogue of events that were best not known in detail.

Instead, Judas asked the question that was really burning in his mind. "We don't have much time. Tell me quickly; have they been questioning you about the Temple attack?"

Bar Abbas grunted. "No, the Romans don't care about the Temple. To them, that is a religious matter. It is a problem for the priests. What the Romans are asking me about is you and the other freedom fighters. They think you are a threat to Rome. But the questioning has not yet gotten serious; these are just guards having a bit of sport with me, and so far I have told them nothing. I pretend to be as stupid as they are, and they are prepared to believe me. But someone betrayed me to them, and that person must have told them enough to get me arrested. Once an officer comes, acting stupid will not protect me."

"Can you hold out against them?"

"Are you crazy?" Bar Abbas hissed. "Nobody holds out! It is just a matter of time!"

Judas fell silent. Bar Abbas could read his mind even in the dark. "Do not think you will be able to have me killed to shut me up, like you did Lazarus. If you don't want the Romans to come after you, you have to break me out of here or you and the others will be my roommates, and we will all be companions hanging on the cross."

Judas smiled bitterly. "Now I think it is you that must be crazy. What a brilliant idea! We all might as well just kill ourselves or crucify each other as attempt an attack on this prison. Maybe you really are as stupid as you pretend."

Bar Abbas' response carried a tone of warning. "You better come up with something, Judas; otherwise you and I will be hanging next to each other on crosses as surely as though we did crucify each other."

They stared at each other in the gloom. "Maybe there is a way," said Judas finally, "but it is a long shot." Bar Abbas muttered, "I hope it has a better chance of success than depending on my withstanding torture."

"Let us think about what the Romans want . . . order and peace and the continued flow of taxes. It is the job of the high priest and the king to keep the population in line to ensure that. That is why Rome appointed first Annas and then Caiaphas to be the high priests and spokesmen for the religious council of the Sanhedrin. To be effective, their authority over religious matters must be unquestioned and un-challenged."

"But, Judas, that was exactly the purpose of our attack on the Tem-ple! We showed all of Israel that the Temple could be freed from its sinful and shameful slavery to Rome's policies. That authority has been undermined by us, just as we planned."

"Yes, Bar Abbas, that's true. But we also created the condition that allows us to use the affront to the high priest's authority as a means to get out of our predicament. Think a moment—the only way to restore any semblance of credibility and authority is for High Priest Caiaphas to capture and execute the perpetrators, or at least their leader."

"Judas, you fool. *You and I* were the leaders." Bar Abbas paused. "And besides, the high priest has no authority to sentence anyone to death. Only Pontius Pilate has that power, and I don't see why he would do that for a religious crime, no matter how much the Sanhedrin wants it."

"*We* know we are the leaders, Bar Abbas, but Caiaphas and the Romans don't know it. We have already spread word that it was Jesus who led the attack, and while he was in Galilee, he remained free. But now he has come to Jerusalem, to the house of Lazarus. We will give him to the high priest. He will be arrested by the Temple guards and charged with blasphemy or with inciting criticism of the priests. We will have to work through the Sanhedrin and Caiaphas, because the Romans have no reason to arrest him. The Sanhedrin will want him executed as a public warning against challenges to their authority—but to do that, they will have to take him for trial before the Roman procurator, Pontius Pilate. And to get a verdict warranting execution, they will have to accuse him of a capital crime against Rome."

"He has committed no crime against Rome. They will have to release him!" cried Bar Abbas. "That leaves me stuck here; how will that help get me out?" he shrilled.

"As a bargain for surrendering Jesus, we will insist that you be freed at the Passover amnesty. Pilate always relies on the recommendation of the high priest to identify the prisoner who will be freed. We will give them Jesus on condition that it is you who is freed."

Bar Abbas shook his head doubtfully. "It seems to me that you are pinning a lot on the incentives of the high priest to punish the Temple attackers, and on his influence with Pontius Pilate." He glared into Judas' face. "And it is you and I who will suffer if your plan doesn't work!"

"Oh, Bar Abbas, we are no worse off, and indeed, you are better off if Jesus is arrested for the attack." Judas counted on his fingers. "One, it shifts the high priest's anger away from you. Two, it moves the attention away from your petty rebellion against the might of Rome toward maintaining the fundamental system that underpins Roman rule and the power of the high priest." Third finger, "It gives them an innocent lamb to vent their revenge upon."

"And fourth, it allows us a chance to continue our work to free the Chosen People from the tyranny of Rome. Once you are free, and suspicion is diverted, we can re-gather our forces to fight the Romans and drive them out of the land that God gave to Moses."

"Well, you are supposed to be the clever one, Judas. Maybe it will work. I can't think of any other way out. But I fear we will both be hanging from a cross before Passover."

"You just make sure you don't give up any information about us. When they sweat you hard, give them Jesus. I will be doing the same at Caiaphas' council. That way we can provide independent corroborating evidence."

As Judas left the prison, he wracked his mind to develop a way to strengthen his hand. Although he had airily dismissed Bar Abbas' doubts, Judas knew his plan was weak. "I have no credibility with Caiaphas or the Sanhedrin; indeed, I probably could not even get in to see them."

Just then, the late afternoon sun slanted through the streets of Jerusalem, and a reflection glinted sharply into his eye. He stopped and stared at it. "Look how that reflected ray of light is so much brighter and sharper than the beam that created it. I must be like that reflected light. I must find a way to magnify and direct my plan into the mind of Caiaphas. And since he won't trust me, it must appear as his idea, or to come from someone he trusts. Yes, it must be presented to him by someone who understands the issues and can speak to him as an equal."

It took only a moment's reflection, running through possible candidates, before the name came to him—Annas, the former high priest! Annas would understand the ramifications of the relationship between the Romans and the Temple. As Caiaphas' predecessor, Annas could approach the high priest as an equal. And Caiaphas would take the private counsel of Annas and present the ideas to the Sanhedrin so it would be his own advocacy and his plan, not the prodding of a suspicious Zealot who would clearly have a hidden agenda. Judas turned on his heel and headed toward the house of Annas.

Chapter 8: Judas and Annas

Annas was meticulous in observing the requirements for welcoming an unannounced visitor. The impending Passover prevented him from offering the normal honey cakes and sweet mint tea that would have been forthcoming at another time of year. Judas' impatience could not have been more evident had he been tapping his foot, so Annas cut short his lengthy observations on the weather. "How may an old man serve you, Judas Iscariot?"

"Rabbi Annas, I come to you for guidance; I am troubled and do not know how to satisfy my conscience."

Annas stroked his beard. "Go on."

Judas hesitated, choosing his words. "I am caught between two paths, both being righteous. But choosing one will cause me to sacrifice the other. You are aware of the attack on the Temple recently?"

Annas became agitated. "Of course I am! Who is not? The whole city is treating Jesus of Nazareth as a hero of Israel. They think this blasphemer is a new Maccabee who will lead the people of Israel against Rome. When he came into the city a few days ago, the fools greeted him as a hero. They do not seem to understand that the only thing standing between them and total slavery to Rome is the Temple and our covenant with God!"

Judas stroked Annas' pride, "I do not understand, Rabbi."

Annas looked at him and thought, "Must I explain the obvious to one who has the wits of a beetle?" Aloud, he said, "The Temple is the symbol of the covenant. It is what sets us aside from the worshipers of idols, including the emperor. It stands between the people of Israel and the Romans. To maintain our identity, the Temple must represent the Romans' control over the people of Israel. That control must be absolute and unquestioning, for if the people think the Temple is a tool of their oppression rather than the link between them and the Lord, Rome will destroy it, and Israel will be destroyed as well."

Annas' expression darkened. "That attack was a blasphemy that no

Jew can abide. Jesus of Nazareth must be brought to justice and made an example. He must be put to death in a public way!" Judas nodded, looking away as though distressed. "That is the basis of my problem, Rabbi. I know where Jesus is to be found. He is nearby and will celebrate Passover tonight in Jerusalem."

Annas leaned forward in his seat and pointed his finger at Judas emphatically. "You must turn him in! He must be punished for his sacrilege."

"I know the horrible sacrilege Jesus has perpetrated, Rabbi, but I also know that the high priest cannot impose a death sentence. Only the Romans have that authority," Judas replied.

"Ah! You are right," said Annas. "But Pontius Pilate cannot afford to allow unrest again in Jerusalem. The case for Pilate is simple: Jesus is causing trouble in Jerusalem. He is a known rebel, and he is endangering public peace at a time when large and volatile crowds are thronging the city. It is entirely reasonable to arrest him."

"Of course you are right, Rabbi. But arresting him is not enough to restore the respect for the Council of the Sanhedrin and to re-establish the authority of the high priest. If Jesus were to be charged with some religious crime, or get off with only slight punishment, he would rise even further in the eyes of the people. To really punish him and establish the enormity of this crime, his rebellion cannot be seen as only against the Sanhedrin; it must be against Rome itself. That makes it a matter for Roman law, and that makes it a rebellion, which brings the punishment of death on the cross."

Annas continued to stroke his beard, running his fingers through the long gray strands idly, his eyes staring at nothing in particular. Maybe this Judas was not as stupid as he first appeared. "You make a good point, Judas. I am sure you have thought about this before coming to me. What is your conclusion?"

Judas set the hook. "Jesus claims to be the Messiah."

Annas' dismissive hand wave stopped in midair. "Ahhh. I see! That is different! The Messiah comes to restore the Kingdom of David and rule all of Israel. To do so, he must overthrow the rule of Rome; that makes his crime not blasphemy, but sedition."

Judas nodded. "Yes, and sedition is punishable by death under Roman law."

Annas' face betrayed nothing, but his words indicated that he clearly understood the path before them. "Are you prepared to identify Jesus of Nazareth to the soldiers of the Temple Guard?" he asked. We cannot risk arresting some other Jesus; that would make us look ridiculous and weak."

Judas nodded. "I will do that, but I have a request in return. The Romans are holding a friend of mine. I want him released under the Passover amnesty. His name is Bar Abbas."

Chapter 9: The Last Supper

Several weeks had passed after my resurrection. We were a somber group that gathered with Jesus for the Seder Passover feast. We knew from friends that we were being hunted by the soldiers of the Temple. From me, the others had learned of Judas' role as leader of the attack. They also knew Judas had spread the lies that Jesus was the leader and instigator of the attack in order to divert attention. We did not yet know that the crime of which Jesus would stand accused was to be sedition and treason against the emperor in Rome. That only became apparent after his arrest and execution.

We gathered at a house that was owned by my Uncle Joseph, where he would lodge on the many occasions when he came to Jerusalem from Arimathea to do business. He often entertained members of Pilate's court, to whom he sold metal products that came from the tin mine managed by my father in distant Britannia. The house was a magnificent two-story building, with rooms downstairs for baths and food preparation. The walled entry courtyard was paved with lovely tiles depicting flocks of birds in flight and animals in garden-like forest settings. The walls around this beautiful space were covered with brilliant lime whitewash, and on sunny days were almost blindingly bright. Lovely rose bushes and small palm trees grew around the perimeter of the walls, and in the center was a small fountain covered with beautiful light- and dark-blue tiles. Uncle Joseph often used the house as a meeting place, because it was more conveniently located to the Temple than our home in Bethany. It was here that Mary and Martha were preparing for the Passover.

Upstairs was a large room that could accommodate the sumptuous feasts expected from those who sought to do business with the Roman and Greek officials and the courts of Pontius Pilate and King Herod Antipas. There we gathered in the late afternoon. The freshly plastered and whitewashed walls reflected the light from candles glowing inside translucent alabaster lamps brought up from Egypt. Once we were all seated, Mary and Martha brought in dishes and cups for each of us, and their movements made the flames flicker. On the floor, the dogs, fish, birds, and animals depicted in the tiles seemed to come alive and move in the shadows.

Before we arrived, Martha and Mary had finished the scrupulous cleaning of the house and conducted the ritual rooting out and elimination of leavened foods. Beginning on the night before Passover, they had searched the kitchen and dining areas, scraping, removing, and incinerating all traces of leavened foods. They toured the apartment armed with candles, feather dusters, and brooms made from rolled-up papyrus, and consigned their scrapings and dusting to the ritual fire in the courtyard. For us, the reminder of the delivery of Israel from the Egyptians provided hope for similar delivery from the domination by Rome.

Our Seder ceremony was led by Jesus, proceeding as it had for a thousand years. The familiar words and ceremonies recalled the escape of the Hebrews from the servitude of Egypt, and the transformation of a group of Semitic tribes from the northern Sinai into the nation of Israel. Like all Jews, our faith was sustained by the recollection of the covenant struck by Moses with God and our selection as the Chosen

People. The Romans were wise to allow us to be ruled by Jewish king and priests, to keep the fervor of the population in check, especially during the Passover, when the people's consciousness was at a peak.

This was a lesson that the Romans had learned the hard way. Recently, Pilate had introduced statues of the emperor into the Temple, a blasphemy that cut to our very identity. The results of this act were fresh in Pilate's mind. A mob gathered outside the palace, demanding that he remove from the Temple the statues he had snuck in and erected under cover of darkness. Why did we take this sycophantic attempt to curry favor with the emperor so seriously? By placing the emperor's statues in the Temple, Pontius Pilate declared the emperor's divinity and his equality with the god of the Jews. Moreover, the act affirmed the empire's polytheism and the equality of all the gods.

The Jews declared only one true god, and under the Law of Moses, all other gods, including the emperor, were false—not inferior, but false. The uprising was a treasonous political act, punishable by death. Threatened at Pilate's command by Roman soldiers, the mob had quietly lain down in the street and bared their necks to the legionnaires' swords, preferring to die rather than permit this continuing and obvious blasphemy of our holy place. The event unnerved Pontius Pilate and he backed down, for if he executed the peaceful demonstrators, his legions could not control the predictable backlash.

Pontius Pilate knew that if he slaughtered these protesters, far worse trouble would erupt, and the consequent failure of his primary responsibility—to keep the region peaceful and the taxes flowing to Rome—would not be lessened by the argument that he had only been trying to honor his emperor and uphold his status as ruler over all. Pragmatic above all, in Rome, tribute trumped theology, so the whole affair was treated as a minor religious issue, inflamed by the passions of the Passover.

As we began our Seder, eating the unleavened bread and drinking the unfermented wine, we all knew we were fugitives. Jesus, in particular, knew that the false accusations of his involvement in the Temple attack would not be easy to overcome. However, we counseled him to not worry too much. The crime of which he was accused was against the Temple, not against Rome. The high priest could make trouble for him and us, but nothing would come of it without Roman involvement. And the last thing Pilate would want while Jerusalem was filled with pilgrims was a controversial trial over a purely religious matter. Such a trial was likely to inflame the masses of Jewish pilgrims in the over-stuffed town at a time when religious fervor was high and anti-Roman sentiment already inflamed. Everyone remembered the previous explosions during the Passover.

We thought Jesus might be arrested and tried by the Sanhedrin, but that nothing would come of it. He could prove that he had not even been in Jerusalem. And his eventual release would remove the onus from the rest of us. Even if he were not released, we were sure that Jesus would sacrifice himself by going to prison to protect his innocent disciples. We were so naive—a bunch of country bumpkins convincing ourselves that the outcome we desired was inevitable.

What we did not understand in our naiveté was that High Priest Caiaphas saw himself moving against Jesus and his followers as a way to forestall a massacre. Were we a bit more sophisticated, we might have understood the situation better and realized the peril Jesus faced.

While we were offering assurance to each other, Caiaphas had called his council to the Temple. He began with a quick description of the situation. "Because of Passover, Jerusalem is stuffed to near-breaking, and the mood of the people is ugly. The burden of Roman taxes is crushing them. They are ready to raise their fists against Pilate and the Temple. And the success of the mob last year has emboldened them."

Caiaphas slapped his hand loudly on the table top. "The Romans will not tolerate another incident like that! Pilate will have to prove he is strong. He cannot allow last year's defeat to be repeated. If there is trouble and he fails again to act strongly to quell any disturbance, the whole of Israel will see his weakness and will likely erupt. Rome would send in the legions to put down such a rebellion without mercy, and thousands would die on the cross. The people of Israel will suffer more even than they do now. And we will be held responsible for not controlling our people."

Caiaphas looked around the room and saw that all there understood the peril they faced. "What can we do?" asked one.

The high priest spoke deliberately. "We must give Rome a sacrificial lamb to satisfy their need to look strong. We must sacrifice a Jew to protect the Jews. Jesus stands accused of attacking the Temple, threatening to destroy it. He has declared publicly that the kingdom of Caesar is not the kingdom of God, and therefore the emperor is not divine. As Jews, we must agree with him; but to the Romans, these are crimes not just of blasphemy, but of treason!"

There was murmuring around the room. "We see your point, Caiaphas, but . . . he was not there, there are no witnesses to his being there. We cannot condemn him for a crime unless we can prove he committed it; our own oaths require that we act justly. If we fail in that responsibility, our own souls are forfeit."

"We will act justly," said Caiaphas softly. "This will be on the head of Pontius Pilate and the Romans."

"Nevertheless, Caiaphas, we must have proof. How will you prove that Jesus of Nazareth led the attack on the Temple?"

"We have a witness—one of his followers who is willing to identify him as the leader in return for his own release and the release of a friend. We will send our Temple guards to arrest Jesus of Nazareth and bring him here for trial. Then we will turn him over to the Romans for punishment in accordance with the law. And we will truthfully tell Pilate that we found Jesus guilty of blasphemy in this court."

And so it played out. After our Seder, Jesus and a few followers strolled in the garden and settled for a while in the darkness of an overhanging tree. Sleepy from the wine, Peter fell asleep and was gently snoring when the Temple guards, led by Judas, came for Jesus.

Loyal but foolish Peter stupidly pulled his sword to defend Jesus, which confirmed the guards' suspicion that we were Sicarii. Thank heaven it was night and the full moon had not yet risen—our identities were hidden in the shadows, and we were able to escape. Jesus surrendered, of course, as we had expected, although he knew that he was delivering himself into the hands of wily and vicious enemies.

Protected by the dark, we followed at a distance. We expected the Temple guards to take Jesus to prison for trial in the morning, for Jewish law requires that trials take place in full light of day. But instead of going to the traditional court on the grounds of the Temple Mount, they took him to the house of Caiaphas. It became clear that matters were far more serious than we had anticipated; not only was there to be a trial at night, an illegal trial, but it would take place on the very night of the Passover, a feast day. The double violation of Jewish legal processes meant this was to be a mock trial, with what looked like a certain outcome.

In relying on the testimony of Judas, Caiaphas overreached. Judas testified that Jesus had threatened to destroy the Temple, a double offense of blasphemy against God and treason against Rome. But there were those—a minority—in the Sanhedrin who were independent of Caiaphas despite his undeniable power and influence, and who keenly felt their responsibility to God and the Jewish people. They refused to convict Jesus on the strength of a single uncorroborated accusation. Judas claimed he could bring other witnesses, but the very secrecy of the trial stymied this, so the charges could not be proven. There were no other witnesses present who had seen the events that led to the charges, and the illegality of the proceedings meant that Caiaphas had to rely on the resources he had in the room.

Seeing his attempt failing, Caiaphas tried to get Jesus to impeach himself. "Are you the Son of God, the Son of the Blessed? Are you the Messiah?" Some in the hastily assembled group of twenty-three scribes, lawyers, and elders of Jerusalem's Jewish community protested that the question was itself a blasphemy, but Caiaphas had stacked the court with his sycophants. Jesus remained silent, but his refusal to deny the accusation was enough. Caiaphas announced that Jesus had spoken blasphemy. The majority of the court agreed: Jesus deserves the death sentence.

All this I learned later, from my uncle Joseph, who was one of those present.

Chapter 10: After the Crucifixion

The events of the next days played out painfully, just as Judas and Caiaphas planned. Initially, it looked like Pontius Pilate might not play his assigned role, because the defense that we had attributed to Jesus was strong. There was simply no evidence, no witness, that he had been present at the taking of the Temple. Judas, of course, was not in a position to provide corroboration, for that would have signaled his own involvement. Lacking evidence, Pilate ordered Jesus scourged, hoping to wrest a confession from him. Afterwards, he was led out onto the balcony of the Roman court for display to the mob below. I was there.

Jesus was a pitiable sight. Head wounds bleed immoderately, and his face was covered with streams of dried, caked blood. His torturers had forced a crown of thorns from a rose bush down onto his head, and beaten the long thorns until they pierced his scalp. Jesus' eyes were hollow and desperate, vulnerable, weeping, and bleeding. His eyebrows twisted above his nose in a quizzical, hurt expression of incomprehension at the injustice of the pain inflicted on him. We could not see his arms below the top of the bicep, because he stood behind a wooden barrier, but they were clearly bound behind his back. The muscles and sinews of his neck stood out in strain, bearing the pain. His face and neck, browned by the sun, contrasted with the smooth, pale, hairless skin of his chest and the rounded softness of his shoulders.

His long brown hair, matted with blood and sweat, was plastered down over his forehead, and trailed down over his shoulders and back, parted in the middle and held tightly by the thin twist of thorny vines. His beard, looking like the careless growth of a day laborer, grew back on his neck and curled thinly around his chin.

Bar Abbas was freed in the Passover amnesty, eliminating the risk that he would be tortured into confessing his and Judas Iscariot's roles in the attack on the Temple. Instead, Pontius Pilate reluctantly ordered Jesus to be crucified in the face of the accusations that he was trying to spark a revolution against Rome, although even Pilate admitted there was no proof of his guilt. In doing so, he forestalled what he imagined would be a Jewish uprising—a fear fed by the crowds Caiaphas organized to raise that fear in the procurator. Caiaphas was initially satisfied that the perpetrator of the blasphemous attack on the Temple had been eliminated, although he continued to smolder at the challenge to his authority.

It was fear that brought Jesus' disciples cautiously together several weeks after his arrest and execution for sedition and treason. The day was overcast, and the wind blew a haze of dust from the desert across Jerusalem. The weather kept the street traffic subdued, and provided a reason for us to scuttle on the edges of the streets with our faces muffled. Our fear was stoked by the knowledge that, while High Priest Caiaphas had the peak of his anger slaked by the crucifixion of Jesus, he remained mindful that there were others still at large—us.

We gathered once again in the house in Jerusalem where Jesus had led our Seder meal, and the sight of those walls and appointments refreshed in our minds the events of that night. Mary and Martha brought forth the plates and cups we had used that evening, except for the ones that had been used by Jesus. These Mary kept separated as a kind of memorial.

Our council was led now by James, the brother of Jesus. After our simple meal, provided by Martha, James spoke right to the heart of our fears. "We are all at risk now. Caiaphas has issued orders that all the disciples of Jesus are to be arrested and brought before him on charges of blasphemy. He has sent out the Temple guards and hired bounty hunters to seek us out and bring us for trial before the Sanhedrin. We are protected solely by the fact that most of us are from Galilee, and hence not personally known in Jerusalem."

"Must we then all flee, James? Where can we go that we will be safe?"

James replied, "I have thought about this a great deal. It is my opinion that we must scatter, for if we stay together, there is a risk that we will be arrested together."

James went on. "I will stay here in Jerusalem as long as I can, because my face and name are not known. But my plan is to go over to Egypt and seek refuge in Alexandria. There, the long arm of Caiaphas cannot reach. I suggest that each of you strike out, certainly beyond the borders of Judea, and even beyond the lands of Israel. We can remain united by sharing our common understanding of the things we learned from Jesus, and we can search out the Jewish communities to shelter us. Perhaps, over time, we can convince many that we are not blasphemers and apostates, but rather, through the force of example and teaching, that we are followers of a prophet who will save Israel from the distortions of the high priest and the blasphemy of worshiping the emperor in Rome."

Although we all felt fear, as time went by and nothing happened, the urgency of James' recommendations was muted, and most of us remained in Israel, cloaked by our anonymity. Over the next few years, we found that Jesus' message of charity and piety resonated with many Jews, so the population of those who were coming to be called "Christians" grew rapidly. Communities formed, gathering in small groups, establishing synagogues, sharing weekly meals, and providing the kind of mutual help that strengthened all. This extended to assistance given by each community to the widows and orphans of its members.

Those of us who had lived through the life, trial, and death of Jesus were frequently sought out to tell our stories, and soon secondhand versions of those stories began to circulate, often with highly imaginative accounts attached. So many Christian synagogues emerged that we found it necessary to appoint assistants to lead the meetings and explain the teachings of Jesus to the flock. The teaching function was especially important in the growing number of synagogues populated by Jews coming from outside Judea, for whom Aramaic and Hebrew were not mother tongues, but who conversed mainly in Greek, and who were skeptical of the rituals and rules of the Temple.

Our complacency, which had grown as Caiaphas' attention appeared to focus on his relations with the Romans, was shattered on the day the bounty hunter, Saul of Tarsus, brought his captive before the Sanhedrin for trial.

Chapter 11: The Trial of Stephen

I suppose it is part of human nature to believe that because something has not yet happened, it will not happen. Three years went by after the death of Rabbi Jesus, and the small group that followed his teachings grew substantially. Much of this growth was the result of the outreach of my sister Mary. Her disgust with the hypocrisy and venality of the high priest and those who used the Temple rituals as a means to sustain power and enrich themselves was enhanced by her anger at the institution that had brought about the execution of her beloved Rabbi Jesus. The Jewish immigrants that came from around the Roman Empire had no deep bonds to the Temple either, and it was from them that much of the growth of our little sect drew, spreading to eleven synagogues in Jerusalem alone.

After long discussion and consideration, the original followers, gathered in council, decided that these new followers of Jesus' teaching needed ministering by those who could better understand their language and customs. After some search, we selected from among these converts seven Greek-speaking deacons, chosen for their devotion to the teaching of Jesus and for their ability to win new members to the rapidly growing population of Christians. Mary argued that this was appropriate, as most of the newcomers spoke Greek and would be best served by having a deacon minister to them who was familiar with that language and their special needs. Their primary duty was to see to the care of widows, a growing number of whom arose as a result of the rapacious policies of the Romans and the penury and starvation they caused.

There were many groups of Jews at that time that rebelled against the heavy hand of the Temple. The Essenes withdrew into the desert near the Dead Sea and established their own community, rejecting the Temple even to the point of disputing its calendar and the dates of the various Holy Days. Protected by their distance from Jerusalem, they developed practices and community rules of their own.

Many of the Greek members of our growing community, though not attracted by the asceticism and isolation of the Essenes, also felt a deep dissatisfaction with the Temple. As our numbers grew, factions developed, and tensions grew as well. We Jews of Judea were raised in the Temple tradition, adhering out of habit to the rituals and holidays with which we had grown up. Our language is Aramaic, and we think of ourselves as the orthodox Jews enlightened by the teachings of Jesus. The Greek-speaking Jews, who increasingly filled our synagogues and over time established their own, had their own traditions. The tensions between the two groups over interpretation of Jewish law were exacerbated by linguistic differences, and gradually our two camps became separated into multiple synagogues. Those of the Aramaic speakers were ministered by one or the other of Jesus' original followers, while the Greek speakers turned to the deacons to provide services to their communities—arranging the community meals and distributing food and clothing to the widows and orphans of their flock.

One of the Greek-speaking deacons was named Stephen. For him, the story concocted by Judas Iscariot and Bar Abbas of the attack on the Temple, which had led to the trial and crucifixion of Jesus, took on a significance that made the facts almost irrelevant. Judas and Bar Abbas had hoped the attack on the Temple would spur an uprising that would lead Israel to throw off the yoke of Rome's pagan oppression. Its failure, and their desperate attempt to save their own lives and shift the blame, resulted in the story that the attack had been led by Jesus. That story was widely believed, but those of us who were there and knew its falsity had no incentive to dispute it now.

But for Stephen, the attack had a different significance. For him, it marked the end of the dominance of Judaism by the Pharisees and the high priest. It ended their authority to interpret the Law of Moses. For the Hellenized Jews, raised in such places as Syria, Rome, and Spain, there was no particular reverence for Temple pronouncements. Accepting that Jesus was the Messiah, Stephen reasoned that the attack on the Temple was a point of separation between the Mosaic Law of the Temple and a new covenant that expanded the scope of being Jewish beyond the strict requirements set by the high priest and the Temple rules. Caught up in the spirit of the attack on the Temple, Stephen preached that Jesus had come to destroy the Temple and replace the Law of Moses with a New Covenant that reached far beyond the selection of the Jewish people as the sole Chosen People.

This was heresy, indeed, and the synagogues split into factions, which on inspection were largely based on whether the members were Aramaic-speakers or Greek-speakers. The former were incensed at the implied rejection of their special status as Jews, while the latter were more open to the idea that Jesus' teachings opened the door to their full inclusion in this new cult. The debate drove a deep wedge between the two groups, and the friction brought out other differences that had been rankling below the surface. The Greek groups felt they were getting short treatment in the distribution of food and alms to their widows. Their resentment against this perception of unfairness made them less inclined to adopt Jesus' admonition to forgive their enemies, and this in turn bred a return resentment.

Meanwhile, the high priest naturally perceived that Stephen was another one of those difficult followers of Jesus preaching against his authority and that of the Temple. He summoned his enforcer, Saul of Tarsus, to arrest Stephen and bring him to the Sanhedrin for trial.

Was there ever a more self-righteous person created on Earth than Saul of Tarsus? Has anyone ever adopted such a mantle of rectitude and certitude about events in which he did not participate?

Even after all the time that has passed, I find it hard now to contain the anger I feel at this master of hypocrisy. Where do I begin? I could start with his role as bounty hunter for the high priest. This is the man who hunted down and arrested loud-mouthed and intemperate Stephen; who brought him for trial before the Sanhedrin not just once, when he was able to talk his way out of the charges against him, but twice. And when the high priest still could not convict Stephen of heresy his second time before the Sanhedrin, Saul watched passively while the mob, inflamed by the prosecuting rhetoric of the high priest, stoned to death a man who could not be convicted under the law. Stephen was not the only one to suffer. James, the brother of John—not the brother of Jesus—was beheaded at the behest of King Agrippa, the grandson of the old Herod. Peter was arrested and imprisoned.

Several years passed after the stoning of Stephen, our outspoken deacon. Our community in Jerusalem spread the messages of Jesus, layering atop the Law and the traditional practices of Judaism the messages of charity for the poor and the forgiveness of transgressions. These teachings attracted many to our synagogues; people were drawn both by the messages and the charity, especially as it was delivered to those left widowed and orphaned by the cruelty of the Romans and our own kings.

Stephen's tragic death raised a debate within our community. His stoning came about because of his view, which we all shared, that Jesus was the Messiah, but more important, that Jesus' message of charity and forgiveness represented a break with the stern "eye for an eye" underlining the Law of Moses. The messages of love, charity, and forgiveness were appealing to Gentiles, and many sought to convert to our beliefs. They were put off, however, by the stern view that their conversion required they subject themselves fully to the Torah and the Law of Moses. This, of course, required that male converts had to endure the pain and terrible risk of circumcision.

There came a time when we in Jerusalem were visited by Greek-speaking converts from Damascus. Their leader was a man whose parents in Cyprus named Joseph, but we called him Barnabas. He was given this name because he had sold all his possessions and donated the proceeds to support our community in Jerusalem. He was a good man who fully embraced the message of Jesus to love his neighbor, and he was much admired by all of us for his piety and charity.

Barnabas came before us to plead the case for the gentile converts. "Like you, we are Jews. And like you, we believe that Jesus is the Messiah. Like you, we believe that if we follow his teachings, we will be counted among the saved at the final judgment that is nigh.

"But we are Jews, not Israelites. Our ancestors did not escape from Egypt with the tribes of Israel. We did not wander with Moses in the desert, and we were not waiting at the foot of the mountain in the Sinai when Moses struck the covenant between God and his Chosen People.

"We come from places as diverse as Crete, Syria, even Rome. Our language is not Hebrew or Aramaic; we speak Greek and Latin. We have never worshiped in Jerusalem, although we pay our dues to the Temple. The Law Moses brought down from the mountain and the covenant he made with God were for the Hebrew tribes of Israel, not for us.

"Stephen taught that Jesus represents a new covenant. The coming of the Messiah was the fulfillment and completion of the old covenant, in which God promised to send a Messiah. Stephen's great insight was to understand and teach that being a Jew no longer means being an Israelite. It is time to be separated from the Law of Moses."

Jesus' brother James, his mother Mary, and my sister Mary were appalled. I believe that if this rank heresy had come from anyone but Barnabas, they would have turned him over to the Temple for trial immediately. My sister was particularly vehement in rejecting the argument. "Jesus was a Jew! It is absurd to hear you speak of his teaching representing anything but a call to be better Jews. The sign of being a Jew is accepting the covenant of Moses and Abraham. Being unwilling to undergo the sign of this covenant means they are unwilling to be Jews."

I found myself torn. The vehemence of my sister was actually a bit disconcerting and even perversely amusing because, as a woman, she had not experienced the ritual of circumcision. I doubted that she could imagine how it would feel to a grown man.

I think her vehemence was a product of the personal love Mary had given to and received from Jesus of Nazareth. She could close her eyes and see and hear him in a way that these foreigners could never experience. They saw Jesus not as a human being, and by their interpretation, they raised him from being Mary's beloved to some sort of divine symbol.

Mary had seen and heard the power of Jesus, but I had experienced it more directly when I emerged from the tomb at his behest. So I was inclined to accept that Jesus represented more than a beloved rabbi. Yet, as a person who bore proudly the mark of the covenant, I was hard-pressed to now accept the view that it was no longer a sign of God's special relationship with the people of Israel.

In any case, Barnabas was dismissed and his pleas rejected. He returned to Damascus. James and Mary Magdalene were pleased with the outcome of this challenge. They had prevailed. Their authority as keepers of Jesus' teachings and heritage as a Jew and an Israelite had been affirmed. We all knew that their and our credibility rested on our personal relationship with Jesus, and the evidence stood before any challengers in the forms of James, the two Marys, and me.

Our supremacy did not last long. As I learned later, Barnabas had kept from us a major secret: his knowledge that Saul had become a follower of Jesus. The secrecy was impressed on him by Saul, who understood rightly that if we knew Barnabas had come to us at Saul's behest, we would have believed he was a spy sent by our persecutor. With secrecy, his safety could be preserved from our animosity.

I cannot look into Saul's heart and determine the genuineness of his conversion. The tale of its circumstances stretches my credulity. He was traveling with a group when the conversion occurred. Saul led a prison convoy, taking Christian Greek-speaking Jews, whom he had arrested, from Damascus back to Jerusalem for trial before the high priest and the Sanhedrin. One of these prisoners was Barnabas.

The desert route between Jerusalem and Damascus takes you first east from Damascus across the north end of the Dead Sea, then south through the land of the Ammonites, continuing through Nabataea along the Roman desert highway to Petra, then turns west, skirting the highlands into Jerusalem. It was on this highway that, according to Barnabas, Saul was subject to a miraculous vision. According to Saul's account, he was struck down from his horse by an enormous thunderclap, and Jesus appeared to him, declaring him an apostle and instructing him to be his follower. In Saul's vision, Jesus addressed him by the Greek name of Paul.

The prisoners and guards in the entourage also experienced the terror of the thunderclap and the flash of almost unbearable light. But no one heard voices or saw anything other than Saul sprawled on the sandy rock of the desert. The prisoners escaped into the mountains that bordered the road and were pursued for a short way by the guards. Barnabas, however, heeding the message of charity and love that had brought him to Jesus, stayed to help his stricken captor.

Saul was in dreadful shape, according to Barnabas' description. His clothes were almost blown off, his hair and beard were singed, and he was blind and deaf. Unable to continue to Jerusalem, the party turned back and returned to Damascus. There, Barnabas, acting as Saul's caretaker, put Saul in the hands of a man named Ananias, who cared for him until he recovered his health. It was weeks later, when Saul had recovered his sight and hearing, that he told the story of the voice of Jesus exhorting him to cease his persecution of Christian Jews.

I have lived all my life in desert country. To me, this description of Saul's conversion to Jesus sounded very much like he had been struck by desert lightning. I knew a man from Bethany who had been hit by lightning while traveling in the desert east of the Dead Sea. He appeared to have survived unscathed after a short period of deafness and blindness, but his mind was ever after deranged, and he was prone to violent ravings. Did this happen to Saul and explain his sudden conversion? I believe so.

In any case, by claiming that Jesus had appeared to him and declared him to be an apostle, equal to those of Jesus' original disciples, Saul effectively neutralized the privileged positions claimed by James and Mary. Indeed, because his revelation had been more recent, Saul could claim more current knowledge of Jesus and his intentions.

On the strength of his conversion, and with the credulity afforded him by the testimony of Barnabas, Saul traveled to Jerusalem and sought the most credulous of those who had been closest to Jesus during his life—Peter. If he could convince Peter of the validity of his conversion, Saul could attain the legitimacy he needed. Peter was a simple man, and easily influenced. Though not the head of the Jerusalem sect, because he was an apostle, Peter's approval gave Saul enough legitimacy and cover that he felt he could proceed with his preaching.

Saul artfully courted Peter, stroking his vanity by citing Peter as the most beloved and reliable of Jesus' followers, eclipsing even James, the brother of Jesus, and totally ignoring Mary. Declared by Saul to be the rightful heir to Jesus' teachings, Peter became a follower of Saul's vision, and for all future recipients of Saul's preaching, Peter's name was invoked. Saul preached that Peter was the rightful leader of the Gentile followers of Jesus.

How did Saul persuade Peter? It was pretty easy. Peter was a simple fisherman from Galilee. Saul was a Pharisee, learned in the scriptures, and knowledgeable of the prophecies. I believe he was quite mad as a result of being hit by lightning, but that really has no bearing on the events. The cataclysmic nature of his conversion made him believe that a similar cataclysm would soon affect the whole world, and that Jesus' appearance to him in the thunderclap presaged his return to render the Final Judgement. The case that Saul made to Peter rested on the books of the Bible that were written after the Hebrews' return from Babylon and the construction of the Second Temple. Saul believed and preached that Jesus as the Messiah would rule in "the last days," and according to the prophecies of Zechariah, that his rule would extend worldwide. Saul further pummeled the prophecies of Zechariah to identify the prophet's "two anointed ones"—Jesus being one, the priestly messiah. Saul flattered Peter by denoting him to be Zechariah's second one—the "royal messiah." Through this belaboring of the prophets, Saul was able to convince poor, simple Peter that *he* was the leader of the followers of Jesus, not James.

Saul convinced Peter that his mission to the Gentiles fulfilled the prophecy of Isaiah and Zephaniah that "all men would turn to the Holy One of Israel and serve him with one consent," because "in the coming 'Day of Yahweh' he would shake all the nations of the earth." To justify the relaxation of Mosaic Law for the Gentiles, he cited Isaiah, who said that "former things shall no more be remembered."

Peter was no match for these sophisticated blandishments. Unschooled in the scriptures, he was easily swayed by Saul and totally accepted his position, so much so that he went so far as to abandon the Torah's dietary rules until he was even rebuked by Saul.

All this occurred over a period of only two weeks, and might have continued. However, word spread in Jerusalem of Saul's presence in the city. When those convert Jews who had been served by synagogues headed by the Greek-speaking deacons heard that Saul was in Jerusalem, they threatened to kill him in revenge for the death of Stephen. Saul was secretly escorted by Peter and Barnabas out of the city. Despite his flight, Saul felt Peter's approval had bestowed on him the legitimacy he needed to preach his version of Jesus' teachings to those who knew nothing about his bounty-hunter past.

In my mind, the greatest sin of Saul of Tarsus was his incredible hypocrisy. Having first been the instrument of putting Stephen to death for declaring that Jesus' teaching and attack on the Temple represented a break with the Judaism represented by the high priest and the Pharisees, Saul then became a fanatical advocate for that very position. He even had the nerve to come before the council of Jesus' disciples to argue this.

Whatever else one might say against this man, he believed deeply in the Jewish faith and the special relationship between Israel and God. He saw the repeated rebellion of Jews against Rome as an ultimate threat to Israel, and he saw no outcome in which rebellion could succeed. He knew that the patience of Rome was not infinite, and that at some point, the armed might of the Empire would be unleashed against Israel, ultimately destroying the Chosen People.

In Saul's fantastic view, the salvation of the Jewish people would come only when the entire Roman Empire became Jewish. But as a Roman citizen who came from Tarsus, a Greek city, he knew the version of Judaism that was rooted in the Temple in Jerusalem could never be accepted by the vast majority of the Empire's population. In its place, Saul argued for a New Covenant that would be acceptable to Gentiles.

The Hebrews of Jerusalem were appalled by Saul's proposal, and in the vicious dispute that followed, the Greek-speaking synagogues felt so threatened that they and their members fled to Antioch. There they adopted a greatly modified form of Judaism. The Torah's strict dietary laws were relaxed to conform more closely to the culinary tastes of the Greek palate. Most important, Gentiles were allowed, and even encouraged, to join the synagogues. Saul decreed that, consistent with his adopted view of the New Covenant, circumcision was not necessary to participate in the community, substituting baptism for that painful ritual. As a result, many adult Gentile men who might otherwise have demurred were brought into the community.

Or perhaps I could begin with Saul's continued hounding of and threats to Mary, the mother of Jesus, and my sister, Mary of Magdala. His threats to bring them before the high priest to receive the treatment meted out to Stephen ultimately led us to counsel that they flee to avoid that fate. Maybe Saul's campaign against the two Marys was in part a consequence of his overt and aggressive misogyny. I don't know where that arose in Saul's life. Perhaps it emerged from his having adopted too many characteristics of the Greek community in Tarsus, where he was raised. He never married, and he always viewed women as a temptation to be resisted, if possible by avoidance of their company. In this, Saul reflected a widely accepted view among certain sects of the Jewish people, in particular the Essenes, who favored a radical celibacy and a rejection of what they called "the sins of the flesh." But I always thought his misogyny was based on his personal preference for the company of men, rather than any philosophical or religious basis.

In any case, Saul scorned women and disregarded their thoughts and opinions. He was especially rancorous when he found himself contradicted or, in his opinion, somehow made to look foolish or wrong—and if a woman were the source, he was almost unhinged. So the more he made things up about Jesus or invented events that never happened, or put words in Jesus' mouth that he never spoke, the more he found the true witness of the two Marys contradicting him. This drove him almost wild; for Saul, it did not matter whether something was true or false in reality—it was sufficient to make it true that he wished it to be true.

And so it came to pass that Saul used his authority as the policeman for the high priest to threaten my sister and the mother of Jesus with arrest and trial on charges of conspiring in the plot to attack the Temple that Judas Iscariot and Bar Abbas had attributed falsely to Jesus. We all considered the threat sufficiently credible that arrangements were put in place for them to flee. As a result, the two people with the most intimate connections to Jesus, who had in their heads the closest understanding of his life and teaching, were banished from

Israel. Accompanied by John, the son of Zebedee, Mary, Jesus' mother, went to Ephesus. My dear sister Mary Magdalene embarked from Alexandria and sailed to Gaul, where she lived out her life.

However, all these dogmatic disputes had little immediate effect on me. It was Saul's misogyny and hypocrisy that affected me, separating me from my beloved sister Mary, and driving me to conceal myself in the Jewish community in Caesarea. Over the years, Saul (who changed his name to Paul in an effort to identify more with the Greek communities in which he preached, and more importantly, in my view, to emphasize the break between his Jewish faith and the version called Christianity that he was busy creating) traveled throughout the Greek and Roman world. He claimed falsely to be one of the original followers of Jesus, though they had never met. He nevertheless wrapped his preaching in language and teachings supposedly from the mouth of Jesus, but that actually had never been spoken.

Meanwhile, all kinds of outlandish versions of Jesus sprang up. In part, I believe this was due to the severe erosion of the authority of the Temple and the high priest who, despite failings on the political front, at least kept the Torah and the Law of Moses more or less consistent. But because of the obvious and cynical control exercised by the Romans over the high priest, and the personal corruption and inadequacies of the appointees to the position, the Jewish people largely disregarded the pronunciations and dictates that emanated from the Temple.

For many of these "wandering" Jews, Jesus became, if not a Golden Calf, at least an object of veneration. Like any such, believers began to attribute many magical powers. One group in Alexandria, no doubt influenced by the religions of Egypt, began to argue that Jesus was the Son of God, sprung directly from divinity much like Osiris was sprung from the Egyptian Sun God, Ra. And stemming from this thought, Jesus was imagined, like Osiris, to be a god who had become human.

From this adaptation of the Egyptian beliefs into the Christian tradition, a great many threads emerged. Was Jesus always God? Or did he become God at birth? Or at his baptism by his cousin John? Perhaps Jesus was just a man who had attained secret knowledge, no doubt picked up when he was living as a young man in Egypt with his parents.

If Jesus was god, how could he die on the cross? The Jewish religion has no belief in an afterlife, but does believe in bodily resurrection, specifically at the end of times. Perhaps Jesus rose from the dead as Paul was saying, and this was an indication that the end times were coming?

Consistent with all these feverish imaginings, a cult of the ancient goddess was being transformed from Artemis to Jesus' mother, Mary, who settled in Ephesus after being hounded out of Jerusalem by Saul. The Greeks were certainly adept at imbuing their current pantheons with the trappings of more ancient ones, changing only the names to accommodate their current religious fashions.

And Paul went hither and yon, speaking authoritatively and totally inventing the life and teachings of Jesus. He created out of whole cloth a system of rules that he imposed on the various Greek-Jewish communities he encountered throughout the world.

Chapter 12: The Jewish War – Beginnings

If you were ever to doubt the existence of evil in the world, the behavior of Gessius Florus would convince you otherwise. His predecessor in the office of procurator, Albinus, had tolerated banditry and widespread bribery as long as he was given a cut, but Florus' reign as procurator was one of disgraceful greed, rapacity, heartless cruelty, and duplicity. If Albinus extracted his ill-gotten wealth like teeth pulled from the mouths of individuals, Florus' reach went down the throat to extract the pluck. To satisfy not only his own insatiable greed, but that of Rome, the procurator stripped whole cities, virtually encouraging the entire citizenry of his dominion to become bandits, provided that he got a portion of the loot.

And then the first tiny drop of rain fell, which, like Noah's flood, spread and deepened and destroyed the world.

The first drop of rain in this storm had a name: Lazarus. A generation had passed since the death of Jesus, and I was now a respected elder and rabbi, shepherding a small synagogue in Caesarea. Roman Emperor Nero had legally ceded control of the city to its Greek population. Our synagogue was on a plot of land that abutted one owned by a Greek man who kept and slaughtered chickens for his non-Jewish customers.

Aside from pursuing these activities in a non-kosher way so as to be maximally offensive to us, his Jewish neighbors, this Greek had a particularly unpleasant and combative demeanor, which was compounded by his intense antipathy toward his Jewish neighbors and his desire to acquire the land on which our synagogue stood. He objected to our use of the footpath down an alley that partly crossed his property and served as the only approach to our synagogue. He felt, perhaps with some justice, that our celebration of the Sabbath interfered with his commercial activities with his Gentile customers. Like many disputes between warring neighbors, there were then a series of trivial tit-for-tat incidents that inflamed both sides. The Greek dumped trash on our property, we returned the favor, and our younger members endeavored to make their passage as noisy and dusty as possible.

I went with John, a tax collector, to see this Greek, whose name was Philip. We attempted to arrive at some arrangement that would satisfy our need to pass and his wish to conduct his business. "Are we not neighbors, both seeking to conduct our affairs? Surely we can reach an amicable solution. We would be prepared to buy your land." I named a price that was many times the value of the little strip of alley we sought.

His beard wagged like a dog's tail as he furiously rejected our offer. "I will not be driven off my land by you Jews at any price!" he shouted. "The emperor has given this city to the Greeks, and you need to learn that you cannot dictate to us." Despite the high price, he haughtily rejected our offer and drove us from his premises with many insults. Within days, laborers appeared and constructed an extension of his building right up to the boundary of his land, cutting the narrow path that led to the synagogue even further so it was almost impossible to pass.

Some of our younger hotheads attacked the construction workers, who fought back fiercely. The violence brought the affair to the notice of Procurator Florus, who summoned us to his palace. John and I went on a Thursday and appealed to him to force the Greek to cease construction. Naturally, we went expecting to pay a bribe, and so it was. In return for a payment from us of eight talents of silver, Florus promised to order Philip the Greek to halt the construction. But instead of honoring his commitment, that evening Florus departed from Caesarea with our silver, and we were left to work out the dispute as best we could.

The following day was the Sabbath, so no action was contemplated until the next day, but even that short respite was not to be. While we were praying in the synagogue, Philip came right to our entrance, upended a filthy chamber pot, and proceeded to sacrifice a chicken on it to honor Caesar. The initial squawking of the bird drowned out our Sabbath prayers, but that was nothing to the awful disturbance as the headless chicken, spouting gouts of blood from its severed neck, was set loose to run into the building.

The events of the next several weeks played out as though they were scripted by the author of a Greek play—I have a hard time distinguishing whether we were actors in a comedic farce, all caricatures to be laughed at for our shortsightedness and stupidity, or a tragedy driven to its hubristic and inevitable conclusion by the foibles of the characters.

Whichever interpretation is given to the succeeding events really doesn't matter; the outcome remains the same.

Act 1, Scene 1: We complained to the local Roman authority, a cavalry officer by the name of Jucundus, about the further transgressions by Philip the Greek, and Jucundus tried to intervene. Though his intentions were honorable, his resources were inadequate, and he was not able to halt the violence threatened by the Greek and his friends. In the face of their continuous threats to the synagogue and to our people, and the inability of the Romans to protect us, we retrieved the scrolls of the Torah from our synagogue and fled from Caesarea to

Narbata, a village about seven miles away that was entirely Jewish.

Act 1, Scene 2: John and I and ten other elders traveled to the city of Sebaste, where Florus had decamped. Upon achieving an audience with him, at the cost of further payment of bribes, John explained the situation and reminded him of the eight talents of silver that had been paid to him to prevent this outcome. Florus became incensed at the criticism. Seizing on the pretext of the sanctity of the synagogue in Caesarea, he accused us of stealing holy objects that rightfully belonged in Caesarea. We were arrested and put into prison in Sebaste, but our confinement was ended when a further exchange of silver took place between our group and the jailers.

Act 1, Scene 3: The population of Jerusalem was outraged when the news of our treatment was reported. Anger was directed at the Greeks of Caesarea, of course, but true fury was poured out at Florus for his duplicity. It is widely said that an honest public official is one who, once bribed, stays bribed. By that standard, Florus had demonstrated his dishonesty and corruption for all to see. Not that he cared.

Act 1, Scene 4: Faced with the anger and hostility of the Jews of Jerusalem, a prudent procurator might have decided to let things blow over for a while. Not Florus. Behaving almost as though someone had hired him to inflame a rebellious war, Florus went at the head of his troops to the Temple treasury, where he instructed them to remove seventeen talents of gold and silver. His haughty explanation was that "Caesar requires it. The procurator has expenses that must be covered for his sustenance."

This was so outrageous that the people actually laughed when it was reported to them. A voice in the crowd shouted out, "Let us take up a collection for the poor man, so that through our charity he will not starve." I was startled to realize that the voice was familiar. The years had made its tone a bit raspier and lower, but there was no doubt in my mind that this was the voice of Judas Iscariot. Like the other followers of Jesus, I thought him dead, for it had been put about that he had committed suicide by hanging himself in remorse for having betrayed Jesus. It came to me that this must have been a rumor initiated by him and encouraged by his zealous followers in order to hide him from retribution.

I recalled the curse I had put on Judas for his special part in the death of Jesus of Nazareth. But even with that plot carried out to divert attention from him and the Zealots, I am sure he feared that, were the high priest to discover the truth of the attack on the Temple, he would send his soldiers after Judas. Judas knew I was alive, a witness to the truth and the conspiracy to crucify an innocent man. Even if his perfidy were not uncovered by the high priest, his sedition against Rome was enough to warrant his discreet disappearance. In any case, he had melted away from any scrutiny by pretending to be dead. Now, like me, he was resurrected.

With loud jeers, Judas and his band of young followers began to pass a basket through the crowd and even collected a few copper coins to mock Procurator Florus. But the humor of the situation was soon exhausted, to be overwhelmed by anger at the injustice. Led by the Zealots, the furious crowd of several hundred Jews rushed to the Temple. The mob initially shouted spontaneous pleas to the faraway emperor to free them from the misrule of Florus. Judas and his band of Zealots quickly managed to turn the chanting against the more proximate target of Florus himself.

Act 1, Scene 5: The conclusion of the opening act of this tragi-comedy should be predictable, knowing what we do about the character of our villain, Florus. If it is true—and it surely is—that the quality of a drama is directly proportional to the iniquity of the villain, then Florus seemed to strive mightily to play that role. One can almost imagine him thinking, "It is my role in this play to act the villain. What can I do that is the most villainous thing possible, which will shock the audience and cause them to gasp in disbelief? What would freeze them in their seats and make them remember me as a truly gifted villain? Let me think! Ah! I've got it!"

Any normal public servant would have sought to mollify the

mob by making empty promises of a "full investigation" that would fix culpability and provide justice. Where any normal person would have gone to Caesarea to dampen the fires of strife that had broken out there, as he had in fact been paid by us to do, Florus instead used the opportunity to make some more money for himself. There was no money to be made in Caesarea; he had already extracted what he could from the Greeks and Gentiles who lived there. The wealth he sought was held by the Jews and the Temple, and they were not in Caesarea. He roused the army from their barracks outside the city, and with a troop of soldiers and cavalry, headed toward Jerusalem.

The people of Jerusalem, forewarned of his approach, sent a delegation to head him off on the road with friendly greetings and a submissive attitude. Florus would have none of that! No profit to be found there! There was no gold to be had in groveling rabbis and apologetic pleadings. Instead, he ordered fifty cavalry soldiers ahead to meet the city delegation, and through their captain, Capito, demanded that they return to Jerusalem. Florus evinced fury at the abuse and insults that the crowd had heaped upon his name, and he accused the people's delegation of mocking him by pretending to be polite and subservient.

"If you were real men, you would stand up to me, be as fearless and outspoken to my face as you are when my back is to you," he hissed. "Make fun of me while you stand before me, and bring your armed might to fight me if you are such lovers of liberty!"

And then, not waiting for a reaction, Florus sent Capito's troops charging into the crowd. These were experienced cavalry, and the horses were accustomed to charging into an enemy infantry formation. The horses reared and kicked and used their bulk to knock down and trample those on foot; the cavalrymen, shouting and creating a fearful din, scattered the crowd and sent them fleeing back to the city. The people of Jerusalem spent that night in the meager shelter of their homes, knowing that, predictable in his unpredictability, Florus was likely to lash out further against them.

Act 2, Scene 1: Sure enough, the next day, Florus took his seat on a dais he had erected outside the palace and summoned before him all the chief Jewish citizens of the city. He looked rested and relaxed after a comfortable night. Those of us gathered before him were less so, anticipating further outrages. We were not disappointed.

Florus began by sounding aggrieved. "I have endured the scorn and abuse of the people of Jerusalem patiently. But yesterday's insults have exhausted my patience! This is not about my own pride and injured feelings. The rabble in your midst that hurled their insults aimed them not only at me personally, but assaulted with their words the authority of my role as representative of the emperor. By doing so, they attacked also the authority of the emperor and Rome itself. This is an act of rebellion, and the perpetrators must be punished accordingly. It is your responsibility to arrest those responsible and turn them over to me."

The high priest stepped forward as spokesman for the city. "Sir, we apologize unreservedly for the insults that were directed toward you. Please be assured that the young people who used such injudicious language in no way represent the people of Jerusalem. Nor is there any intent to vilify Rome or your imperial authority. In any crowd there are going to be young, impudent hotheads—we do not even know who they were. But please know that we are remorseful."

At this point, the high priest made his mistake, and our little play turned from farce to tragedy. "Your Highness, Florus, do you not agree that it would be better for the peace of the nation and the city to pardon the few unidentified guilty for the sake of the many innocent and loyal citizens? To do otherwise will inflame the population even further and spread the feelings of injustice. Surely it would be better to let a few irresponsible scamps go unpunished."

Florus' face reddened and he leapt to his feet, saliva flying. "You dare to threaten me? Do you dare to defy Rome and shelter those among you guilty of this treasonous language? You have the temerity to question my administration of justice! Well, you shall feel the full weight of my justice and the wrath of Rome. Do you forget the fate of

King Mithridates, who led the people of Pontus against Rome? Or of Carthage, which like Pontus, was ground under the heel of the Roman legions? Well, I promise you will remember them until the end of your days, which may come sooner than you think. Your mighty Jewish god will not protect you from my justice!"

Act 2, Scene 2: For once, Florus kept a promise. The savagery with which his soldiers attacked the people of Jerusalem was beyond description. From the upper rooms of the house that had once belonged to my uncle and had since passed to me, I could hear the cries from the streets as the Roman soldiers worked their way toward me. They rampaged through the Upper City, looting and killing without discrimination. They broke through windows and knocked down doors, killing the occupants without mercy. Those who fled from the assault were chased down and hacked to pieces. Unlike the angels of death sent by God to kill the firstborn of Egypt, who passed over the houses of the Hebrews, the Roman soldiers targeted the homes of the richest and noblest Jews of Israel. Resistance meant death, and submission meant arrest followed by merciless crucifixion. The streets were slippery with the blood that flowed from the bodies of the still living and the dead.

The screams served like thunder to track the progress of the coming storm. From several streets over, I could hear the Romans' approach. I quickly gathered up some food, lamp oil and a small lamp, a few clothes, and a bowl and cup. Just as the soldiers reached the next street, I left the house and made my way by circuitous paths to the only place that I could imagine would provide a sanctuary—the Temple.

Under the Temple Mount there are tunnels and cisterns that store water and channel it down to the pools in the old city. The water runs through the tunnels in rivulets and streams to exit into ancient pools far from the Temple itself. Entering the pool at the base of the Mount, I splashed my way through the tunnel's darkness, climbing upward until I found a small grotto in a branching tunnel off the main channel. Here I brought my few belongings, thinking I could hide here for a while until the city above was safe. I wrapped a cloak around myself against the chill of the damp tunnel. This hole, deep under the Holy of Holies, would be my shelter, where I could hide safely.

The tunnels under the Temple served to magnify rather than muffle the sounds from the streets above. I could hear clearly from my cavernous shelter the screaming and shouting. After a time, these diminished, to be replaced by the sounds of the wailing, the wounded, and the victims of the hasty Roman crucifixions. Cautiously, I emerged from my sheltering tomb—this was becoming a familiar habit—and made my way through the bloody streets.

Act 3, It Begins: The smoke hung like a fog over the Upper City of Jerusalem, sliding into homes through broken doors and windows, permeating and emphasizing the carnage wrought by the rampaging Roman army. Survivors wandered through the Upper City, weeping and lamenting and calling down curses on Florus, probably to his great satisfaction.

At my house I was met by a messenger, who called me to join the civic leaders and priests in a hurried council. After a prayer for the dead and dying, the chief priest spoke. "We must stop these demonstrations against Florus lest he view them as further rebellion. We must remove every sign of resistance, even resentment. Only then will he have no excuse for undertaking any further actions against the people. Once we have a period of calm, we can send a delegation to the emperor and ask him to take action."

I rose to my feet. "That is a big mistake! Florus has demonstrated repeatedly that he will not be mollified by obeisance and overtures of submission." I pointed scornfully at the chief priest. "You think you are being a clever diplomat, but you are proposing a pact with the devil! By these actions, you will turn your back on God. You are making a covenant with Rome in the hope that the emperor will protect you. Do you really think you can transform Florus from a ravening beast into a meek shepherd by lying down like sheep before him? Florus would not do this without the approval of Emperor Nero!

"It is obvious what is happening here! Nero is pressing all the provinces for funds so he can raise Rome from the ashes of the fire that consumed so much of the city two years ago. Florus is simply carrying out that mission, and he will never allow us to stand in his way. Which do you think is more important to him? Approval and peace here in Judea, or approval and submission to the will of the emperor who appointed him? What appears to us as blind greed and injustice is to him a duty."

The priests grew agitated at this accusation, for in their hearts they recognized its truth. Still, they objected. One said, "I understand your point, but can't you see we have no choice? Rebellion against Rome is impossible! Florus has made it clear that the only end to that path is the same as that suffered by Pontus and Carthage. Our only option is submission."

I responded, "You have lost your faith in the power of God to sustain his people. Did not King David prevail against the might of the Philistines? Was Daniel not led unscathed from the lion's den? Was Joshua not able to conquer Jericho? These battles were all won by relying on the power of God working through his Chosen People. But when Israel doubts the power of the covenant, God withdraws his hand. We must reject the protections of Rome and return to the protection of God. We must be zealous in our faith in God! We must fight!"

Despite my exhortations and despite significant support from within the group, after some heated debate and finger-pointing, the counsel of submission and cowardice prevailed. Reluctantly heeding the insistence of the priests, the mourners stuffed their fists into their mouths, and the shrieking and lamenting for the dead fell silent. Of course, their passivity had exactly the effect I had predicted.

The unnatural silence served only to annoy Florus by undermining his excuses for continued outrage. Summoning the chief priests and prominent citizens, he once again demanded proof that the people would not rebel. This time, he ordered the leaders to go out of the city and meet the two cohorts of Roman troops now approaching Jerusalem. While the priests were gathering their delegation, Florus sent word to the centurions leading the cohorts that they were to react to the slightest hint of provocation by using their weapons.

Sure enough, being greeted with silence by the soldiers, the delegation began to mutter, and the soldiers, following their instructions, immediately fell on them. The crowd turned in a panic, and many who escaped being clubbed by the soldiers were crushed under the feet of their companions in the rush to flee. The soldiers followed the mob into the city and drove them through the timber market in Bezetha. It was quickly evident to the fleeing populace that Florus had directed the soldiers to reach the treasures of the Temple and the Antonia Fortress.

While these events were transpiring, the debate between submission and resistance among the people had continued, for debates among Jews are never finished as long as one remains standing. I and others continued our exhortations that those following Florus' commands were marching to disaster. The weight of the recent deaths on their minds moved the bolder ones among them. When word came that our prediction had been fulfilled (it did not require a prophet to foresee), those favoring resistance quickly ran to join the retreating crowd.

Humiliated and wounded, the reinforced crowd was receptive to the exhortations of its new members. Instead of fleeing as the Romans expected, we took to the rooftops overlooking the narrow streets and began to pelt the hemmed-in soldiers with stones. The Romans' tactics were not suited to urban warfare. They were able to cover themselves against the stones and arrows with their bronze shields, but they could make no headway against the Jews who had stationed themselves overhead. The falling missiles forced the Romans back, and they retreated to their camp near the palace.

Chapter 13: Finale

Thus began the revolt of the Jewish people against the might of Rome. The Jewish King Agrippa and his wife tried to intervene to prevent and reverse the consequences of the repulsion of Florus' soldiers, but they were unable to stop the headlong lurch of their subjects into full rebellion. As mere puppets of the emperor, they could not sway Florus from his duty to Nero. For this brief time, the various elements and motivations of the people of Israel converged. The plots and conspiracies of one against the others were put in abeyance in the face of the overwhelming need to prepare for Rome's inevitable counterpunch.

The initial response came from the Roman legate in Syria. Cestius Gallus was ordered by Rome to bring the unruly Jews to order, and he was confident that the Roman legion under his command was easily up to the task. His expectation was well founded. The Legion XII Fulminata had a glorious history, beginning with its creation by Julius Caesar and its record in the conquering of Gaul. Since then, it had fought and defeated enemies of Rome in many campaigns throughout the Empire. In particular, it achieved fame when it fought under Marc Antony in the Roman Civil War against the rebels Brutus and Cassius.

The Twelfth Legion wound up in Syria, but by the time of the Jewish Revolt, it had fallen on lean times. Nevertheless, Cestius Gallus beefed up its ranks with auxiliary troops drawn from two other legions and sent it south into Israel to restore order and quell the revolt. Initially, it found success against ill-prepared Jewish forces around Jaffa. Then the legion marched on to Jerusalem, but it was too weak to successfully defeat us. We had taken up our position in the Temple Mount, and the massive walls of the fortifications were beyond the capabilities of a Roman legion that basically consisted of infantry and light cavalry troops.

When it became evident to Cestius Gallus that he could not prevail in Jerusalem with light infantry, he decided to fall back to the western coast, where reinforcements and heavy siege machinery could be brought by sea. Gallus was probably unfamiliar with the difficult geography of Israel. Unlike the flat plains and open desert of Syria, Israel is characterized by ranges of mountains and hills that mostly run north to south. To reach the coast from Jerusalem required the legion to march westward, following one of the narrow passes that run east and west through these upswelling rocky hills.

It was at the narrowest point of their march that the Jewish Zealots waited in ambush. Attacking from the heights, the rebels devastated the Romans from above with massive flights of arrows. The same weakness that had defeated Florus in the narrow streets of Jerusalem now defeated the Twelfth Legion. In the narrow confines of the pass at Beth Horon, the Romans were unable to form into their famous ten-by-ten fighting squads. At the end of the day, the entire legion of 6,000 Romans was massacred. Even the legion's standard was captured, and served as a triumphant signal to the Zealot rebels that God was truly with them.

The Roman defeat reverberated. New recruits flocked to the rebellion, and the victorious Jews armed themselves with spoils from the Roman dead. No one doubted now that, armed with the power of God, Israel would shake off the tyranny of Rome and establish itself as an independent Jewish nation. This faith was reinforced when a group of Zealots stealthily made their way to the hills overlooking the Dead Sea and attacked the Roman garrison in old King Herod's mountaintop fortress of Masada. They killed the entire Roman garrison and put a Jewish garrison in its place.

The Greeks have a word for what came next: "hubris." By this they mean an arrogance that is offensive to the gods. In our case, it meant we imagined the defeat of the Romans signified God's favor and protection for his Chosen People. With this understanding, we naturally assumed the defeated Romans would henceforth leave us alone to pursue our own destiny in the land promised us, via Moses, by God. The absence of the Romans also left a gap in the dissemination of news from Rome. So there was a long period of time when we remained ignorant of the facts that the Emperor Nero had committed suicide, and that a new civil war had broken out. In the space of one year, Rome was ruled in succession by four different emperors. Of these, Vespasian was the general that Nero, before his death, had sent to deal with the Jewish revolt. The turmoil in Rome proved a distraction from his assignment in Israel, and left a vacuum of some three years.

The Jewish people were thereby left free to turn on each other. We fell to with gusto. On one side were we Zealots. Controlling the Temple and the Lower City, we ordered that all sacrifices for Caesar and any of the customary payments to the government be immediately abolished. On the other side were the Pharisees, who continued to seek the forgiveness of Rome and feared the retribution they foresaw. In their fear, the Pharisees sought help from Florus and King Agrippa.

King Agrippa made a lengthy speech in which he emphasized the power of Rome and its defeat of opponents who were far more powerful than the forces that could be mustered in Israel. Convinced that Rome would wreak havoc in revenge for the rebellion, the Pharisees begged Agrippa to send troops to support them. Agrippa turned to Florus, who, as usual, made promises that he did not keep. The two thousand troops that came at Agrippa's behest were mercenaries under the command of Darius the cavalry commander and Philip the general. These forces occupied the Upper City, which had so recently been the site of Romans massacring Jews. Meanwhile, the Lower City and the Temple remained in the hands of the Zealots. We fought each other in the streets of Jerusalem with stones and slings, even in hand-to-hand combat, resulting in days of mutual slaughter. After a week of street battles, we were joined by the Sicarii, and together we drove the Pharisees and King Agrippa's troops out of the Upper City.

Victorious, we pushed on. In a frenzy, we set fire to the house of Ananias the high priest, as well as the palace of King Agrippa. We were tempted to stop and bask in our victory, but I raised my voice to counsel otherwise.

"We must destroy the records of the moneylenders. This will free the poor and the debtors who are yet afraid to join us!" And so it came to pass that we turned to burning the records office where all the data were kept on the bonds of moneylenders and the debts they held. With the debt records destroyed, the poor debtors rushed to swell the ranks of the rebellion.

And so came about the open warfare between us Zealot rebels and the forces of the Pharisees who were supported by Agrippa's troops. But within the camp of the Zealots, there was also discontent. Menachem, our initial leader, was attacked by a faction who thought him arrogant and tyrannical. Supported by the mob, he was caught and massacred, while some of his followers were able to escape to the fortress at Masada. Roman troops who attempted to surrender in exchange for their lives were brutally murdered, and the portion of the Jewish population that still feared the vengeance of Rome was further convinced of their fatal destiny.

Meanwhile, in Caesarea, where the whole thing started, the Greek population massacred the entire Jewish population, killing more than twenty thousand Jews. I was in Jerusalem, or that would have been the end of me, because even the few survivors were rounded up by Florus and sent in chains to the dockyards as galley slaves. This so aroused the Jewish population that the rebellion, which had so far been confined to Jerusalem, rose throughout the country. Cities were sacked by both sides, and wholesale slaughter was the order of the day.

Jews everywhere turned on each other. Whole populations of Jews were murdered by their fellow citizens. Fathers executed their own families in order to preserve them from the horror that would otherwise befall them in the event of their capture by their fellow Jews. Treachery followed treachery as sides betrayed each other, violated truces, formed and broke alliances. Roman forces came and went, often triumphant initially, but in the end finding defeat.

And so passed some three years. During this period, Rome was busy sorting out its succession problems after the suicide of Emperor Nero. After three years of civil war and contending claims, the Senate at the end of the day accepted a new emperor—Vespasian. He came to

Rome with the support of the legions of Egypt, Judea, Syria, and the Danube. Vespasian sent his commander Primus ahead to secure Italy on his behalf. After a major and bloody battle, victory was achieved at Cremona, Emperor Vitellius was defeated, and in December of that year, Primus took Rome. The senate passed a law conferring the powers of emperor on Vespasian, and he arrived in Rome in the late summer of the following year.

Vespasian had been charged by Emperor Nero with the task of ending the Jewish Revolt, but the death of Nero and the succeeding upheavals diverted him from this task. Now, with his seat on the throne secure, Vespasian turned his attention back to the task he had let linger. Titus, Emperor Vespasian's son, was given the responsibility of bringing the now three-year-old rebellion to heel.

As I sit here writing these words, I am able to personally attest to the capabilities and success of General Titus. I have once again had to take to my secret shelter in the small cavern under the Temple. My old home where I grew up with my sisters on the eastern slope of the Mount of Olives has been destroyed, with almost all the possessions that were kept there. I have only been able to preserve the few items that I have kept with me. Here next to me on the table where I write these words—the table that Jesus made for us so long ago—are my few remaining belongings. I have a plate for my bread, and for water I have the cup that came from our household; the same one used by Jesus of Nazareth for that last Passover meal before his arrest and crucifixion.

I can hear the thudding boom of the Roman battering rams as they systematically destroy the walls of the city. In the tunnel outside my little nook, I can hear fleeing Jewish fighters sliding down the waterway, seeking escape. I suppose many of them will seek refuge in the fortress at Masada. To prevent these desperate refugees from taking over my little refuge, I have slid a large stone over the low opening, hiding the entrance from view in the darkness of the tunnel. My little oil lamp sheds poor light, and, in any case, the stone is tight-fitting, so the light is not visible to those passing through the tunnel outside.

It is clear to even the most pious Jews that the God of the Israelites will not intervene to protect us against the Romans. Perhaps He never cared. Or perhaps the despicable behavior of His Chosen People over the short period of our independence from Rome led Him to withdraw his countenance. Who can explain the divine will? In any case, there is now only one outcome possible in this battle. Soon the pounding of the battering rams will cease, and the screaming of the dying will begin. The sack of Jerusalem, the destruction of the fortress on which the Temple stands—these are now inevitable.

I am an old man now, and my head throbs in time with the blows of the Roman battering rams as I put these words down. Perhaps someday searchers will find my little hollow under the Temple and read my account. I don't know why the flame on my lamp is guttering and smoking; there is ample oil remaining. I am so very tired.

Part IV
Christopher Columbus

There was an addendum to this amazing document. It was written in French with the goal of documenting the way in which this stunning book of Lazarus had come into the possession of the Knights of the Temple. Indeed, its discovery underlay the very purpose for which the Knights had been formed.

The two Frankish knights felt their way cautiously down the tunnel. Their flickering torch cast shadows on the rough walls, but shed little light except to ensure that they did not fall into a hole in the floor.

Above them, in the bright sunlight, the triumph of July 1099 had passed. The screaming had stopped, the smoke from the burning buildings had cleared, and the smell of roasted human flesh had drifted away from the synagogue where the few Jewish inhabitants of Jerusalem had sought refuge, only to be burned to death in the fire set by the conquering Crusaders. The piles in the streets of heads, hands, and feet that made the invaders walk cautiously lest they slip in the blood had been removed, and the gutters washed clean. The thousands of bodies had been cleared away into mass graves, the buildings had been looted, and the treasures of Islam had been removed or destroyed.

After a few weeks of protestations that he was unworthy to be king of Jerusalem, Raymond of Toulouse declined the crown and it fell to Godfrey of Lorraine. The tall, handsome, fair-haired descendant of Charlemagne was idolized as the perfect Christian knight, the peerless hero of the whole crusading epic. Since then, over the period of years, kings and nobles had come and gone, ecclesiastical hierarchies had been established, and now King Baldwin II ruled over Jerusalem.

All that took place above in the sunlight, but below, in the tunnels beneath the Temple Mount, Hugue de Payan and Geoffrey Bissot stumbled in the dark. Behind them they trailed a rope to guide their return. By agreement, Hugue stayed to the left wall of the tunnel, and Geoffrey to the right, trailing their fingers along the cold, damp walls. The two proceeded in this fashion until they came to the end of their rope, and then turned to begin their return climb.

Geoffrey hissed, "There is something here, Hugue. I feel a crack in the wall, and there is an indentation like a door." Hugue ran his fingers along the edge, finding a circular outline. "It is very regular and smooth. This is not a natural feature of the tunnel walls." He put his shoulder against the stone, which did not budge. "Let's go back to the others. We need to return with pry bars and better light."

The name on the baptismal certificate was a shock—Gerard de Villiers? Vague memories from my childhood were linked to this name, but I had always put them in the category of fables and myths. Yet here was proof of his existence, and the link back through my family to this French nobleman. The tunic, moreover, identified him as a Knight of the Order of the Temple, an order of heretics accused of the worst imaginable perversions and sins against God and Holy Mother Church.

I carefully shook out the tunic and held it up to the light, for it seemed wonderfully old to me, and I imagined it resting on the shoulders of my ancestor. As the bright light of Chios shone through its threads, I saw that something had been sewn into the shoulder pads. I painstakingly split the stitches and drew out a folded piece of vellum. I smoothed it out carefully on the table. As my eyes became accustomed to the faded inks and the initially meaningless squiggles, I found that the whole resolved itself into a portolan map. Its age was difficult to determine. Such maps had been around for hundreds of years, used by and shared among sailors to navigate across open waters to distant coasts. I could discern a faint notation on one corner in Latin, Greek, and what appeared to be Arabic or Persian, ascribing the map to someone named Piri Re'is, based on reconstructions from far earlier maps. I could not know the original sources, but imagined it derived from explorations as far back as the Egyptians and Phoenicians, perhaps even to Minoans.

There had been many reports among seafarers that a great continent lay to the west across the Ocean Sea, but this map was more than a vague outline of such a landmass. The land it depicted was highly detailed, showing serrated coastlines and the outlets of rivers, islands, and bays. The areas depicted extended far below the equator, and showed the coast of Africa as well as the Portuguese coastline jutting into the ocean. The European portion of the map looked quite accurate, suggesting that the rendering of the land on the other side of the ocean might be equally reliable.

I spent days pondering the technical elements of this inheritance. With study, I could discern the meridian that indicated true north, and from there could judge the latitude lines intersecting the meridian at right angles. What I could not determine from the map was the actual distance from the coast of Europe to the far shore.

To answer this question, I turned to the recently discovered work of the ancients. The books of Ptolemy had been translated recently into Latin, and a copy was on deposit in the library of the monastery. Ptolemy clearly knew nothing about the land to the west, but what was important to me was his estimate of the distance around the earth—from this I could estimate the distances displayed on my portolan map. His estimate yields a circumference of 28,800 kilometers, which means that a reasonable estimate of the distance from the coast of Portugal to the land mass shown on de Villiers's portolan was about 2,000 kilometers.[4]

While the technical aspects of the portolan map fascinated me, the greater mystery lay in the purpose of the map and the manner of its concealment. This purpose was revealed when I turned the map over. On the back, in scratchy Oc, the language of southwestern France, was a long paragraph. The ink had faded after all these years, so it was difficult to discern the words. I could make out a few, and guessed at

---

[4]I have converted the manuscripts measurements into modern kilometers. It is well known that Ptolemy's estimate of the earth's circumference was short by about 40 percent. (Ed.)

some that were similar to Italian: "Knights Templar," "holy cup," and scattered others. I pondered the meaning of all these clues.

After some cautious consultation with Father Pantaleon, combined with his wise guidance through the extensive library of the monastery, I was able to piece together the message that had been sent through time to me. It was astonishing.

It was, of course, impossible for a person with even the most meager education not to know the stories of the Holy Grail. These stories had been circulating for hundreds of years, first when Chretien de Troyes published his poem "Perceval, or the Story of the Grail," and most recently in my own time with "Le Morte d'Arthur" from the scoundrel and brigand Thomas Malory.

It was now clear to me that the spread of the Grail legends at about the same time as the French attack on the Templars and the confiscation of their treasure was no coincidence. The original poem of Chretien de Troyes was not finished by him, but was instead completed by a Templar clerk in the court of the daughter of Queen Eleanor of Aquitaine. Aquitaine included the city of La Rochelle and the part of France known now as Languedoc. It seemed plausible that the Templars, possessing the cup Jesus used at the Last Supper, wished to conceal its reality. By putting out wondrous and magical tales, the Grail could be shrouded in mystery and myth, transposed into a spiritual dimension, and manifested in multiple ways.

After the attack on the Templars by King Philip of France, the Grail receded even further into the realm of myth and the miasma of mystery. By deliberate misdirection, the legends directed seekers to the island of Britain—to the ruins of Tintagel Castle or to the foundations of this church or that church. Meanwhile, the secret of its flight from France aboard the Templar treasure fleet in 1307 was assured. And now, God be praised, my forefather had passed on the secret of its true location to me.

I knew now where my destiny lay. I had been shown the way. For the glory of God and Holy Mother Church, and to honor my ancestor's legacy, I would devote myself to the recovery of the Holy Grail. Like Odysseus shaking off the captivating soft arms of Circe, I now shook off the lovely breezes and soft water of Chios, and I sailed home to Genoa and the stringy embrace of my father.

My return to Genoa (or more accurately, Savona) in 1475 was not accorded the celebrations of the return of the prodigal son. My absence had been that of a fugitive from justice, so my return was more like that of one released from prison. Like many in Genoa, the family business had fallen on hard times with the fall of Constantinople.

Over time, the opportunities to sell our wool in exchange for products from the Silk Road had diminished. My brothers and I could see that the future for the sale of finished wool in the east was drying up, and together we pressured our father to shift his focus to Europe. He was reluctant to change from ways he had known all his life, but he surrendered to our pleadings and the evident need to adapt. Our voyages began to move west from Genoa, sailing through the Pillars of Hercules to England and northern France, where the generally filthy climate creates a ready market for wool cloth.

And so it was that in the summer of 1476, the year following my return from Chios, I shipped out with a Genoese fleet of five ships bound for Portugal and England, carrying a cargo of wool and mastic. Our first destination was Lisbon. From there we intended to sail on to Bristol, in England. Three of the other ships, like ours, flew the flag of Genoa, and one flew the flag of the prince of Burgundy.

My father had entered into a business arrangement with Nicola Spinola, the owner and captain of our ship. Instead of the usual manner of paying for passage in advance, in order to save money, he entered into a joint venture. The captain and his crew would get half the proceeds from selling the cargo once it reached Bristol. In this way, my father reasoned, it would save him the up-front payment, encourage the captain and crew to make haste, and lay off half the risk of any adverse events.

While my father's logic was impeccable, events have a way of tripping the most careful plans. Not being a seaman, my father did not recognize that the ship was barely seaworthy. It was built as a whaler, not a cargo ship, and had seen rough service. The leaking holds let in water that soaked into the woolen bales and created a spongy mess that could not be pumped out. The weight of the liquid thus absorbed forced the ship lower into the water and slowed its progress so we were unable to maintain speed. The other four ships of our convoy were obliged to slow to our pace.

While the wool bales could be dried out on arrival with little loss of value, the whole journey would have been lengthened by many days. I sought to give Captain Spinola the benefit of my years at sea and broad experience. Taking offense at my mild remonstrance, he spurned my advice regarding sail trim and shifting of the cargo. I was treated rudely and sent off the deck with orders to the crew to bar any attempt to return. So our little convoy wallowed through the waves of the Middle Sea while I chafed at the slow speed and the prospect of delayed sale of our cargo.

My concerns about delay disappeared once we entered the narrow channel of the Pillars of Hercules. This was for me a sublime journey; to pass from the Middle Sea to the great Ocean Sea beyond, and to pass through the narrow defile that separates Europe from Africa. More importantly, I was transported by the practical challenges of navigating the channel.

The narrow Strait funnels the wind, but it also funnels the current. Inshore tidal movements can reach three knots, but these diminish as one sails closer to the center of the channel. I inquired of the captain why we did not hew to the central channel to overcome the tidal thrust, but here he revealed a secret of this mysterious place—regardless of the state of the tide, there is a constant east-moving stream in the center of the Strait! So a ship exiting the strait must balance the power of an adverse current in the center with the power of a strong tide near the verges, and the associated risks of sailing with a lee shore. Complicating our transition was the heavy weight of our wet cargo, reducing the maneuverability of our ship.

Despite these challenges, thanks to light winds from the east, our transit was uneventful. I noted in my journal the state of the winds and tides, and drew some sketches of the coastline as we passed, carefully rendering the landmarks, the angle of our tacks and reaches, and the timing of all the captain's commands with regard to the reefing of the sails and movements of the tiller.

Our flotilla turned northwest after clearing the Pillars of Hercules, seeking to make up some time by transiting across the Gulf of Cadiz toward Cape St. Vincent. The winds were favorable, but our fortunes were not. As we sailed past Faro, we sighted what turned out to be hostile sails approaching.

Had we not been so heavily laden, we might well have outrun these attackers, for the captain knew they were corsairs under the command of a notorious pirate named Casenove. Now we were forced to pay the price of being in a wallowing tub. The five ships of our convoy gathered tightly, and the men who were so equipped donned their armor in preparation for the hand-to-hand fighting that would inevitably result from being boarded.

The enemy closed tightly, hull to hull, and the corsairs swarmed aboard, swinging their swords and pikes. Our crew fought bravely, but they were seafaring merchant sailors, not warriors. In a desperate attempt to reverse the battle, our captain ordered fire pots to be thrown from our rigging, but these got caught in the rigging of the corsair ships. The flames intended for the pirates spread rapidly to include our ship, and then spread across the entire flotilla, consuming friend and foe alike. Three of our ships were burned to the waterline, as were four of the pirates'. In the face of these losses, the remaining pirates took axes to the lines that bound them to us and fled, as did the two surviving members of our convoy.

Alas, I was not aboard one of the surviving ships. The flames spread rapidly over the deck, and the terrible smoke choked and blinded me. Like many of my shipmates, to avoid the flames, I climbed over the deck rail and plunged into the frigid waters. Unlike many of those poor souls, I was not burdened by the heavy armor that dragged them under the water to their deaths. Instead, God sent into my grasp a wooden oar. Clinging to it, I was able to stay afloat while kicking my way toward shore.

The shore of Portugal along that stretch consists of high cliffs, with waves dashing through the rocks at their feet sending up huge gouts of water. There is no beach with soft sand on which an exhausted swimmer might find rest from the breakers. So it was necessary that I remain in the water for six hours, swimming parallel to the tantalizing shore, seeking a landing site. Finally, I spied through the waves a strip of beach and kicked toward it. The waves carried me in through the small surf, and I was able to crawl out of the water.

Some fishermen who had seen the smoke of our battle found me. Throwing blankets around my shivering form, they carried me to their nearby village of Lagos. There they kindly cared for me for many days while I regained my strength, for I was as weak as a newborn baby. Thus was I baptized in the holy water of the Ocean Sea.

When I first departed Genoa for Lisbon, I was a proud man. I had sailed the Middle Sea for many years, knew its coastlines and winds, could navigate by the stars and the sun. I could command a ship, knew the names of the sails, and could direct crew to raise and lower them as needed. I fancied myself a sailor.

The Ocean Sea humbled me, and I believe God sent me a signal with the sinking under me of the very first ship on which I sailed on its surface. I took the message that here was a beast that exceeded in every way the fierceness of the Middle Sea. I needed to learn its tricks and its predictable habits. Here, I was a novice.

There were many Genoese living in Lisbon, my youngest brother among them. I had not seen Bartholomew since before my sojourn in

Chios, but the time apart did not affect our warm relationship. He was wonderfully welcoming and provided me with lodging in his house. It was understood that I would help him in his shop. So, for the next six years, when I was not at sea, Bartholomew and I prepared maps and charts which we sold to the sailors and merchants traversing Lisbon's sea lanes.

I had thought that my time sailing the waters of the Middle Sea had made me an expert sailor. And, indeed, the following chapters of my life at sea would not have been possible without them. But my time in Lisbon oriented me away from the well-traveled shores inside the Pillars of Hercules and toward the vast forces that moved the currents of the Ocean Sea. In Lisbon, all focus was on the Ocean Sea.

The next six years found me only intermittently on shore. This was the period when I devoted myself to learning the ways of the Ocean Sea. And in the course of my various voyages, I nursed in my heart a fixed objective—the destination of the Templar fleet and its precious cargo.

What did I know for sure that could guide me? I had the map and the history that had come from my ancestor, Gerard de Villiers. So I knew there was a land far to the west over the Ocean Sea. I thought this a great secret until I discovered in Lisbon that, while the existence of that land was not exactly common knowledge, neither was it a great secret, at least among the sailors who came to our map shop. My map showed many details of the shoreline of this distant land, but gave no clue as to where the Templar fleet might have landed.

And so I chose my voyages from Lisbon carefully. While the exigencies of commerce necessarily limited my scope, I was able to explore a surprising variety of directions. The most careful direction I took, however, was in my choice of a wife. And it was that choice that opened paths for me that would otherwise have not been available.

When I joined my brother Bartholomew in his map shop enterprise, I hoped I would be brought into contact with the elite of Lisbon and Portugal. All of the higher echelons of Portuguese society were bent toward seaborne commerce and exploration, thanks to the nation's location at the pivot between the Ocean Sea and the Mediterranean Sea. The famous school of navigation established by Prince Henry encouraged and sponsored exploration. I hoped that, ensconced in our map shop, these currents would flow through our doors. I expected that the need for our maps, carefully drawn and constantly updated on the basis of sailors' reports, would bring rich and influential nobles and merchants to our shop. I was confident that, given a chance, my evident expertise and natural persuasive ability could elicit sponsorship to organize a voyage of discovery to the west.

Of greatest consequence during this period was my voyage to England and beyond. I departed in February of 1477 with a Genoese fleet of ships carrying cargo to the port of Bristol. The Bristol harbor is wonderfully sheltered at the end of a long channel that allows ships to penetrate from the west to deliver and collect cargoes. This channel forms the mouth of the Avon River, which extends far into the heartland of England and provides a ready road for commerce. Bristol's prominence as a trading center and seaport makes it a natural place for sailors from all over the world to congregate between voyages, and it was here that I made the acquaintance of a ship's captain who captured my imagination. It happened thusly.

If there is one thing I have learned about sailors from my years of mingling with them, it is that they are torn between boasting and secrecy. Often the boasting conceals something true and profound. And sometimes, tales that appear boastful and beyond belief are actually true, at least in part. The tales told by Marco Polo of his journeys in Cathay were initially dismissed as fabulous inventions, until they were later verified by other travelers.

My attention was focused on those who described voyages to the north and west, for these offered a potential source to verify the map I carried secretly, passed down from my ancestor. I knew that Portuguese sailors had covered the southern seas, and that only land lay to the west of Constantinople. So my hopes were pinned to the remaining points of the compass that had been little explored. English merchant ships often sail from Bristol to Thule carrying cargoes of wool, tinker's pots and pans, knives and axes. These were traded in return for cargoes with rich consignments of furs, ivory, and whale oil, baleen, and ambergris. My interest was not only exploration, but also a way of achieving a measure of wealth to underwrite a future marriage that I saw as essential to my plans.

So, sitting in a tavern in Bristol in late January of 1477, I listened carefully to the conversations of the seafarers around me. They came from many lands, and the babble of different languages surrounded me: Scandinavians, Germans, Brits, Irish, and even some Africans. There I saw two men who appeared to be from Cathay, with their straight black hair, broad faces, and slanted eyes. I approached these and questioned them closely, though we shared little by way of language. Nevertheless, through hand signals and pointing, they made it clear that they came from lands to the west, arriving in a ship laden with seal skins. They called themselves "Inuit."

From them, I learned of a ship that was commanded by a captain who was famously familiar with the northern seas. My two new Inuit acquaintances explained to me that they planned to return to their home village as crew on this captain's planned next voyage. The ship would first travel from Bristol to Galway, Ireland, and thence across the sea to a place beyond Thule. I pressed the local sailors for a better description, because "Thule" was a name that was used to refer to many different northern places. I could not discern the name, but it was clear they were not referring to any of the places that the local sailors associated with the name of Thule.

I was aware that many sailors in that region had described trips they had heard of taken by Basque, Irish, and English ships. Many of these sailors had grown rich from taking whales and fish for markets in England and Europe.

I sought out this captain. He was a Spaniard named Pedro Vazques, but all referred to him only as "Captain." When I inquired of his plans, he answered, "My cargo is bound first for Galway in Ireland. But I have heard there is a pressing need for supplies to be taken to the Esquimó settlements in the Arctic seas. This is an opportunity for a very profitable voyage for those who dare. I have sailed those seas before, and I know the routes. I seek a full crew, for it is difficult to find sailors willing to undertake a voyage to these places, especially at this time of year."

I was skeptical at first. "It is midwinter! How do you propose to sail through the frozen seas? I know from other sailors that the water is clear for some distance, but that ice clogs the way before one reaches Thule."

"It is true that ice blocks the way as one travels straight north from Iceland toward Greenlandia, but that is not our destination." And then he spoke the words that made me certain I would accompany him at any cost. "We travel further west, and then north, where the seas are sufficiently clear of ice throughout the year for us to sail."

At the words "travel further west," my soul leapt in my chest. Was this the route that the Templar fleet had taken to the land depicted on Gerard de Villiers' map? I had to see. Maybe this voyage would pave the way for future explorations under my direction.

But, as always, the issue of money raised its snake-like head. I had little. A voyage like this that promised a big payday could go a long way toward enabling my future.

"How do these savages pay for the supplies you provide?" He looked at me as though I were a child, which I found so demeaning that I nearly strode out of the tavern.

But his reply caught my attention. "These savages are experts at capturing whales, seals, and walrus. The skins, tusks, meat, and oil are so valuable that after one voyage a crew can retire to the beach in comfort. In fact, since I have made several of these voyages, I now own the vessel on which I sail. There is no fat owner sitting back in Ireland or England who creams off most of the profit. So there is a larger share of the profit that is available for those who sail in my crew."

"If profit is so generous, why can you not find a full crew? I would think sailors would be clamoring to sail with you."

The captain sipped from his ale and wiped his beard. "There is money to be made in voyages that are less risky. The northern seas into which I plan to sail are not familiar to most sailors, and they rightly fear the unknown. They reason that the promise of riches is not enough to counter the risk of death, so they find their smaller rewards on more conventional journeys."

I then asked the primary question that is in the mind of all sailors. "How do we get back?" He laughed. "Don't you worry, young man. That I can get us back is self-evident, and for proof, all you need to understand is that I am sitting here with you, and those two Inuit over there are here as well."

With that, I resolved to accompany him on his next voyage. Although he was polite, it was clear that Captain believed I would add little value to his crew, despite the wide experience I had on the sea. "I will take you aboard as an able-bodied seaman, and you will get a proportionate share in the proceeds from the journey. But your experience sailing in the Middle Sea, and on those coast-huggers that go between Portugal and England, will be of little use in the northern seas."

I protested and described my navigational skills and my ability to steer by compass headings. "That is exactly my point, young sailor. Your compass headings will be of little use where we are going. The lodestone loses its mind there, spinning in all directions. Sometimes it even points south." I gaped at him like a schoolboy at these words.

"Now, I suggest you spend the next days gathering the warmest and driest clothing you can find. Get the Inuit to help you find some furs, and do not neglect boots, gloves, and hoods. Winter in the northern seas is not for the underdressed." He left me with a laugh, and so I went off in search of clothing unlike any that I needed in Genoa, Chios, or Lisbon.

We sailed in February, first to Galway, which, like Bristol, lies at the end of a long channel and provides sheltered mooring. There we filled the holds of our carrack with trading goods—metal axes, knives, wheat, and wine. On top of these items, we loaded great amounts of lamp oil, for in February, days in Galway were short. I was assured, though I could scarcely believe it, that we would not see the sun at all during much of our voyage.

"How then can we take readings? If there is no sun at noon, how can we measure our latitude?"

"Don't worry, Christopher," I was told. "We will be in eternal night. The North Star will be visible all the time. We can actually be more accurate with our sightings because we can take them at any time without having to wait for a noon sighting."

We sailed for ten days across the open ocean, the longest period I had ever spent without sight of land. Our course took us to the northwest. I watched closely as the captain took his measurements. The sun was low in the sky at noon, and sank lower with each succeeding day as we moved north. At noon, the captain measured the angle to the horizon using his hands and fingers. He revealed his calculations to me—an open hand at arm's length measured twenty-two degrees between the tip of his thumb and his little finger. A closed fist was eight degrees, and the width of a finger measured two degrees. With these calculations, it was easy to determine our progress north and south, and on the evening of the tenth day, estimating our speed, he ordered us to strike the sails, for he reckoned we were near land.

A weak sun rose the next morning, and after a few hours, the lookout sounded the sighting of land—the cape that marked the southernmost tip of Greenlandia. "These waters are full of rocks and shoals," our captain explained to me, as he directed the ship in a wide angle around the headlands. Once past the tip of the cape, we bent a sharper northerly course that brought us close to the shore. When I questioned the captain about the dangers of our proximity, he revealed that his challenge was to sail far enough to avoid danger, but close enough to pick up the warm current that would carry us northward.

Now the captain posted a crewman at each side of the bow with lines to plumb depth. In addition to the visible dangers of icebergs and pack ice, the waters concealed rock pinnacles and shoals. We stood well off the land that was visible about twenty miles to the east and cautiously rode the current that edged between the shore and the pack ice that was visible to the west.

We carried on for several days, moving cautiously to avoid the large ice floes. The days were very short, and the sun barely emerged from the horizon. Fortunately, the sky was clear and bright with moonlight that reflected off the ice for our lookouts. And the most wonderful and mysterious light filled the night sky, brightening the earth to the point that objects cast visible shadows. These colored lights flickered and shifted like clouds in a most enchanting way. The captain replied to my excited inquiry that these lights were common this far north.

The sound of ice breaking off the shore and collapsing with a dull boom into the water constantly filled the air. On one occasion, the captain spotted a dense fog bank dead ahead. He immediately doubled the deck watch and ordered two crew members to blow on a ram's horn in different directions, to listen for echoes and to count the seconds between the blow and the echo. From this he was ingeniously able to judge direction and distance to the ice mountains that floated invisibly about us in the fog.

These mountains of floating ice were both a blessing and a curse. While they threatened to sunder our little carrack, they also afforded a source of fresh water. Small boats were sent out with empty casks a number of times to collect water from the icebergs. I was warned that on these sojourns it is easy to walk up on a bear lurking in the snow, for the only thing visible against the white is the black triangle of its eyes and nose. I was assured that in these winter months the bears were sleeping, so the danger was slight, but I maintained vigilance.

While in Galway, I had not fully credited the captain's warnings about the cold, but now I was astonished at the almost unbelievable and unending cold. How could anyone or anything survive in this frigid place? It was amazing that the ice covering the sea in every direction could nevertheless be navigated. Our ship passed through a narrow strait only twenty-eight miles wide between the coast of Greenlandia and a nameless island to the west. This strait lay at the incredible latitude of 78 degrees north. Beyond it was an expanse of open water that the captain called the North Water. He assured me that it stretched for hundreds of miles. As we made our way north from the strait, he explained that we had just made it through the strait in time before a frozen ice wall shut off access to the North Water. We were now locked into the North Water until the spring would bring a thaw to the ice wall and release us for our return trip.

For several months, sea ice would not be a problem, although there could be no relaxing in the face of blinding blizzards. But we faced another danger for which my Middle Sea sailing experience left me totally unprepared. In these sheltered waters, tidal flows were enormous because they were magnified by the narrow channels and bays that lined the shores on either side. Tides of ten feet were considered mild, with thirty-foot tides being common. But in some places the tides reached fifty feet or more, flowing like rivers so anchorages became perilous, for a strong tide could push our carrack onto the rocky shore.

We made port at a number of Inuit settlements and undertook to trade with the natives. They were very glad to see us, and we spent a number of days haggling before we traded our cargo for the furs and walrus tusks offered in exchange. I was happy to acquire for myself the skin of one of those white bears, for its fur makes a wonderful warm coat, though it is so heavy that it must be cut into pieces for wearing. Seal skins also afford the Inuit with the warm gloves, coats, and hats that allow them to survive in these frigid places, and we loaded our holds with pelts.

At each of our stops, I questioned the natives closely. Did they know of any settlements of white Europeans? Had a fleet ever passed through these waters heading west? The replies to my search for signs of the Templar fleet were uniformly negative. While there had been, from time to time, short-term settlements of Europeans, these were Norwegian trappers and fishermen who established brief camps and then moved on. Could a fleet have passed through here and proceeded through some passage to the west? The Inuit were unanimous that any such attempt would be blocked by impenetrable ice. With my own experience on this voyage, I could only agree.

By this time, several weeks had passed and the sun began to appear again over the horizon. Although none would ever claim that the weather turned balmy, the weak sun was sufficient to begin melting the ice wall that bound us in this ocean. And so, with the memories of the wonders I had seen in this northern sea, we made a slow and careful journey south and east, and returned to port in Galway and Bristol with our holds full of furs, ivory tusks, and whale oil. The voyage was highly profitable for my purse, though disappointing for my search. Still, I had thereby eliminated the northwesterly direction of the two directions that were possible, and the remaining way was clear: search to the southwest.

While I was busy between my commercial voyages looking out for a wealthy shore on which to beach my ambitions, international events provided guidance for my ambitious navigations. Conflicts between Spain and Portugal over the succession to the Portuguese throne supplanted the king's interest in supporting Portuguese voyages and exploration. These conflicts were resolved in the usual diplomatic way. The Spanish monarchs, King Ferdinand and Queen Isabella, agreed to marry their eldest daughter to the five-year-old Portuguese Prince Alfonso. The result was that power over the Portuguese kingdom shifted substantially toward Spain.

With this royal example before me, I resolved to do likewise. I was convinced that I had been chosen by God to find the Templar treasure fleet, and with it the Holy Grail. But to this point, God had not strewn funds and reputation in my path. Consequently, since fortune had not smiled on me, I resolved also to pursue success the old-fashioned way—through marriage. A prudent marriage might open the doors to the royal court, or at least to some coffers that might fund my search.

I approached my brother Bartholomew for his views on my plan. He was not encouraging.

"You know, Christopher, you are not a very desirable catch." He examined me with a critical eye. "I suppose you are a decent enough looking fellow." I stood taller than average and at the age of twenty-nine, I retained my health and my hair remained dark. My active life at sea had given me strength and a certain air of confidence. And I believe that my gray eyes are one of my best physical features.

"But you are a foreigner from a family of commoners. You have little wealth and no position, so you bring nothing to the family of a potential spouse."

I protested that his evaluation was too harsh. "Surely there is some family with an unmarried daughter that would find me to be a suitable husband!"

Bartholomew stroked his pointy little beard and pretended to think, though I could see he was smiling behind his hand. "Well, perhaps there is a strategy that we might implement to find a suitable bride. What you need, Christopher, is an older woman; one who is more than usually plain, but of a virtuous nature. She should come from a good family that is a bit down on its luck and would be happy to shed the expense of maintaining an unwed daughter. Such a family would probably not be able to afford much of a dowry."

I interjected. "It is not money or wealth I seek through a marriage, although that would certainly be nice. The more important element is access to business ventures that allow me to sail to the west, and acceptance at the royal court in Lisbon. As a Genoese merchant and sailor, I have no standing; but as the husband of a Portuguese woman of rank, doors will open. That is what I seek. I know that if I can gain the ear of the king, I can persuade him to support my voyages."

And so my search for a wife began. It was not long before we found the ideal candidate. Her name was Filipa Perestrello e Moniz, and at age twenty-four, she was on the verge of spinsterhood. Her virtue was unassailable, for she lived in the Monastery of All Saints in Lisbon. Also impeccable was her status as the daughter of a nobleman who, fortunately from my perspective, was dead.

His name was Bartolomeo Perestrello, and he was descended from a family of Italians that had come to Portugal a century before. He was a seaman and well known in Portugal, being part of the school of Prince Henry. In fact, he had been a member of the expedition that had discovered the Madeira Islands in the Ocean Sea forty years before I came on the scene. As a reward, he had been appointed by Prince Henry to be governor of the island of Porto Santo, a smaller one of the Madeira group. The position was hereditary, and on the death of the father, the title had passed to Filipa's brother.

I inspected her secretly one Sunday as she emerged with her mother from Mass. Filipa was not hideous, though painters would not clamor to render her portrait, at least not without payment. Her best features were her dark hair and her large, dark eyes, clearly inherited from her mother. Of the two, the older woman was actually the more attractive. Otherwise Filipa's looks were typical of many Portuguese women her age. She was a bit thick about the middle, but she walked with a dignified gait. When the sun caught her at an angle, a slight moustache was evident, but not so substantial as to detract from generally pleasant features. Bartholomew whispered in my ear, "She's not too bad, eh? What do you think? Could you bring yourself to lie with her?"

"Well, all cats are gray in the dark, Bartholomew." He snickered. "What do we know about her family?"

"She is the daughter of a Portuguese Knight of Santiago. This makes her a member of the households of Prince John and Prince Henry. Her family can be of immense value to you, Christopher. A marriage would give you access to the very highest levels of Portugal."

I protested. "Bartholomew, I do not have the means to marry a woman of that stature in society."

"Christopher, don't worry. Since the death of her father, the family has had to rely on slender means. A marriage would remove the need to pay for her residence in the convent, and at her age, that could be a burden that lasts a lifetime. Your low status is actually a benefit to the family, because you are not in a position to demand much of a dowry."

Bartholomew and I subsequently made contact with Doña Moniz, Filipa's mother, after Mass the next Sunday. The discussion was not very different from the commercial negotiations with which we were familiar. Instead of a bale of cotton, the merchandise in play was Filipa. Strangely, in this case, I was the seller and her family was the buyer. How much would the family pay for me to take their daughter off their hands?

Doña Moniz turned out to be a charming woman. It had been several years since the death of her illustrious husband, and although she still dressed in the black of mourning, her demeanor reflected no sadness or melancholy. Her long, dark hair curled over dark eyes that glinted with humor and a bit of mischief. She smiled often and readily laughed coquettishly behind her fan. Filipa was one of four children. Two younger sisters were married and lived in Spain. A brother served as governor of the Madeira Island of Porto Santo. This island was Don Perestrello's reward for his part in the discovery of the Madeira Islands, forty years before, and had passed to the family of his widow. It was clear to me that great advantages would come my way with a marriage into this family.

And so it came about that in the last month of 1479 I was married to Filipa Perestrello e Moniz. I brought to the arrangement a bit of money from my share of the voyage beyond Thule, and this provided the capital to initiate a venture in the Madeiras, where Filipa's brother had assumed his role as governor. With Filipa's mother, we took sail and residence on Porto Santo, which lay about thirty-five miles northeast from the largest of the islands in the group. We were technically guests of Filipa's brother, the governor, but in practice, we were all part of the family enterprise.

Porto Santo was chosen as the family residence because, unlike the larger island, which is mountainous and unsuitable for anything but grazing, Porto Santo is relatively flat and sandy. There is not an abundance of water, so it was necessary to choose a crop that needed little. The terrain showed promise for the cultivation of sugar cane, grown from stock brought from the coast of Africa. It also proved a convenient location for the importation of Negro slaves from Africa to work the cane fields.

My role in the land-based side of the enterprise was minimal, although I watched closely and learned the ins and outs of such plantation agriculture. I was a merchant and a seaman, and to me, wealth was created by transporting goods from their originating source to markets. But in agricultural endeavors, the source of wealth derives from the availability of cheap and plentiful labor. To our east, across a few leagues of sea, lay the coast of Africa, and it was from here that our labor source derived. The African slave, acquired in plenty from Arab traders on the coast, was a cheap and productive source of labor. The males were strong and able to work long hours. Combined with a supply of the females, the work force could replenish itself and even grow. With strict oversight and a manager's eye to keeping low the expense of maintaining the herd, the production from the fields could be as bountiful as the Garden of Eden.

But I am no farmer. My interest is in the sea, and I chafed at being effectively a prisoner on this remote island, far from the centers of power and money that could provide the wherewithal to satisfy my yearning to sail west. And so I took to the sea.

In the Madeira Islands, I relearned the lesson that I had first learned on the Nile River so long ago. Sailing southeast to the coast of Africa, my ship could benefit from the current that swept from north to south along the African coast. The return trip required that we tack far to the west before our sails could fill with prevailing winds that bore our craft to the northeast and back to our port in the Madeiras. Our sailors called this maneuver the *volto do largo,* and without it, they could not return safely from exploration voyages along the coast of Africa.

Using this knowledge, we undertook a voyage that was my contribution to the family venture. It was under my command that a ship sailed from Porto Santo to the Guinea coast, and then returned after tacking to the far western ocean with a cargo of sugar cane and African slaves. These became the foundation upon which the sugar economy of Madeira was founded. Filipa's brother and mother were industrious in managing this enterprise, and it prospered.

This long reach into the Ocean Sea demonstrated to me that sailing west was not a one-way voyage. I became more determined than ever to pursue the treasure of the Templars and its promise of the Holy Grail.

Thus I made my contribution to the success of the colony on the Madeiras. But having done so, I found myself virtually imprisoned. This isolated little piece of land far out in the Ocean Sea was like banishment. I saw my dreams of a voyage west diminishing each day with the setting sun. I needed to find a royal patron to give me license and certify my future claims to rewards, which I was sure would be mine based on a successful voyage west. Cast ashore on Porto Santo, I was like the classic sailor marooned on a desert island, waiting to be rescued.

After two years on Porto Santo, we were able to shift our location to the slightly less bucolic environs of Funchal on Madeira Island. In due course, Filipa gave me a boy child, whom we named Diego.

My time was not completely devoted to these agricultural and commercial endeavors. Doña Moniz was a naturally warm-blooded woman of substantial beauty that lingered strongly. Widowhood was a burden that severely taxed her, and the fact that we were in constant proximity created temptations to which she and I eventually succumbed. For my part, temptation from this beautiful and vivacious woman proved a relief from the wooden and passive inaction of my wife. Filipa's piety extended to the marriage bed, which she regarded as a distasteful duty from which no pleasure should be derived. Her mother, however, proved to be a different story.

Doña Moniz's affection for me extended beyond the physical pleasures of our relationship. In some ways, she saw me as a reminder of her dead husband because of my passion for the sea.

My mother-in-law, seeing my interest—indeed, my fixation—on these matters, gave me access to all of her husband's navigational charts and maps, pilot books and notes about the routes along the coast of Africa, including the Azores. My gratitude to Doña Moniz cannot be overstated, for I gained much knowledge about navigation on the open seas from her husband's manuscripts. I roamed the shores of these islands over the seasons, and kept a journal of the shifts in winds and tides, and the migration of sea birds and fish, that prevailed in these parts of the Ocean Sea. I spent hours by the seaside.

For example, I noted that, in normal weather, the waves broke more heavily on the western side of the island, and the prevailing wind blew from west to east. I noted the litter that washed ashore, including plants and trees that were unfamiliar to my European eyes. I calculated that the sun set two hours later in Madeira than it did in Genoa. Extending that knowledge made me realize that the distance around the earth was far longer than had been estimated by Ptolemy. All these things served to confirm the secret knowledge from de Villiers' map that a distant land lay to the west, tantalizing me.

On the other hand, that which I had most wished for from my alliance with the Perestrello family was their connections in the Portuguese court. While the time I spent in the Madeira Islands was pleasurable, and my travels from there to Africa were instructive, no progress was made in obtaining that royal sponsor that was the necessary foundation for my future. The closest I came was an audience arranged by my mother-in-law with King John II in Lisbon in 1483.

I was taken by surprise when Doña Moniz informed me of the audience, and I had little time to prepare a strategy. One of her relatives, the canon Fernando Martins, provided the entrée to the royal court.

In hindsight, the approach I took in my audience with King John was flawed. Clearly, I could not reveal the map that had been provided by my ancestor, for its source—the convicted heretics of the Knights Templar—could condemn me to the inquisitor's chambers. I certainly did not wish to reveal that there was a clue to the vanished treasure fleet of the Templars, for that would have provided the basis for a dual blow against me. I could be accused of heresy and subjected to the Holy Inquisition, and while enjoying the tender ministrations of the Dominican friars, be forced to reveal the route to untold wealth. And under torture, the odds are good that I would also reveal that in that treasure trove was the cup Jesus used at the Last Supper. No. That was not a path for me to venture down.

Instead, I determined to appeal to the king's faith in the Holy Scriptures. Clothing myself in piety, I presented to the king and his advisors the view that I could sail by the words of God as propounded in Genesis. "And on the third day, he united the waters and the earth's seventh part and dried the six other parts." It was by appeal to the Word of God that I sought to convince King John to support and fund my expedition to the west.

Alas, I had not counted on the king's prior exposure to these topics. Through Fernando Martins, his father, King Alfonso, had been in touch with one of the greatest frauds in Christendom, Paolo Toscanelli, astrologer to the Medici in Florence and a friend from Canon Martins' youth. With the fall of Byzantium fresh in his mind, the old king had written to Toscanelli, inquiring whether the way west would be a faster route to the Orient than sailing east around Africa. Toscanelli replied with a fabricated map that argued for the westward route, but I could see by comparing it to the map in my possession that it was nonsense. In any case, King Alfonso had already committed Portugal to the eastern route of sailing around Africa to Cathay. As a result, ten years later, his son John had no interest in an exploration to the west.

Although the King of Portugal was unfailingly courteous in his rejection, I could tell from his advisors' scornful evaluations of my proposals that he thought me a charlatan or madman. He was kind enough not to reject me to my face, but instead referred me to a panel of "experts" who were less subtle. These "luminaries" knew nothing about actual sailing, but excelled at drawing lines on a map. Their foremost expert, José Vizinho, a Jew touted as a scientist, went so far as to assert that "the radius of a circle traced on a map is not the path of the sun," and he even raised doubts about my sanity. In any case, I was sent away by King John with as firm a rejection of the westward expedition as made no difference. It was a shameful episode that left me profoundly depressed.

One good thing came of this fiasco; I now had in my possession a plausible map from an undeserving but well-respected scholar showing a western route to Cathay. I could argue that this was expert support for my pleas to fund voyages to the west. I no longer had to dissemble and hide my reliance on a secret map; I could use Toscanelli's map as cover for the real map from de Villiers. There were two problems, though. The most immediate was that maps are state secrets. I could not reveal that it was in my possession in Portugal, for by surreptitiously copying the Toscanelli map from the royal archives, I was in violation of the law. Humiliated and in peril, with a false map only useful outside Portugal, it was imperative that I depart the country.

The second problem with overtly relying on Toscanelli's map was that it was wrong. By hitching myself to it as a cover story, I was also obliged to defend the idea that the circumference of the earth was much smaller than I knew it to be. Thus the lie compounded itself; I was now obligated to defend, in public, what I knew to be incorrect. Moreover, I would be forced to reveal my false calculations, leading to convoluted inconsistencies. Of course, I did not quite understand this conundrum until I found myself standing before experts in the court of Spain.

The question of my destination on leaving Portugal was settled sooner than I had expected. Filipa was taken by God and a fever in 1485. Suddenly I was a widower. Although I was not under immediate threat of arrest, with responsibility for a small child, I could not take the risk of a sudden visit from the king's troops. So it took little thought to settle on Spain as my destination. My mother-in-law provided the means for me to embark on the next chapter of my journey, now moved not so much by affection for me as concern for the future of her little grandson, Diego. Two of Filipa's sisters had married men who lived just over the Portuguese border near Huelva in Spain. So little Diego and I took our leave of Portugal and the Madeira Islands, and headed for the court of Aragon.

Of course, nothing is as easy as it first appears. Spain was only recently arising as a country out of the shards of its various principalities and regions. The path to a royal audience was akin to finding one's way through a swamp by jumping from one tuft of grass to another, with frequent slippages, retraced steps, and humiliating discomfort. I was nearly penniless, responsible for a small child, and probably a fugitive. My future appeared bleak. My spirits were as low as at any time in my life, and I began to question the plan that I believed, until that point, had been placed before me by God.

Nevertheless, I resolved to resurrect myself in imitation of Our Lord Jesus. As a sailor, I knew that to raise an anchor or a sail, one must patiently draw the rope hand over hand, one pull at a time. This became my model. As I met people, I evaluated their suitability to advance my cause, cultivating those who appeared helpful, and discarding those who were not.

My first task was to shed the burden of caring for a six-year-old motherless child. Consistent with that, I needed lodgings that were suitable for my meager resources. While I was devoted to Diego, I could not care for him and also pursue my mission. Through the intervention of Filipa's sisters, I was able to solve both objectives with the same solution, the assistance of the friars at the Monastery of La Rábida, outside the port of Huelva.

The monastery of La Rábida lies at the northern end of a small peninsula that extends southward like a fish hook from the eastern bank of the mouth of the River Odiel, where it empties into the Mediterranean Sea. Passing the mud flats that form much of the beach, one turns sharply to reverse direction and approach from the south. The monastery stands on the side of a small hill dotted with widely spaced pine trees separated by low grasses. Under the shade of the trees, a few ungainly hoopoe birds hop about, stabbing the ground with their long bills, pursuing insects and snails in the grass while swallows and colorful bee-eaters swoop above.

Cresting the hill, the gate and walls became visible. Beyond them,

I could see the tidal flats of the River Tinto where it emptied on the eastern side of the peninsula into the waters of the Mediterranean Sea lapping the shore. The white walls surrounding the monastery and comprising the interior walls of the structure reflected the hot summer sun, but a cool breeze from the water mitigated the heat. It was apparent that the structure had once been a fortified place, situated at a strategic point at the mouth of two rivers and a natural harbor. I learned later that it had begun its religious life as a convent, but had recently been taken over by Franciscan monks.

Having passed the night in the nearby village of Palos, Diego and I arrived at La Rábida in the middle morning before the late June heat became stifling. Holding Diego's hand, I descended the hill and rang the bell that hung near the gate. A few moments passed before the door was opened by a friar who ushered us through the vestibule into the meeting room. There I produced for the abbot the letters of introduction given to me by my wife's sisters.

My departed wife's relatives thereby started me on a path that I could not have foreseen. At the monastery of La Rábida, I came to know two Franciscan monks who would have profound influence on my future.

The first was Father Antonio de Marchena. Unlike many of his pious but woefully ignorant brothers, Marchena was a learned man, and, more importantly, he was passionately interested in nautical studies. He was the rare type of man who drew his knowledge from observing the world about him, rather than relying on ancient texts or received wisdom. Though pious, he believed that the power of God could be discerned as well through the study of nature and the cosmos as through Scripture and the books of the ancients.

As Custodian of the Monastery, Father Antonio was responsible for receiving travelers and pilgrims. Under the duties of his office, he was persuaded by my sisters-in-law to accept Diego and me as guests, and so we took simple rooms with the monks. Diego was schooled daily by the monks, and there I remained for the year 1485.

I spent my time in a mixture of despair and boredom. Monastic life held no appeal, and the daily prayer cycle, though uplifting, became more of a spiritual binding than liberation. Still, I was pleased that Diego was receiving schooling, and that our physical needs were met through the kindness of the monks and the support of my in-laws. Little did I realize that this sojourn would prove the key to my eventual success.

It was the custom of the monastery that each resident confessed his sins prior to attending Mass on Sunday. This made me quite uneasy, for I concealed within my soul the secret that had come from my heretical forefather, and I feared being compelled to reveal it. Nevertheless, since it was not my personal sin, I felt able to clean my conscience each week. It was through these weekly confessions that I came to know Father Juan Pérez, the monastery's prior.

Father Juan's simple brown-hooded robe and knotted rope belt made it easy to mistake the person underneath to be equally simple. At confession, when he folded his hands in his lap and directed his full attention at me, it felt as though my soul had been flayed open and laid bare like a filleted fish. His gentle questions were like rapier thrusts through my dissembling words.

"You are a man with a secret, Cristóbal Colón. You hide it well, but I know what secrets look like. A shift of the eyes, a change in the pace of the rise and fall of your breathing, a slight coloration of your cheeks. Are you a Jew, Master Cristóbal? Or a *converso?* Have a care, sir, for our Dominican brothers are on the lookout for such as those. Their Most Catholic Majesties, King Ferdinand of Aragon and Queen Isabella of Castile, have created the Tribunal of the Holy Office of the Inquisition. The Dominican friars have developed ways to identify those who retain secret adherence to their old faith; secrets do not last long under their hands. And be warned, Master Cristóbal. Secrets attract attention."

I was taken by surprise, for I had imagined that I was able to remain concealed behind my carefully cultivated image of a bluff seaman and merchant. I dissembled, and he knew it.

I feared Father Juan would denounce me to the Inquisition on the basis of his suspicions. I felt it necessary to inquire about him, to see whether I was in serious danger. To this end, I cautiously approached Father Antonio de Marchena, for he was a man who straddled the worlds of piety and nature. He explained the lay of the land to me as we strolled through the fragrant gardens one evening.

"The marriage of King Ferdinand and Queen Isabella in 1474 brought together the kingdoms of Aragon and Castile and ended decades of wars. In Castile, civil war and unrest had raged since the death of Isabella's father, King Henry IV. The succession to the throne of Castile was disputed and undermined by privileges granted by the old king to those supporting the claim of his daughter Joanna to the throne. Isabella, as half-sister to Joanna, was supported by most of the Castilian nobles once she married King Ferdinand of Aragon, for in their opinion, the marriage barred the undue influence of the Portuguese. So the terms of the marriage contract acknowledged Isabella as Queen of Castile and Leon, but gave her no power in Aragon, while barring Ferdinand from exerting any control in Castile. Thus, although the marriage brought the two kingdoms together, in practice they remained separately controlled."

I was puzzled. "Father Antonio, I appreciate greatly this lesson in the history of Spain, but what has it to do with Father Juan?"

"Patience, Master Cristóbal. I am getting there."

Father Antonio continued. "You must remember that the queen was but nineteen when she married her second cousin, Ferdinand, who in his turn was only eighteen. Although they were better suited by age to rule than Joanna, who was only nine at that time, there was great uncertainty as to the security of their claims to their respective thrones. It was only once the pope ratified their marriage that they began to gather support from the *hidalgos* and could legitimately collect taxes."

"This is when Father Juan rose to prominence. In his youth, he was a page to Isabella before she became Queen of Castile. He trained as an accountant and worked in the state accounting office of Castile. He was instrumental in convincing the nobles created by King Henry that they could retain their titles and financial grants. This was critical to their support for Isabella over Joanna. In his later years, once Queen Isabella's grip on the throne of Castile was secure, he wearied of court politics and decided to become a Franciscan friar. To honor his commitment to the religious life, and in gratitude for his years of service to her, Isabella appointed him to be her private confessor. And, later, she appointed him as Prior of the monastery at La Rábida.

"So you see, Master Cristóbal, Father Juan Pérez is no simple country priest; he has powerful connections in the court of the queen, and he remains her trusted confidant and advisor. Do not treat his suspicions lightly."

I turned over his words in my mind. Here, in this country monastery, I had come upon a man with powerful connections to the royal court. If I could win him to me, he could be the instrument I needed to present my plans and get funding for a westward voyage. Yet, I could not tell him of my true conviction based on the map and the story of my heretical ancestor, for this would surely bring the Inquisition to my door.

I determined that my best course was to conceal the greater crime beneath the lesser one. I revealed to Father Antonio under the seal of confession my theft of the Toscanelli map from Portugal. As a Spaniard, he rendered swift and gentle absolution for my sin. But my revelation to him opened a door. By revealing my sin of theft, I also revealed that I was no simple sailor and merchant. And this revelation led in turn to my discovery that, like Father Juan, Father Antonio de Marchena was no simple country priest. As a Franciscan monk, he had been deeply exposed to the works of the Franciscan philosopher and theologian Duns Scotus.

Duns Scotus taught that truth can be found in the study of nature. Followers were encouraged to lift their heads from the Scriptures and discover truth by examining the world around them. Father Antonio consequently showed a curiosity and inquisitiveness about the workings of nature that separated him from those who believed that truth was only to be found in the pages of the Bible. He was an avid student of cosmology, and he had acquired from a Dutchman a pair of polished glass disks in a tube that extended his vision far into the heavens.

Antonio's interest in scientific inquiry became the basis for lengthy talks between us. We would sit in the afternoon shade where the breeze was funneled through the colonnades. Our conversations ranged over many subjects, and he pressed eagerly for stories of my travels and the strange and wonderful things I had seen and heard. Although he never broke the seal of my confession, he could not avoid the knowledge of my passion to undertake a voyage to the west as a means of reaching the East. We became good friends, but I never did reveal my true secret, for although he was a learned man, he was still a priest. I could not trust him not to reveal my links to the heretic Knights Templar. I was acutely aware that his knowledge of my possession of the Toscanelli map was protected by the seal of confession, but my deeper secret certainly was not.

As my friendship with Father Antonio deepened, it was natural that his friend and colleague Father Juan would join us and be drawn into our discussions. And so it came to pass.

The two priests were receptive to my expressed hope to reach the Indies by traveling west over the Ocean Sea. I, of course, revealed nothing about my secret map or the knowledge of the location of the Holy Grail on an intervening landmass, for these would have made me appear delusional and suspiciously heretical. But revealing my secret was not necessary to entertain discussions that proved both interesting and valuable. I was referred by these learned men to many books written by scholars and church authorities, and I read them carefully, sometimes making notes in the margins and copying passages into my journal. The upshot of my studies was to confirm some things I already knew—the earth is round and spherical, and the sea is navigable—and one thing I knew to be false, but found convenient to expound, that between the end of Spain and the beginning of Cathay is only a few days' sail. I was particularly taken by reading the Book of Esdras in the Hebrew Bible, which said that six parts of the globe are habitable, and only the seventh is covered by water. So just as the Toscanelli map provided scientific cover for my plans, so the Book of Esdras provided religious cover to ensure its orthodoxy.

While I found my discussions with the two priests entertaining, and my reading edifying, I chafed as time passed and I found myself no nearer to a patron who could be a source of funding to equip a voyage of discovery. The priests were the type of people that, once having conceived a problem and its solution, feel little incentive to undertake an empirical test. But they were, at heart, practical men who had survived and prospered in the devious politics and arcane world of princes and kings. I knew their many relationships throughout Spain were the key to my future voyages. When I expressed these thoughts and my utter reliance on the friars, I was grateful to find that they directly turned their thinking from the heavens to the earth, and from salvation to secular pursuits.

At first there was some debate between them as to the best way forward. Their circles of relationships overlapped imperfectly, though to a considerable degree. I was secretly amused to observe them subtly—though clearly—trying to demonstrate to each other the superiority of their connections. This was a game I encouraged, being as I was the beneficiary of their little contest.

So we sat in the cool of the afternoon, after the priests had finished reading their daily breviary, and I listened as they debated the merits of approaching this nobleman versus that one.

After lengthy discussions, during which I paced impatiently, agreement was reached. We would first attempt to win the patronage of Don Enrique de Guzmán, the second Duke of Medina Sidonia, and the most powerful and richest grandee in Spain. This was a nobleman with a practical eye, and his success was evidenced by his wealth. He had personally financed voyages to Africa, and he even owned his own shipyard at nearby Lepe.

Father Juan wrote letters of introduction, praising my experience, skills, and visionary ideas. The three of us sailed from Huelva the short distance along the coast to the port of Santa María, and then traveled by horseback. The road to Medina-Sidonia runs almost due north from Cadiz, about 40 kilometers, so we arrived late in the afternoon. We took lodgings in the village for the night, and rose early in the morning to make the climb to the castle in the cooler part of the day.

High on the hill, the castle of Medina gleamed white in the sun. Medina-Sidonia had been a fortified place for as long as human memory. Its commanding position was atop the first set of hills from the coast, and it overlooked the flat plains that extend from the foot of the mountain all the way to the shores and the port of Cádiz. From its battlements, a watchman could see and warn of any approaching threats that might come from the coast. Over the centuries, Phoenicians had been attacked by Romans, Romans had been attacked by Visigoths, and Visigoths had been attacked by Moors. Most recently, the Moors had been driven out in bloody battles by Christian forces under the command of Count Juan Alonzo de Guzmán of Niebla. As a reward for his Reconquista of this important fort, de Guzmán was rewarded with the title of Duque de Medina Sidonia. It was with his son, Enrique, that we sought our audience.

We climbed the rising road to the shade of its gates, where we were met and welcomed by members of the duke's staff. We were ushered through the great hall of the castle and into a comfortable but sparsely furnished study richly adorned with carpets from Anatolia. Despite the warmth of the sun outdoors, the stone walls kept the inside of the castle cool, and a small fire flickered in the hearth.

Don Enrique was standing near the fire. He was a man of about fifty years old, with a smooth forehead under a hairline that receded well back onto his skull on either side of the center. The remaining dark hair extended down the sides of his face before turning gray just below his ears and ending with a pointed beard and moustache. His eyes were dark and large on either side of a long nose that hooked sharply like the beak of an eagle. His erect carriage reminded me of some of the Italian grandees I had seen in my youth, but that impression dissolved when he spoke to greet us, for he had a most pronounced and annoying stutter.

The duke's slow speech encouraged listeners to underestimate his acumen, but I needed only a few minutes to detect that his stutter concealed a rapidity of thought that was quite outstanding. Indeed, his slow speech made it necessary for him to carefully pick his words and gave him time to consider them carefully. I will spare you the details of the over-long conversation necessitated by Don Enrique's speech impediment. Here is the gist of it.

Don Enrique was not a man to be motivated by considerations of royal grandeur; he was no king or prince. Nor was he a man to whom care needed to be taken to remain theologically pristine. This was a man of commerce, to whom voyages meant cargoes and profits weighed against risk and cost. And so my plea to him was couched in such terms. I proposed a voyage that would sail easily to the west for a few days before making landfall in the Indies. There we would purchase such cargoes as could be sold for handsome profits in Europe—spices, silks, carpets, and jewels. Based on the Toscanelli map, with which he was already familiar, and his knowledge of the circular winds and currents of the Ocean Sea, the risk was low, the payoff high, and the capital investment in ships and men small in relation to the potential reward. He was quite taken with the whole idea.

As ever, though, there were political problems to overcome. The separated nature of the two Spanish monarchs' realms divided their maritime interests. King Ferdinand of Aragon was focused on the waters of the Middle Sea, which washed the shores of his kingdom. It was Queen Isabella, with her Castilian crown, who was focused on the Ocean Sea. Spain was barred by a treaty with Portugal from gaining any footholds on the Guinea routes. Indeed, the voyages to Africa undertaken by the Duke of Medina Sidonia with Isabella's tacit assent were really pirate ventures that violated the treaty.

Such was not the case with expeditions across the Ocean Sea. Such a voyage could not be condoned as a private venture, so Don Enrique felt it necessary to decline his support for my plans.

Disappointed with the Duke of Medina Sidonia, but buoyed by his acceptance of my proposal in principle, we returned to the monastery at La Rábida. Our next attempt was to approach the Duke of Medinaceli, Don Luis de la Cerda. This worthy was not as rich as his peer, but he had the advantage of being higher in rank at the royal court because he was a direct descendant of the first kings of Spain. Dozens of his caravels were anchored in the port of Santa Maria, where we had disembarked for our earlier visit to Don Enrique. So, once again armed with letters of introduction and recommendations from the Franciscan monks of La Rábida, I embarked in the autumn of 1485 to Cádiz and then onward to Medinaceli.

I emphasize the date of my departure to meet Don Luis. While my hopes had been raised and then dashed by Don Enrique, I saw this new opportunity as a second chance. Had I been listening carefully, I might have heard the door quietly swing shut and lock behind me. My entreaty to Don Enrique had let the cat out of the bag about my plans. They were now known to the royal court. This meant that any enthusiasm Don Luis might have brought to my proposals could not proceed without the assent of the queen, just as had stymied me earlier. I was trapped between the hope that Don Luis would embrace the opportunity I laid before him, and the need for approval from the throne of Castile. But Don Luis offered me hope. As I soon discovered, those whom God most wishes to punish, He first fills with hope.

It is said that men's fortunes are governed by a seven-year cycle. Knowing this, Joseph was able to predict seven years of famine and seven years of abundance, and then prepare for famine by storing away provisions during the good years. The seven years that followed in my life from my arrival at the castle of Don Luis to the fruition of my ambition were not so clear cut.

At first, all appeared promising. Don Luis listened carefully to my proposal and, I am sure, consulted also with his peer, Don Enrique.

Like Enrique, Don Luis was impressed with my idea and promised his support in the form of ships and men.

But then, like his peer, Don Luis requested permission to underwrite my expedition from the court by writing a letter to Queen Isabella. In the letter, he made it clear that he was prepared to shoulder the expenses and the risks, in return for the rewards that might come. He reassured me, saying that since this would not burden the Crown's finances in any way, he was confident of a rapid and positive reply. Leaving Medinaceli, I descended the steep hill and carried on to the southwest toward the royal court. I carried the letter to Córdoba along with letters of introduction to the court. And so I was again dependent on the decision of the queen to underwrite and approve my expedition.

The initial responses to my proposal to sail to the Indies by traveling west across the Ocean Sea were positive. The monarchs clearly recognized the political difficulties of attempting any other course. Their way around Africa was blocked by the Portuguese, and overland was simply infeasible, given the distances and the need to cross territories of other sovereigns who, even were they willing, would exact tribute and could hold caravans hostage. Only the way west was open.

But not yet.

While I chomped at the bit and wandered the streets of Córdoba, the young queen and king were focused on cementing control over their kingdoms. Together, they went from town to town, city to city, dukedom to dukedom, staying a week here, a month there. Queen Isabella made sure her face was familiar in every corner of Castile. By doing so, she forced the people of each place to acknowledge her position and her power. The exercise was then repeated, though less intensely, in Aragon, for the security of King Ferdinand. Only once they were sure their respective monarchies were secure did they return to Córdoba and the business of the court.

Even on their return, did Their Most Catholic Majesties turn their attention to my project? Barely! On the day I made my first presentation, I was ushered into a room where the monarchs sat on a slightly raised dais. I gazed curiously at them, especially Queen Isabella, for I knew she held the power over my future. I hoped I might charm her a bit, coming on as the handsome sailor from exotic lands.

The queen at that time was no winsome girl, though. At thirty-five years of age, she had waged war to win her kingdom and endured court intrigues beyond my comprehension. She looked at me quite impassively as I laid out my plan. I tried to emphasize the huge benefits that would derive from my success and the low costs to the Crown in the event of my failure. Her narrowed eyes, set in a long oval face under arching eyebrows and hair parted in the middle, seemed unimpressed, though not hostile. My handsome appearance did not appear to stir her; her breathing did not alter under the square bodice of her golden dress.

When I looked over at King Ferdinand, I saw that he likewise appeared unmoved but also not hostile. No smile appeared on his slightly feminine lips, lurking above a weak chin that descended into a chubby throat. But nor did he frown or look at me negatively. I wonder in hindsight whether he even listened to me, perhaps dismissing the whole affair as another boring audience that he undertook out of royal duty.

At the end of our audience, Queen Isabella addressed me directly. "Your proposal is interesting, Señor Colómbo. Regretfully, we find our attention and energy are consumed at this time by our continuing struggle to remove the stain of Islam from our kingdoms. Until that task is complete, we must set aside or delay other adventures, regardless of their appeal and ultimate benefit. However, your proposal shall get careful consideration by members of our court who have the knowledge and skills to properly evaluate your claims. Once we have completed our immediate efforts to fully restore Christian rule, we can receive their recommendation."

My ideas were thus not dismissed out of hand, but instead my plans were directed to a commission of advisors for evaluation. This was worse than outright refusal, for it froze me under their jurisdiction. Had they simply rejected me, I could have sought other patrons, perhaps in England or France. I had been around long enough to know that referral to a commission is the kiss of death. By this means, any decision was deferred indefinitely and could easily die of old age. In the rare event that the members of the commission actually entertained the plan before it, it was usually only to reject it. It was a game, and everyone understood the rules.

For my part, I was condemned to appear before the worthy scientists and clerics to answer their questions and receive their criticism—criticism I knew to be generally valid, but which I could not accept. Their main complaint was that my calculation of the circumference of the earth was much too low. Of course I knew they were right, but if I accepted their way, I exposed myself to having misled Don Luis and Don Enrique. Both had supported my plan on the basis of a short voyage beyond the Canary Islands and the Azores.

But the greater danger from acceding to their criticism was the identity of a member of the royal commission—Father Tomás de Torquemada. Though the commission was nominally chaired by Father Talavera, it was Torquemada who was the real power. This Dominican friar had the appearance of a gentle person, walking about with his hands piously folded, and mild in his speech. Yet his quiet demeanor concealed a fanatical Catholicism and a cruelty that became legendary. Born into a Jewish family that had become Catholic, he carried inside him the zeal of the convert. He had become a priest and confessor to Queen Isabella when she was a girl, and her trust in his judgment was total. It was on his advice that the young queen agreed to marry King Ferdinand of Aragon and consolidate the two kingdoms.

Perhaps to overcompensate for his *converso* family, Torquemada became the foremost instrument of the Inquisition that most persecuted them. He had convinced the pious and impressionable Isabella that among the *conversos* were many false converts who worked diligently to undermine the religious foundations of her kingdom. Indeed, he maintained that they were more dangerous than Moors, for these hidden Jews were stealthy and wealthy, and held positions of power.

The day I first appeared before the royal commission to present my proposal, I was accompanied into the hall by Don Luis and Father Juan Pérez. Supported on either side by nobility and clergy, I struggled to conceal my trepidation. I also hoped to conceal my secret knowledge behind the Toscanelli map. I expected to be thoroughly questioned about the technical details of my plan: days at sea, expected provisions, distance and route to be sailed, speed of the ships, returning voyage, and other such mundane matters that I could easily handle. These were important questions, and I was prepared to deal with them. And, indeed, those questions came, but not at first.

Talavera opened the proceedings. "Señor Colómbo. We are charged by Her Most Catholic Majesty to evaluate your fitness and ability to undertake a voyage that has never before been contemplated. You propose to sail west over the Ocean Sea in the exact opposite direction from the land of your destination. We are expected to believe that this will lead you to the Spice Islands and the sources of gold, silks, and wealth that will enrich Spain and Their Majesties. You ask for ships, crew, and provisions to undertake this fantastic voyage at a time when the kingdom is struggling to find funds to pay for wars against the Moors right here in Granada. Why should we spare the tiniest coin to indulge your fantasies?"

"My lords, you are right to be skeptical. The sea is a mysterious place. Seen from shore, it can shift from being unpredictable and dangerous in one moment to inviting and delightful the next. The tales that most likely reach your ears are those of harrowing experiences and disaster; storms and pirates and shipwrecks and death. These things do indeed happen. But I stand before you as someone who has spent my entire lifetime sailing both the Middle Sea and the Ocean Sea. I have experienced all that the sea has to offer, good and bad, fair winds and foul. I have had ships sunk under me and survived—and, by the way, the sinking was not done by the forces of the sea but by the hands of men sailing ships of their own."

"That is all very well, Señor Colómbo, but there are many experienced sailors about. What makes you so special?"

"My lords, I am no common sailor, tugging on a rope when ordered to do so. I am a navigator. I can guide ships far out of sight of land and return to a selected port. I have studied the currents and harbors and coastlines of all the lands bordering the Middle Sea. I know the patterns of waves and winds and their variance across the seasons. I have frequently sailed far out into the Ocean Sea and guided my ships back to their desired landfall in the Madeira and Canary islands. I have sailed the coast of Africa and voyaged to the far north where the sea is covered with ice. The sea can throw little at me that I have not already experienced and mastered."

"And, my lords, you will discover by asking those familiar with me, that I am known as a mapmaker. I have studied the maps of the world and constructed many maps of my own."

Talavera spoke. "We have indeed inquired of your past, Señor Colómbo. We know that you have presented your ideas to the Portuguese, but were rejected. Why should we recommend approval to the king and queen when your proposal has already been examined and found wanting?"

"My lords, the Portuguese king has already staked his throne's future on a passage to the Indies that lies south, along the coast of Africa. He has rolled his dice, and there is no profit for him to roll again until he sees the outcome of his first throw. If Portugal is successful, Spain must either sink into second place or seek an alternative path to the Indies. That is what I offer.

"I am sure your inquiries also revealed that I continue to be welcome at the court of King John. He has invited me to return to Lisbon in the most friendly terms to renew my proposal. While I am happy for his friendship, I have not accepted his invitation. I believe that his real motive is not to seriously consider my plan, but to block Spain from adopting it."

I could see from Talavera's face that my response had made its point, though it was probably insufficient to sway him completely in my favor.

Next was the turn of a cowled Dominican friar who leaned forward over piously folded hands. "By your own testimony, you have traveled widely in the regions of the earth occupied by the heathens who defile the Holy Land as well as our neighboring territory in Granada and the lands across the nearby sea. How are we to know whether your wild speculations are not the product of heretical teachings and devilish sources? It is in the study of the Bible and the holy words of the prophets and saints that truth is to be found. By your words, you seem to place far more faith in your own knowledge and experience than in the word of the Lord and the teachings of Holy Mother Church. If we scratch your surface as seaman and merchant, will we perhaps find a heretic? Or a Jew? Or a *converso*?"

I replied calmly, for I had anticipated this line of questioning. "I am no heretic, Padre. Indeed, my first thoughts were stimulated by my study of the Bible. In the book of Esdras, where the creation of the world is documented, we read 'And on the third day, He united the waters and the earth's seventh part, and dried the six other parts.' So the Bible reveals that the earth is made of six parts earth and one part water. Saint Augustine has confirmed the holy status of Esdras as a prophet and his words as true descriptions of the world."

I warmed to my defense. "My experiences as a sailor merely confirm the glorious truth of the biblical account. The writings of many other ancients are not in opposition to the biblical truth. Ptolemy and Aristotle were pagans, ignorant of the teachings of Christ, but their writings confirm the truth of Esdras. Sir John Mandeville and Marco Polo have described journeys that, whether they are true or false in their details, confirm that the Biblical description of the earth is correct. So I will sail by the Book of Esdras and carry the truths contained in the Old Testament in my heart."

When at the end, it came to Torquemada's questions—although being the last questioner is normally the prerogative of the chairman of a commission—a chill spread in the room. Although he spoke softly, his questions felt to me like the back of a sharp knife slowly scraping off the scales from a living fish. He asked no questions about my proposed voyage, instead probing my background and family. How had I come to Spain? What of my parents and ancestors in Genoa? Had I relied on in any way or been exposed to un-Christian and heretical sources about the nature of the world?

I was in a better position than many who faced the Inquisition's probing. I was not anonymously accused of heresy, witchcraft, or devil worship. I did not possess a cat, which had been declared the manifestation of witches and sorcerers. I possessed no property that could be confiscated and handed over to enrich the Church or the court. And I had been brought into the presence of Torquemada, not in his role as Inquisitor, but as advisor to the king and queen, though the boundary between those roles was highly permeable.

But for me, undergoing an examination about the nature of the world by someone who viewed it in solely biblical terms was a perilous undertaking. And my need to conceal the reality of my plan, its source in the depths of the heretical Knights of the Temple, my stolen map derived from pagan sources, and my secret goal of finding the Holy Grail left me frightened and insecure. Torquemada was a man who could sniff out deceit, and his temperament made him naturally suspicious. Not only was my plan in peril, but my very life could be forfeit as well.

Fortunately, I was able to fall back in my answers to the teachings that I had gained at the knee of Archbishop Paolo Fregoso long ago. I am a true believer in the teachings of Holy Mother Church, and said so in response to Torquemada's probing. Father Juan and Don Luis stood by my side, vouching for my piety. As a sailor, I have learned through experience that the sea and sky have little regard for man's beliefs; only knowledge and understanding of the winds, waves, and currents count when survival is at stake. All those forces are commanded by God, and while the prayers of sailors in distress may be mercifully heard, it is also said in the Bible that He helps those who help themselves. The sailor who relies solely on the Bible to navigate the seas is more certain to arrive quickly on heaven's shore than on a safe landfall. But, keeping these thoughts inside me and answering truly the Inquisitor's questions, I managed to depart with my fingernails on my hands and my bones unstretched.

I did not spend all my time pinned under the sharp eye of Torquemada and the royal commission, thanks be to God. Torquemada was a busy man whose attention was mainly turned toward ferreting out false *conversos*. Likewise, King Ferdinand and Queen Isabella's main task was healing the wounds that remained from the war of succession that still divided the loyalties of much of Castile. And once they had that task in hand, they turned their goal toward removing the remaining foothold of Islam in Granada. My voyage was very far from the top of their priorities.

Here in Córdoba, my distance from the sea was as great as the absence of attention I was granted by Their Royal Highnesses. I was as far from the sea as I had ever been in my life. From the day of my first presentation to the Spanish court back on January 20, 1486, I was considered to be "in the service of the Crown." The good news was that I was given an allowance that enabled me to find quarters and feed myself. The bad news was that I was no longer free to depart; I was required to remain at the behest of the royal commission, and if they deigned to notice me, the king and queen. So in Córdoba I remained.

At first I spent my days hanging around in the court, hoping to make the acquaintance of someone who could break this wall that surrounded me. During this time, I pursued a number of strategies. My hopes rose when I was able to convince the new Archbishop of Zamora, Father Diego de Deza, to support my cause. As tutor and confessor to the young Prince John, his stature could help get further audiences with the king and queen. Unfortunately, achieving access required that they be present in Córdoba, and that was rarely the case.

Through Father Diego, I was admitted to the company of the Archbishop of Toledo, who also represented Spain in the College of Cardinals in Rome. This was a powerful connection indeed, and like

Father Diego, the archbishop was sympathetic to my plight. Cardinal Don Pedro Gonzáles de Mendoza was an unofficial prime minister to the king and queen, and his recommendation of approval could carry great weight. But he was a realist, and, though sympathetic, he laid out for me the problem the court was facing. He explained that the crusade against the Moors was using almost the entire royal treasury. Taxes from across the country were going to finance the war. I protested that the voyage I proposed would cost the Crown nothing, as the Duke of Medinaceli, Don Luis de la Cerda, was willing to fund my expedition. The cardinal gently pointed out that Don Luis was no longer in a position to afford such a venture, as his wealth was now obligated toward taxes to fund the war. I riposted with the objection that my voyage could bring such wealth and treasure to Spain that its finances would be quickly brought back into order, but the cardinal only smiled. "The money for the voyage must come now, while uncertain rewards may come sometime in the future. Such is the nature of these decisions that the present certain cost overburdens the possible future returns."

Another tactic was proposed by my brother Bartholomew, who remained in Lisbon and pursued matters on my behalf in Portugal. He maintained relations with the court of King John II. By dint of repeated requests, he managed to arrange an audience for me to renew my pleas for support to the Portuguese. I gave this great consideration, but in the end declined to make the journey. I thought such a visit would put my relationships in Spain at risk with small prospect of success, given my previous attempts in Lisbon. I was now in the pay of the Spanish Crown, and a presentation to the Portuguese court might easily be regarded as treason. Moreover, there was the little matter of my theft of the Toscanelli map.

Bartholomew continued to work on my behalf, writing to the King of England and the King of France, but none of his attempts proved fruitful. And so I dawdled in Córdoba. The last words of Queen Isabella repeated in my mind: "Once the matter of Granada is settled," my plan could be reconsidered.

Nevertheless, I soon found myself quite happily occupied in Córdoba. This city in Andalucía is justly famous for its fragrant blossoms, its sturdy mules, and its beautiful women. I was generally reticent in approaching the latter, having found that it is better to be the pursued than the pursuer, for beautiful women become accustomed to yearning suitors, and tend to spurn ardent approaches. But an appearance of indifference to their beauty often presents them a challenge that leads them to initiate a relationship. None of these stratagems were relevant to my situation, as it turned out.

Like many of my fellow Italians, I took quarters in the district of the Hierro Gate across the stone Moorish bridge that leads to the left bank of the Guadalquivir River. There I made the acquaintance of two brothers named Barroia, who ran a nearby pharmacy on the street between the synagogue and the Church of the Savior. Many of the expatriate Italians living or visiting in Córdoba gathered informally there to hear news from home and speak to others in their mother tongue.

In the shade of the afternoon, the Barroia brothers would put out tables and chairs and sell coffee to their *paisans*. Sitting often in their marvelous courtyard, half-drunk from the heavy scent of Andalucían blossoms, I came to befriend another idler, a young man named Diego de Harana, who proved both sociable and generous, though he was not a rich man. A member of the tribe of Basques from northern Spain, Diego was affable and demanded little in return, being neither prying nor gossipy.

After our acquaintance evolved into friendship, he introduced me one day to his wife, Costanza, who came to the shop with him to purchase some items. Like Diego, Costanza was outgoing and friendly. The result was an invitation to supper at their house, which I gladly accepted—both for the courtesy offered and for being tired of the meager fare afforded me by my allowance from the court.

The dinner set before me was sumptuous, and the other guests who were our dinner companions were not tedious. Least tedious of all was the cousin of my host, a girl of twenty named Beatriz. I had been long out of the company of women, and I am no ascetic monk. Beatriz Enríquez de Arana captured my eye and my heart. Her brother Pedro, like Beatriz an orphan cousin adopted by the Harana family, was also friendly to me. Indeed, the whole family welcomed me, and I felt a greater kinship with these people than I had ever felt with my birth family in Genoa.

Had the prophet not already written the Song of Solomon, and just now looked down to earth, the sight of Beatriz de Arana would have moved him to put down that sublime passage. This was no serene Madonna with upturned eyes gazing toward heaven, but a dark-haired beauty with flashing Spanish eyes and a teasing smile. As I write these words, she appears before me, her skin like fine alabaster, the arc of her jaw curving like the crescent moon from her delicate ears adorned with turquoise dangles. Her chin is strong and underpins a mouth framed on either side by the slightest of smile lines, which as she ages will doubtless evolve into laugh lines. When I saw her last, her mouth was curved into a gentle and confident smile as she bid me a fair voyage and a safe return to her. Her nose is a straight, sharp drop from between her arched eyebrows. Ah! And those eyes! Her gaze is half curious and half knowing, as though she has examined you and come to a tentative conclusion that wants only the confirmation of experience. And once I experienced her love, it was never to be forgotten.

I was smitten, and Beatriz returned my love. With little courtly business to occupy my time, I devoted myself instead to courting Beatriz. As we became more intimately acquainted, she came to know a version of the mission I pursued. Her eyes would sparkle with excitement at the stories of my travels, especially those voyages to the exotic ports of Egypt and Constantinople. I revealed to her my goal of sailing west to reach the lands of China and the Spice Islands.

"Imagine how I could transform the world, Beatriz. We are held in bondage by the Venetians and the Turks, who control the way east. Between them, they suck the marrow from our bones, leaving just enough so we do not wither away entirely, leaving them no one to feed on. Portugal has found a way around the Antipodes, but it is a dangerous and expensive voyage. And when they reach the Indies, what do they have? They are just a mouth being fed by an expensive trickle of spices and goods that make their way to Goa and Ceylon from their real source in Cathay. If we could trade directly with the spice producers and avoid the greedy Arabs, we would become rich beyond imagination! I would strike a mighty blow for Christendom by breaking the source of so much of the Arab wealth, mostly taken from our coffers. That treasure could be spent in driving back the tide of Islam that has swept all the way into Granada."

Beatriz smiled tenderly at my enthusiasm. "Cristóbal, you must use these exact words to convince the king and queen to sanction your voyage. Convince them by offering the one thing they desire more than all else—removal of Islam from Granada."

I slumped back into the cushion. "I have done exactly that, sweet Beatriz, and they have responded with favor. But the treasury is so strapped by the current battles. The nobility and the merchants cling to their wealth as a hedge against the possible fall of the kingdom to the rivals for the throne. They provide just enough that, should Ferdinand and Isabella be able to cement their hold on Castile and Andalucía, they will not have appeared so withholding as to earn future wrath and retribution. In the meantime, the king and queen are so occupied with obtaining and retaining their loyalty and prosecuting the war in Granada that they are continuously absent from Córdoba, and I am out of their thoughts."

I could read in her eyes her confidence that I would be able to succeed in my petitions to the monarchs and in my voyage. Our love was deep and genuine, and I knew she felt for me as I did for her.

But I never spoke to her of my true quest for the Templar treasure or the Holy Grail.

As Beatriz was an orphan, I sought the permission of her brother and cousin to ask for her hand in marriage. I was not an attractive match for the lady; I was fifteen years older than she, I had no fortune or castles, and my only income was a slim allowance from Queen Isabella. But in return, Beatriz had no rich dowry. I was clearly not attracted to her for her fortune, for she had none. It was obvious to Beatriz's relatives that this would be no joining of dynastic fortunes, but a love match. And so they left the decision to her.

I went to her on a Sunday afternoon to offer my hand in marriage. It was a lovely day in Andalucía, which is more perfect than a lovely day in any other place. I was confident that Beatriz loved me as I loved her, as sure of her affection for me as I am of God's love. I was not prepared for her rejection of my suit. It is too little to say that I was crushed and bewildered.

"Is it because I have a son from another woman? Or are my prospects so dim that you foresee a life of penury? Have you been laughing at me behind that ridiculous little fan?"

She took my crestfallen face between her warm hands. "I love you, and I will always be true to you, Cristóbal. But if we marry, it will put you into grave danger. I cannot do that to you."

I cried out, "What are you talking about?"

"Think a moment" she replied softly. "My grandparents were Jews, so my brother and I are classified as *conversos*. Even though we are true and faithful followers of the Catholic Church, our lineage puts us under suspicion. Did you not realize the reason that my brother and I are orphans? Our parents became Catholic, but as children of Jews they were arrested by the Inquisition and subjected to its fierce trials. They survived the immediate questioning, and there was never a finding of heresy, but both Mother and Father died within days of their release from the hands of Torquemada's inquisitors."

I was well aware that children of those questioned by the Inquisition were viewed with suspicion. Often those who were left orphaned when their parents perished at the hands of the Dominican priests became outcasts, refused care even by their own relatives lest the finger of suspicion then point at them. The Harana family showed great courage to take Beatriz and her brother under their care, even to the point of their adoption.

"And, Cristóbal, you are at risk in any case. You are unknown; your parents and family are foreign. You have traveled the world, including places where the people follow the teachings of Mohammed. You propose radical ideas of sailing west to reach the East. To the Inquisition, you carry all the signs of potential heresy."

"Beatriz, my dear, you are being overly excitable. I have already been interviewed by Torquemada himself, with no problem."

She flashed at me. "Don't be a fool! You had a mild conversation with Torquemada on a matter that was brought to him in his capacity as an advisor to the queen. There was no accusation; no cause for suspicion. For him, the interview was a formality required to satisfy the court, and his questions to you about your family and background were *pro forma*. He was not acting in his role of Chief Inquisitor."

She went on. "At this moment, you are nothing and you have nothing. You are an outsider with no real links into Spain. You are a petitioner to the court, which has granted you only a pittance to live on. There are no lands for the Inquisition to appropriate, no spider web of connections to those with wealth and power that can be traced from you to them; in short, there is nothing but your life that can be taken from you."

I was nonplussed by her candor and hurt by her frank evaluation of my situation, but I could not deny the truth of it. Her face softened as she put her arms around my neck and spoke gently into my ear. "If we marry, Cristóbal, those defenses you carry will disappear. You will be burdened with all the baggage that I would bring to our union. And if the Inquisition should come for me or my brother, you would also be arrested. Because you love me, I would become your weakness. By threatening me, the Dominicans could gain the power to make you confess to anything they want. The torturers would not need the lever to stretch you on the rack; I would be the lever to make you confess your secrets."

I looked at the wall, through the window, at my feet, anywhere but into her searching eyes. After a long silence, I whispered, "So you know I carry a secret, Beatriz."

"Of course I do, you silly man. Any woman can tell when a man is keeping something from her. Usually, the secret is a mistress; but in your case, I expect it is something else, something that gives you the confidence to pursue your dream of reaching the East by sailing west."

At that point I almost succumbed to the temptation to tell her the truth; that I was only using that goal as a cover story for my real mission, to follow my ancestor's map to the Templar treasure and the Holy Grail. But I quickly rejected that idea. Her own words indicated the risk of arrest and torture by the Inquisition. Should that happen, her ignorance of my private quest would be her salvation and mine.

"I love you and trust you, Cristóbal, but I will not marry you."

Despite her refusal to be my wife, Beatriz and I lived together as a married couple would. My son Diego left the care of the monks and joined us in Córdoba. Beatriz cared for him and me like a true mother and wife and, in due course, she bore me a second son, whom we named Ferdinand after the king. We were not criticized for our arrangement by her brother, who understood perhaps better than anyone the reason for her refusal to marry me. He was just happy to see his sister cared for. And so, in my domestic life, I was content.

In my public life, on the other hand, I was a frustrated man.

I spent the three years after arriving in Córdoba dancing a merry dance before dukes and kings, duchesses and queens. I smiled and bowed and told stories of my seafaring adventures to drunks and imbeciles because they had noble friends or relations who could influence King Ferdinand or Queen Isabella. I was pleasant to the lisping Castilians who cavorted through the court buildings like maggots on a dead cat that had been left too long by the side of the road. I even bedded a noblewoman (before meeting Beatriz) who assured me of her affections and her closeness to Queen Isabella. Three years! And I was not getting younger. Finally, in the last months of 1490, Talavera's commission issued its verdict. It went against me on many grounds, calling me mad and pointing at my "colossal" errors. According to its recommendation to reject my proposal, I was guilty of far underestimating the circumference of the earth. The commission pointed to biblical contradictions to my assertion that much of the earth consisted of dry land, rejected the idea that survival was possible below the Antipodes and, all in all, poured scorn on every element of my ideas.

And yet, there remained some hope, for not all the members of Talavera's commission were aligned with its conclusions. Several members of the commission approached me quietly afterward and assured me that they were in support of my proposal, but were cowed by the opposition from the clerics, especially Torquemada. And these secret dissenters (for the report was falsely presented as a unanimous decision) had sufficient sway with Queen Isabella to persuade her to keep open the possibility of a favorable reconsideration.

1491 turned to 1492, and I turned with it from thirty-nine to forty years old. My hair, which in my younger days had been a nice reddish auburn, became pure white almost overnight.

During that time I generally affected a pleasant demeanor, though I was not afraid to assume a haughty air when appropriate. I was like one of those creatures that can change its colors and conceal itself to fit into its environment. That stratagem, which required me to become fluent in the local dialect, allowed me to camouflage the foreignness that was evident when I spoke Spanish.

My intention was to project a sense of confidence and competence to those I encountered and an appearance of noble heritage. For in truth, I keenly felt my nobility in the blood of my forefather, Gerard de Villiers. But to all appearances to the people of Córdoba, I was a simple Italian seaman with grand ideas and little status.

In January of 1492, an event occurred that brought the royal eye back around to me. Granada fell to Spain, and the war against the Moors, which had lasted for centuries, was   over. The flag of Spain was raised above the Alhambra. My hope was renewed that the king and queen might now turn their attention to me.

At the end of any war, the first survivors to emerge from the safety of their lairs are the merchants. Well, I am perhaps a bit unfair. Coming from a merchant family, I understand the alluring scent of commercial opportunity that arises from the corpse of war. But the truth is, all who have stifled their hopes for the future while battles were fought view the end of hostilities as the dawn of opportunity.

Thus it came about that a strange alliance of church and commerce came together to press my case before the royal court. The good Franciscan friars of La Rábida joined forces with the Duke of Medina-Sidonia to once again urge the queen to reconsider my proposal, even in the face of the Talavera commission's negative recommendations. For the Franciscans, it offered the potential of bringing Christianity to the East. And for the duke, the scent of profitable commerce wafted before his sniffing, acquisitive nostrils.

We gathered in the monastery outside Huelva to plot a strategy. The monks brought together all their expertise and even included experts from outside the monastery. And so it came to pass that Martín Alonso Pinzón and his brothers came into my life—a most consequential event, though I did not realize it at the time.

As I look back on my relationship with the Pinzón family, I am not sure whether they were sent to me by God or Satan. Without them, my voyage across the Ocean Sea—that might very well end in my death—would probably not have happened. On the other hand, the arrogance and self-appointed superiority that all the brothers—especially Martín—exhibited led to many disputes and accusations. More about that later.

For the group gathered at La Rábida, the reputation and influence of the Pinzón family was an essential element of our plans. Our little group was determined to once more bring my voyage of exploration to the ear of the sovereigns. We believed we had representatives that could respond to any criticism. Our strategy was to appeal to Queen Isabella and to rebut the recommendations of the Talavera commission. I, of course, was the leader and inspiration for the voyage, and would serve as the admiral for the ships that participated. The Pinzóns would provide three ships with crews and serve as the captains. The Duke of Medinaceli would supply the ships, fund the voyage, and provide the necessary supplies. The abbot of La Rábida monastery would be the liaison with the royal court in Córdoba. The cousin of my beloved Beatriz, Diego de Arana, was also part of our group and later served as Master-at-Arms on our voyage.

In truth, all we lacked was the royal assent. But I needed more than that.

Our little band of supplicants made its way to the sovereigns' headquarters in Córdoba, from whence their campaign against Granada had been directed. We traveled by road from Huelva to Seville, and then boarded a barge from Seville to Córdoba. We poled against the current on the Guadalquivir River, assisted by a small sail in the afternoon, when the wind blew upstream. Until it reaches Córdoba, the river is navigable, but there it encounters some rapids. The ancient Roman bridge that crosses the river just above the rapids, before it makes its sharp bend in the middle of the city, was our disembarkation point.

From the river, we climbed the muddy banks to the side opposite the Alcázar. From here we could see the massive walls of the fortress looming over the silent water wheel that had been ordered shut off by the queen because its creaking annoyed her. On the other side of the Roman bridge, which had spanned the Guadalquivir River for a thousand years, the Alcázar's protective walls shaded us from the hot sun as we walked under its north side. The crenellated walls of the ancient Visigoth fort loomed above us, providing a bit of welcome shade in the hot afternoon.

After a short wait in the anteroom, we were joined by the Abbot of La Rábida, who lived in Córdoba in his capacity as advisor to the queen. We were soon after ushered into the presence of King Ferdinand and Queen Isabella. We greeted the monarchs in order of our rank, with the Duke of Medina Sidona making his bows first, followed by the Abbot of La Rábida. The Pinzóns were next, and I brought up the rear along with Diego de Arana. I swore to myself that if I ever entered this room again, it would be as a hero in my own right, and the purpose of that meeting would be to confer honors and nobility on me. But for now, I was a foreigner and a supplicant, dependent on the good will of these Spanish rulers.

So once again, we went through the dance that had become so familiar to me. "You greatly underestimate the distance across the sea to the court of the Great Khan." Yes, I know that in my heart, but my voice responds with quotes from the Bible, citations of Ptolemy, tales of seafarers, the writings of Marco Polo. Besides, Your Highnesses, we are not really going to Cathay, but instead seeking the treasure fleet of the Templars and the Holy Grail; but I cannot admit that to you, nor to the others on my team.

"The provisioning of such a voyage would be a huge expense at a time when the coffers of the kingdom have been greatly depleted in order to prosecute the wars against the Moors in Granada." Yes, but those wars are now over, and Spain has prevailed. It is time to make the investments that will make Spain a rich and powerful country. The returns to the kingdom from a successful voyage would make Spain the most powerful nation in Europe, because it would establish a trading route that is not controlled by the King of Portugal or the Sultan of Constantinople. Trading margins would be so much larger without the taxes and levies imposed by those monarchs.

"Your demands for reward in the event of a successful voyage are too great. You ask to be appointed Admiral of the Ocean Sea, Viscount of any lands discovered by your expedition, a tenth of all riches derived from those lands, and hereditary titles and ennoblement. Your demands reveal a hubris that is offensive to us."

I expected this. "Your Highnesses, I and my crew will be taking the risks of a voyage that has never before been attempted. If we are not successful, our deaths are almost certain, and the only cost to the Crown would be pensions for the surviving families and the loss of the ships. But if, God willing, we succeed, the wealth of the Orient is at your feet. Then the compensation to us will seem trivial indeed."

"As monarchs, we are empowered by God and seek in our actions to magnify His glory. You present us with a frankly commercial undertaking that seeks only wealth and power. We suspect that God will not bless a mission based on those motives."

The Abbot of La Rábida stepped forward to respond. "Your Highnesses are right to keep in mind the glory and mission of God, as do we. I am the evidence of our pious intent, for I am the Abbot of La Rábida. The establishment of regular commerce with Cathay will allow the holy monks to act as missionaries to the heathens and idolaters, with millions there waiting to hear the Word of God. Moreover, there is a possibility that our voyages of exploration will allow us to find the Christian kingdom of Prester John noted in the writings of Sir John Mandeville. The Portuguese have not found it because although they speak pious words, they are in fact on a purely commercial mission that stops at the coast of Goa. In any case, reports are that they are looking for Prester John in Africa. But we will press on to the very coast of Cathay, and with that opening, the missionaries will be able to search directly for the Fisher King where most sources locate him, near India or Cathay."

In my head, I longed to blurt out the truth—that all this was nonsense, and the true goal of our mission was far more important than trade with China. If half the legends of the power of the Holy Grail were true, its possession would transform the lives of those who held it, from eternal life to untold levels of power to command the heavens. The drone of the back-and-forth between the abbot and the king receded as I contemplated the impact this revelation might have.

My reverie ended with a start as I suddenly felt eyes probing me. I realized that Queen Isabella had fixed a gaze on me unlike anything I had experienced in previous meetings. I feared she could read my mind. I became quite nervous and tried to hide my discomfort by looking here and there, fixing my eyes on her husband and the abbot—anywhere but in her direction. Then I realized that this probably made me even more shifty-eyed, feeding whatever suspicions might be in her head. When I dared to peek at her from lowered eyes, I was relieved to see her once again looking bored and sleepy.

In any case, the day started as it had in previous presentations. The objections of the Talavera commission were replayed, as were our responses to their objections. I was surprised that the monarchs could not recite them from memory, like children reciting the Lord's Prayer. But now the tedious dance was finally to come to an end. Queen Isabella rose and left the room while King Ferdinand announced the decision.

"We have carefully considered your proposed voyage, Señor Colón. We have sought expert advice from the most learned men in our kingdom. You and your supporters have been given multiple opportunities to persuade us of the merits of your proposal. It is our final decision now that we cannot justify the expense and risk necessary to support your proposed voyage, Señor Colón. Frankly, sir, we are affronted at your demands. While we might be willing to approve your voyage, your demand for hereditary titles and shares of any wealth reveal a hubris we cannot condone. We are aware that you have invested a great deal of time and effort into this endeavor, and we are thankful for your persistence and patience. Our focus must be on restoring the true faith to those lands and people closer to home."

So that was that. All those wasted years and all that wasted effort, living as a near-pauper, clinging to hope. We left the Alcázar by the same route as we had entered, except that hope had been replaced by bitter disappointment. To say my spirits were low would imply a level of happiness that was far above the depth of my actual feelings.

But at least I had a decision. There was no longer a reason for me to linger in Spain. My brother had suggested that I might find friendlier ears at the court in France. And England was rumored to be investigating a possible voyage to be undertaken by a fellow Italian who went in that country by the name of John Cabot. So when I was asked by my colleagues of my plans, that was what I told them: I am off to seek better results in France or England.

The voyage downstream toward Seville was a faster affair than the journey we had started with such hope that morning. Instead of sailing west across the Ocean Sea, we were poling slowly into the setting sun on the crest of a muddy and slow-moving river. My mood was as dark as the mud into which the bargeman thrust his pole.

The river takes a number of wide bends as it flows downstream from Córdoba. As we approached the village of Almódovar del Rio, where the river approaches the road between Córdoba and Seville, we heard a hail from the bank. A man on horseback leading a second horse called out, and our bargeman poled us out of the sluggish current to the bank. The messenger had been sent from the Alcázar, and my heart leapt with the news. Queen Isabella wished me to return.

I fetched my belongings from the barge and mounted the messenger's second steed. We turned our backs to the afternoon sun and rode back toward Córdoba.

I questioned the messenger regarding his instructions and the circumstances of their delivery. He knew little other than that the queen had summoned him and ordered him to catch up with my barge and bring me back to her. The surprising news (other than the summons to return) was that Queen Isabella was alone at the time her instructions were given.

I was unsure of my purpose as I approached again the room where our petition had been denied. As I reached the entrance, I was intercepted by Luis de Santángel, the chief financial advisor to the Crown. He drew me aside, and with his hands folded under his cassock, murmured that I had him to thank for my recall. It appears that after my departure, he had shifted the focus of the queen from defeating Saracens and saving souls. As we had earlier without success, he made the case that approval of our proposal cost the Crown almost nothing if we failed, but would reap immeasurable wealth if we succeeded. The queen appeared to finally absorb the concept that Spain had little to lose and much to gain.

I questioned Señor Luis closely as to the attitude and expressions of the queen during his discourse with her. He told me her mind appeared to be elsewhere, but appearances to the contrary, she attended closely, making him reiterate his argument. Finally, she agreed to send the messenger to call me back.

I entered the room and was startled to find myself alone with Queen Isabella. I had expected to find her surrounded by her usual entourage of advisors, sycophants, and clerics. Even her husband the king was absent.

Queen Isabella sat at her ornate desk and pretended to examine some papers there. I knew this was a technique intended to keep me standing nervously and to signal that she was in command. I had used the same method at times, and it worked exceptionally well with junior seamen and low-ranking officers. But I was forty years old with gray hair, and the years had scraped most of the barnacles off my hull. So I broke the silence with a sweeping bow and a greeting. "Your Majesty wished to see me?" Queen Isabella maintained the charade of examining her papers for a moment longer, and then deigned to raise her eyes.

"Ah! Señor Colón." She assumed an air of surprise, as if she had not been the one who summoned me to return. "It seems we see you so often petitioning our court as you did this morning." Not mentioning that my pre-noon petition had been once again rejected, she capably and quickly summarized the details, including the pros and cons of my proposed voyage. Well, at least she had been listening.

With little to lose, I boldly inquired whether anything had occurred since that morning that might have changed her negative decision and prompted my recall. She gave a slight smile and admitted that her chief financial advisor, Luis de Santángel, had urged her to reconsider. "We have considered your proposal many times over the past years and, as you are painfully aware, have each time determined against proceeding. You have made your case alone and with a consortium of colleagues, but the case does not vary with the telling."

She leaned forward, and her eyes locked with mine. This was disconcerting, for in past audiences, she barely deigned to notice me. "But this morning I noticed a difference in your demeanor, Señor Colón."

I was shocked that this time she did not use the royal "We" and braced for I knew not what. "It was not clear at first, and only after you departed did I understand that something about you had changed. At first I thought it was merely a sense of despair or futility or exhaustion that emanated from your eyes and posture. But after your departure, perhaps my senses sharpened."

Queen Isabella leaned back and languidly pointed her finger at me. "Señor Cristóbal Colón, you carry in your heart a secret. And before you leave here this afternoon, you will reveal what it is!"

I found myself unconsciously taking a step back from her. I tried to recover my balance. "Your Highness, all men carry secrets, especially once they reach my age after a lifetime of mistakes and regrets. I have spent enough hours in the confessional box of churches around the world to have revealed these sins under the seal of confession. I pray that the Lord God in His mercy has forgiven me."

The queen smiled. "Do not try to divert me with the stories of your undoubtedly many sins, Señor Colón. I am not talking about them. Remember, I am a woman surrounded by men. I have risen to the throne of Spain in a world that is dominated by men. Many of those men wished me ill or thought me weak because of my gender. I assure you; I did not survive their many plots or succeed to this throne without being able to read the thoughts and feelings of those around me. When a man's expression changes; when he changes the subject; when his eyes shift away or hold mine too long; when a response to a question is unduly slow; when a silence drags on; then I know that the mind is seeking to escape an uncomfortable subject—in short, a secret. And these signs I detected in you this morning. Moreover, the level of your demands from King Ferdinand and me suggests that you have a higher purpose than simply opening trade routes, desirable as that may be. You foresee discoveries that are proportional to the rewards you seek from us. So, tell me. What is the secret purpose that you carry, Señor Colón?"

I cursed myself, recalling how my mind had wandered during the morning audience while the abbot had droned on about the opportunities for converting the heathens. It must have been then that my face had carelessly revealed my soul to this sharp-eyed woman.

I tried again to dissemble. "Your Highness, I do have a confession. The map on which I rely for my proposed voyage is stolen. The Toscanelli map was shown to me in confidence while I was at the court in Lisbon. I took it without permission, and so I am guilty of theft. It was dishonorable of me, but the map is now to be put to use for the benefit of Spain."

Queen Isabella laughed. "Nice try, Señor. I have known for months that you obtained the Toscanelli map through nefarious means. And you know that everyone in Spain knows it as well. So do not try to distract my attention with something that I already know. No, your secret is more important, and I think it lies at the seat of the confidence you exhibit in your plan to sail west. Tell me what it is, Señor Colón. I do not like to resort to threats, but if you do not reveal your secret to me, I promise you will reveal it to Father Torquemada!"

I was torn. There seemed no way to wriggle off the hook on which I was now impaled. If I persisted in maintaining my secret knowledge, derived from heretical sources and implying the possibility of discoveries that seemed to contradict the Scriptures, I would probably face torture that would wrest those secrets from me in any case. On the other hand, I risked the same accusation of heresy if I revealed my secret knowledge. But perhaps I could conceal my source.

As a sailor, I must often trust my fate to the prevailing winds and waves. I made the decision. I wanted the Queen of Spain to be my ally, not my foe. "Your Highness, I will now place my life in your hands. I have indeed been harboring a secret, and it is the greatest secret in Christendom. My voyage is not to seek the treasures of Cathay, but to obtain the greatest treasure of all—the Holy Grail. And I alone know its location across the Ocean Sea!"

Before the queen could react to what must have seemed to her to be a desperate and preposterous claim, I continued. "Let me remind

Your Highness. As you know, many of the Knights Templar fled from France to Spain, and under the protection of King James II in 1317 they were adopted into the Order of Montesa."

"I know I appear to be a common sailor, Your Highness, and that is no accident, for I have deliberately assumed that guise. But the truth is, I am descended from a French nobleman. He is the source of my knowledge. He has passed down to me a map. Alerted to their impending arrest and imprisonment, the treasure fleet of the Knights of the Temple sailed from La Rochelle before that Order was falsely accused by the King of France with heresy. In their cargo was much of the wealth collected by the Order, but their most prized possession, and their most secret, was the cup used by Jesus at the Last Supper, and then used to capture the blood flowing from His side as he died on the cross."

Queen Isabella looked around the room like someone seeking to escape a lunatic. "Bear with me, Your Highness, for I know all this must sound like the ravings of a crazy man. I know it is commonly said that, on meeting a person for the first time, one can tell if he is insane if, within the first fifteen minutes of conversation, he brings up the Knights Templar or the Holy Grail. But I assure you, if you give me your ear, you will be convinced that I am not insane.

"The Templar treasure fleet sailed from the port of La Rochelle following a map that was prepared for them. The map is based on ancient sources that the Templars discovered in the Holy Land, and shows the details of a land mass easily reached by sailing to the west. This land was the fleet's destination. The French nobleman was my ancestor, and in his belongings, passed to me through my parents and grandparents, I found the map. It is now in my possession."

Queen Isabella picked idly at a plate of dates, but I could tell that her feigned boredom was a pretense. I had her interest.

"And what is this land, Señor Colón? Is it the Spice Islands and the riches of Cathay and the Indies that you have been offering to us?"

"What does it matter, Your Highness? If it is, a successful voyage would bring Spain both the treasures of the Orient as well as the treasures of the Knights Templar. If it is not, is not the potential to find the Holy Grail by itself worth the voyage?" I could see that her piety was beginning to overtake her financial considerations. I piled on.

"Your Highness, it is well known that the loyalty of your nobles is weak and can be easily swayed. But if you were in possession of the Holy Grail, there could be no question that you have been chosen by God to rule over Spain with your husband, King Ferdinand. The Holy Father in Rome would have to recognize, affirm, and protect the heavenly choice."

I dropped my voice a bit. "But you should not reveal the secret agenda of this mission, Your Highness. If your opponents in Spain were to learn of this search for the Holy Grail before it proved successful, you could be accused of heresy by your own Holy Inquisition. And, on top of that, foreign enemies could use the knowledge to Spain's detriment. The French could claim ownership of all the riches of the Templars based on the old claims of King Philip. And the new King Henry in England faces constant rebellions from the remaining Lancaster forces. Possession of the Holy Grail would cement his hold on the throne of England. Revealing the Grail's location—and let us not forget the temptation of the treasure of the Templars—would generate such a maelstrom that our venture together could be swept aside." (Notice how I had shifted the conversation such that the queen and I were now plotting together.)

"I humbly suggest to Your Majesty that you keep the Grail search secret and conceal that purpose under the guise of my initial proposal for a voyage to the East. That proposal is already known and has attracted little attention from those who might otherwise intervene."

Queen Isabella gazed at me with her fingers under her chin. "Let us suppose we agree." Ah! I had her! "How can we be guaranteed that were you, against all odds, to find the Templar treasure and the Holy Grail, you would not simply keep them for yourself? Or sell to whichever party offered you the most reward?"

"Your Highness, what more could a sovereign offer me than that which I have already asked of Spain? A noble title for me and my descendants, a portion of any wealth I find, rank as Admiral of the Ocean Sea?"

"Yes, all very well for you. But we need some equity in your findings, lest we be at your mercy. I think I will put some personal funds into your expedition. That will secure our title to your findings. Yes, that way we will be secure in our ownership rights."

Queen Isabella called out, and Luis de Santángel entered the room. Evidently, he had been waiting outside the door—and for a moment I feared he may have overheard my dialogue with the queen. "We have decided to grant Señor Colón his request for our approval for his voyage to the Indies by sailing west. In addition, we have determined that financial support will be afforded from our personal funds. You shall therefore raise the necessary funds and provide all assistance needed to acquire three ships, crews, and supplies for this voyage."

Santángel's response was immediate. "Your Highness, the Pinzón family stands ready to provide ships and crews once payment is available. I am prepared to raise the funds needed for this expedition. I can approach my contacts among the Genoese and Florentine merchants. In fact, my good Genoese friend Ferdinando Pinello lives here in Córdoba. Your Highness knows he can be trusted, for you have had previous dealings. He is easily able to advance sufficient money for three caravels, crew, and supplies. Naturally, he will wish the advance to be held against some security, but this need not be onerous. I am sure he would be satisfied with the pledge of some jewelry."

Queen Isabella agreed to the arrangement, and matters were put in motion from that moment. "We go to Granada to celebrate the victory of our wars against the Moors. Join us there."

The festivities were impressive. The King and Queen of Spain entered the city through the gates in the protective wall that had been built nearly 500 years before. The solemn procession marched into the Alhambra with banners and flags flying, carrying statues of the Blessed Virgin and various saints. Drums rolled and trumpets blared. The king and queen took seats on ivory thrones in the Alhambra fortress and received the notables of the city, who pledged their loyalty to their new monarchs. The royal couple then withdrew to the nearby town of Santa Fe. To me, Queen Isabella said, "Return to me in a few days and we will have the documents completed."

And so, on April 17, 1492, I followed them to Santa Fe, and in the presence of King Ferdinand and Queen Isabella, I signed the formal agreement granting me all "…those things requested by Don ('DON!') Cristóbal Colón as a manner of recompense for what he has discovered." Five simple paragraphs agreed to all the matters I had specified, contingent on my successful return. Not bad for someone who until recently had been a failed, nearly penniless supplicant and viewed as a common sailor from Genoa!

The next months were filled with the tasks necessary to send a fleet to sea. My first concern was that the Pinzón family, who would serve as captains of two of the three ships in my fleet, should recognize my authority and direction. This was not a certainty, for these were men accustomed to being in charge.

Early meetings were not auspicious. Despite their earlier appearance at my side in Córdoba, the two younger brothers of Martín Pinzón, Vicente and Francisco, were skeptical about, if not hostile to, the whole idea of the expedition. Vicente was the youngest, erect and arrogant in the bloom of his youth, and very conscious that his straight aquiline nose and dark eyes were handsome and pleasing to ladies. Francisco, the middle brother, no leader, was accustomed to following the instructions of his older brother or, indeed, any source of authority. From their perspective, the voyage would be at best a serious money-loser, and at worst a death sentence for them and their crew. Moreover, I was to them an unknown Genoese sailor. They regarded with disdain the seaworthiness of the two caravels and their crews that I had commandeered with my grant of royal authority. There was little I could say to argue against this view, since I agreed with their assessment; but at this point, I had no choice. Neither they nor their crews felt like putting their lives in my hands. However, their view changed, if reluctantly, when Martín joined the discussions on his return from a business venture that had taken him away from Huelva.

Martín Alonso Pinzón was cut from a different cloth than his brothers. A mature gentleman, he appraised the world from calm dark eyes that looked out below the fringe of straight hair concealing his forehead. His small mouth pursed like a slightly open clamshell above his smooth chin. In Martín, the blood of three generations of sailors flowed strong. He knew the sea both near shore and in the blue waters of the deep. He was so well-regarded in the region around Huelva that his willing participation in my venture was essential.

Although he was first a seaman, Martín was also a canny man of business. Along with his brothers, he had amassed a considerable fortune from trading ventures. More importantly, he owned several ships, and these were crewed by loyal and experienced sailors. He shared with his brothers the disdain for the ships and crews I had commandeered. In truth, I did not disagree with them, but felt these were the best I could arrange, given my resources and authority. Martín cast aside these limitations by offering to provide two ships of his own, along with experienced and seasoned crew. In addition, he was willing to invest a considerable sum of his own money into the venture. Naturally, these concessions would not be granted without a consideration.

I was in no position to haggle. After some discussion, I agreed that the Pinzóns would take a half-share of my interest in the venture. I would retain the role of admiral, while Martín and his brothers would serve as captains of their two vessels.

Through their connections, the Pinzóns brought into our venture the well-known navigator Juan de la Cosa. This man was widely regarded as one of the most knowledgeable deep-water sailors of the time. He was also well known as a mapmaker, and I had seen his work while working in my brother's shop in Lisbon. I had even met Juan many years before when I visited El Puerto de Santa María. He had visited the Canary Islands and sailed the coast of Africa many times. I felt at the time we could not have found a better addition to our fleet.

Martín Pinzón and I traveled to Huelva to meet with him. We found him living aboard the *Marigalante*, a ship that he owned.

The *Marigalante* was (I use the past tense because the gallant ship floats no more) of a different construction than the two caravels provided by the Pinzóns. This was a larger vessel, known as a *Não*, with a short, wide, very high hull. The hull was exceptionally strong, reinforced at the waterline and further protected with eleven fenders raked fore and aft. Protection from the waves for crew members was in the form of a small, low deck with gunwales. Slightly above the quarterdeck was a small cabin that I determined to take for my quarters during the voyage. From fore to aft, the ship was bowed like a bow, with a high forecastle and a high stern covering the cabin and the ropes on either side that guided the tiller. Here also was the cooking area, just under the lip of the cabin ceiling, but open to the elements so the smoke from the fire, nestled in a protective bed of sand, could escape. The decks of all three ships were sloped, higher in the center line and rounded down to the rails, so that the seas would inevitably sluice them off.

Through Pinzón's intervention, Juan de la Cosa joined our company and added to our fleet the *Marigalante*, which he renamed the *Santa María* in honor of its home port. This completed the complement of three ships authorized to my use by Queen Isabella and King Ferdinand. To the hands of these experienced seamen, I was able to delegate all the aspects of provisions, water, equipment, and the many small details needed to complete a successful voyage.

The only real issue was the planned duration of our journey.

It was now that my secret knowledge—that there was another mass of land between the western end of Europe and the eastern shores of Asia—would complicate the calculations of time, distance, and provisions. If our reckonings were to rely on the traditional measures derived from Ptolemy and Marinus of Tyre, we would have to provision for an impossibly long voyage. But I knew from my ancestor's map that the distance we would need to cover was far smaller. I needed to somehow get the calculations down to approximately fifty degrees of longitude. If I subtracted from the total of the earth's 360 degrees the area of land calculated by Aristotle, Pliny, and Seneca, and added an estimate of the extensions of land beyond Cathay revealed by Marco Polo, plus the distance between Spain and the Canary Islands, with a bit of hand waving I would be able to reduce the estimated distance for our journey to about sixty degrees of longitude, or about 3,600 nautical miles. This matched nicely with the calculation that derived from my ancestor's map.

By using deliberate and, if I may say, masterful deceit, I was able to reduce the planned distances and times needed to sail to the Indies to a plan suitable for a journey to the land shown on my map. Sailing from the Canary Islands to the easternmost point on the map at a reasonable speed, the voyage could take us as little as one week. If we met adverse winds, that estimate might double and maybe even triple. So, optimistically, I could begin to search for landfall after seven days. Pessimistically, it might be as much as three weeks. In the event, it turned out to be a bit over four weeks. But the provisions we had aboard, though stretched, proved sufficient for the voyage.

At last came August 2, 1492, the day we departed on our great adventure. One by one, each of the ships was warped alongside the quay and a gangplank run out. After lengthy farewells to their families on the dockside, the eighty-seven crew members filed aboard their respective ships, thirty-nine on the flagship *Santa María* under the command of her owner, Juan de la Cosa; twenty-six on the *Pinta*, captained by Martín Alonso Pinzón; and twenty-two on the *Niña*, which was commanded by the youngest of the Pinzón brothers, Vicente. Francisco Pinzón, the middle brother, was master of the *Pinta*, under the command of his older brother Martín. High on the stern of the *Santa María*, the flag of Spain was unfurled and hung limply in the lee of the port of Palos.

We floated on the ebb tide along the river Odiel and anchored for the night near the sand bar at the mouth of the river, awaiting the morning wind off the shore. At the eighth hour on the morning of August 3, our lateen sails filled with a gentle breeze stretching their canvas, and we began to make way with a nice curl under our keel.

It took us six days to reach our first destination, the Canary Islands, where we limped in on August 9. Any prudent seaman knows it takes time to accustom a crew to a ship, and to identify the weak links in a ship on a long voyage. In this case, the weak link was the rudder of the *Pinta*.

Our ships, though generally well cared for, were not new. Once we were on the open sea, the side pressures that pushed against the rudder to enable steering proved too much for the fastenings that held it in place. As a result, within three days of our departure, the Pinta's rudder came loose from its fastenings. Fortunately, the ingenious Captain Martín Pinzón managed to reattach the rudder, though in a weakened state. On the fourth day, the rudder jumped its fastenings once again, and this time Captain Martín responded by fashioning two steering oars from the extra spars we carried and lashing them to the sides of the caravel in order to maintain an unsatisfactory steerage way. Fortunately, we encountered no significant weather, and with fair winds, our little flotilla managed to raise the island of Lanzarote in the Canaries. Then, finally, we arrived at the island of Grand Canary.

I ordered Martín to lay offshore, because he was unable to steer finely enough with his damaged rudder to warp the *Pinta* into the harbor. Indeed, I was so worried over the seaworthiness of the *Pinta* that I contemplated the option of finding another vessel to replace her. However, Martín and I, well assisted by the crew, repaired the rudder and some weak spars. These repairs made the *Pinta* generally seaworthy once more. While we were refitting and victualing, I ordered that the lateen main sails of the ships be replaced with square sails, making them easier to maneuver. At this time, I also ordered that each mainsail be painted to display the simple red cross of the crusading Knights of the Temple. I hoped this device might be spotted from the shore by any descendants of the original expedition that had sailed from La Rochelle almost 200 years before.

We remained in the Canary Islands for some weeks, loading water, firewood, and food aboard the three ships. During this time, we learned from a passing ship that the King of Portugal had sent three warships to capture me and my little fleet. I suspect this was done out of some envy that I was sailing under the flag of Spain, although in truth, I had given Portugal a fair opportunity. I suppose it is like dogs with a bone—nothing so arouses a dog's ire as the prospect of another dog taking a bone, even if the first one had no interest in it.

Spurred on by the prospect of conflict with the Portuguese vessels, we were stimulated to quickly complete our repairs and loading. Finally, on September 6, 1492, we weighed anchor and continued our voyage to the west.

The first few days of sailing were in light winds, and we made little way, but then a good wind began to blow from the northeast. While I was happy with the wind, it created a following sea, and our little vessels buried their noses into the waves, first climbing and then pitching and rolling down into the troughs. Thus, while the wind was favorable, the sea slowed our progress.

On the following morning the wind held, but the sea calmed a bit and we were able to make better way. The log was heaved at regular intervals; the knots in the attached rope were counted against the time it took for the sand in the glass to run out, and thus I was able to calculate our speed through the water. I converted the English distances to the more familiar and lesser Portuguese leagues and posted our distance for each day and night traveled, thereby keeping the crew informed of our progress. At noon each day I measured the distance of the sun over the horizon, and thus kept on a steady course west along the meridian.

At sea, the days soon merge into one another, filled with the routines of changing watches, shifting sails, cooking and serving meals, sleeping as one can. Nevertheless, there are many hours spent just idly watching the waves pass under our keel, searching the horizon and the nearby waters for anything that breaks the monotony of the waves. Our three ships stayed close together, and in this way provided visual interest for one another.

On one night, the dark sky exploded in streaks of light as stars fell out of the darkness. The men were afraid it was a sign of God's disfavor, for sailors are a superstitious lot. Martín Pinzón calmed them with assurances that this heavenly phenomenon happened every year in late summer and was a sign God sent to mariners promising that the way ahead was clear—for only in clear weather could the lights be seen. This quieted the crews.

I was very glad that Martín Pinzón was able to exert this kind of soothing effect. Ships are small communities, and moods are contagious. Left unchecked, they can quickly turn from fear to sullenness to resentment to anger and mutiny. Like a father, a captain must know when to be stern, when to give way, and when to turn a blind eye. The respect and trust for Martín Alonzo Pinzón was essential to the success of our voyage.

As night followed day and then again night, we sailed along a calm and following sea. The crew and all of us were encouraged on the fourteenth day after departing Gomera in the Canary Islands, when we encountered westerly winds. After weeks of sailing before easterly winds alone, this happy breeze meant we were likely to find winds capable of blowing us back to Spain. Our lateen sails allowed us to beat into these winds and maintain our westward course. We often saw weeds and flotsam in the water before us, coming from the west, blown by wind and current. These signs were carefully scrutinized by captains and crews, and we concluded that they were land-based plants. Land could not be far ahead.

On the night of the September 17, the sighting of the North Star showed a different reading from that of the compass. This worried the men considerably, for they feared it meant that we were lost. In the privacy of my cabin on the *Santa María*, I tensely consulted my ancestor's map. There it showed a rosette indicating the need to adjust sightings because the true course was that of the compass. We had sailed so far west that the position of the North Star in the sky had changed. The next morning, I made a great show of consulting the compass and re-affirmed that our course was true. When the word passed among the crew, there was a visible relaxation of tension aboard.

On one day, we saw dolphins in the water around our bow wave. The men cast fishing lines over the side and captured a large tuna. It provided all the crews with welcome meals of fresh meat, which lifted the men's spirits admirably. On various days, we also saw some birds that we speculated had flown from nearby land, as well as a whale and large amounts of seaweed. The latter slowed our way, but we passed through it, borne by the favorable winds.

We were bitterly disappointed when, on September 25, what we had all taken to be land ahead resolved itself into a cloud bank as we approached. Our disappointment was keen, and the crews began to worry that our voyage was doomed.

Their concern was raised further by the depletion of the water in our holds. We had been sailing for about two weeks, and the remaining water was sufficient, with care, to just carry us back to Spain. If we continued westward, it was not certain that we would find land and be able to replenish water before we ran out. This caused the men great discontent, and they muttered and cast unhappy looks at their officers and at me, so that I feared they might rise in mutiny.

The captains and I gathered in conference. It was again Martín Pinzón who took the lead. We pulled the ships tightly together, and he addressed the combined crews with great sternness. His harangue wisely mixed praise and threats, relying on the old adage of the carrot and the stick. Our success in coming this far unscathed he attributed rightly to their praiseworthy adherence to duty and the bravery of the crew. He then brandished the stick, assuring the listening sailors that, in the event of the slightest sign of disobedience or resistance to orders, he would not hesitate to summarily hang the perpetrators. He closed by noting that portents of land ahead were positive, citing the numerous birds, land-based vegetation, and weather signs.

Our priest spoke next. This priest had been recommended to me by Father Juan Pérez, from La Rábida, as a pious man of faith. This he was, but he was also committed to the Holy Inquisition. He brought his skills and techniques with him to practice upon the crew, making them fearful and hesitant. The captains were frightened to confront him, so it fell to me to rein him in. He did not take this kindly, for he was accustomed to servile obedience. I very much suspect that Father Pérez chose him for my crew at the insistence of Torquemada, and perhaps King Ferdinand, to keep an eye on me. But the abbot probably also acquiesced in order to get him out of La Rábida monastery. In any case, his looming presence was useful in quelling the resistance of the crew.

The next day, we altered our course slightly, steering more west by southwest to compensate for the leeway we had been experiencing since our departure from the Canary Islands.

A s the days went by, our course took us further south. The late-September weather was delightful, with steady breezes to fill our sails. The days were warm and sunny. At night, balmy temperatures made it pleasant for the crew to sleep on the deck between watches. The sea turned from the dark gray and cold green upon which we had floated when leaving Spain to a clear and translucent blue and green. Gazing far into the depths, we could make out the forms of fish, and of turtles rising to the surface to catch their breath. Were it not for our constant worry about water and provisions, the voyage could not have been more idyllic. But even these fears were alleviated by occasional rains that were captured in sails rigged to sluice the water into waiting barrels. The men continued to catch some fish, and once we brought aboard a porpoise that provided welcome meat.

It had now been more than two months since we had departed from Huelva, and our voyage was beginning to stretch into its fifth week since we had sailed from the Canary Islands. The sun had moved south on its seasonal trek, and the calendar had moved from September to October. The weather remained wonderfully pleasant, with warm, sunny days followed by nights cooled by the winds that filled our sails as we parted the seas on a west-by-southwest course.

Nevertheless, the days stretched worryingly one after the other with no land in sight. Surely my forefather's map was not false? Our pace was reasonably brisk across the water, but I had expected landfall by now. How badly had I misjudged the distance? Were the wise men in the Portuguese and Spanish courts correct in their estimate of the circumference of the earth? I checked and rechecked de Villiers' map, measuring distances, reviewing my log, and recalculating speed and distance. I was wracked with worry, and I prayed silently night and day for a hail from the masthead signifying land.

I smelled land before I saw it. When I caught the first whiff of smoke I assumed it was from the cook fire below the deck, but it was quickly apparent that the source of the smell was being carried to the ship on the wind. I saw crew members suddenly lift their heads and sniff the breeze, for the scent of woodsmoke is unmistakable.

As we continued on our westerly course, added to the smoke there came the characteristic smell of beached seaweed rotting in the sun. Now, all the crew was aware that land could not be far off.

At about ten o'clock in the evening, staring across the sea to the west, I thought I detected a flicker of light. I was unsure, but quietly summoned Pedro Gutiérrez, King Ferdinand's majordomo. Looking carefully, this gentleman confirmed my sighting, which was like a little wax candle whose flame moved up and down. I spotted the light intermittently over the next few hours.

Later that night, in the middle of the midnight watch, came the cry of "Land Ho! Land Ho!" from the masthead of the *Pinta*. So often disappointed, the men were prepared to once again find a false sighting had been made. But this time it was true! Martín Pinzón clambered into the rigging and confirmed the sighting. Roderigo, the sailor who had made the sighting, was from the town of Triana, near Seville. He found himself clasped in the embrace of his mates as they danced on the deck, from both joy and profound relief.

From the deck of the *Santa María*, we spied in the weak light of the moon the low form of an island, barely protruding above the horizon line created by the sea. Over the hours of the morning and afternoon watches, we sailed nearer. The line of white waves breaking gently against the shore became visible, and then some low trees crested a small strip of sandy beach, bordered on either side by mangroves like the ones I had seen in my voyages to Africa. By now, evening once again was closing in. I conferred with the captains, and we all agreed it would be prudent to lay offshore for the remainder of the night rather than run in the dark to an unknown shore. We determined that when morning came we would send in launches to sound the bottom and detect any reefs or shoals that lurked in the shallows. And so we heaved to and struck our sails for the first time in weeks. The anchors were dropped into a sandy bottom as darkness fell.

I paced the deck, far too excited to sleep. The moon waxed gibbous and the sky was clear with a brilliant array of stars scattered densely across the firmament. I could hear waves breaking gently on the unknown shore. The sea glowed with an unearthly luminescence that cast a green tinge to its reflection on the slanting prow. Across the water, it illuminated the shapes of the *Niña* and *Pinta*, bobbing gently in the slight swell.

I was both excited and frightened. On one hand, de Villiers' map had proved to not be a mythical invention and had led us truly to land. But I did not know what lay ahead in this land. Had the Templar fleet succeeded in traversing the wide Ocean Sea? Or had they perished in the crossing? Even if they successfully found land, had they, too, come to this very spot among all the possible landfalls they might have made?

The chances of that seemed so unlikely that I knew I could not expect such a stroke of providential luck. I knew with certainty that we must sail the coast of this land with flags flying and the Templar cross displayed on our sails. But what if the descendants of the original crews had forgotten their origins after almost two centuries? Had they married women from this land and had children by them? If they existed, would the descendants of the Templar crews who had sailed from La Rochelle in 1307, now so long ago, see and recognize the device on our sails and realize that my ancestor's promise had been fulfilled? Perhaps the tale of that voyage from France by now would have receded into the mists of myth, and become like some of the legends I had heard from native tribes in Africa about the origins of their world. Or perhaps they were all dead, and their secret had died with them.

In these latitudes, the sun rises and sets near six o'clock, morning and evening, although we were several weeks past the fall equinox. I was awake long before that, dressed in scarlet coat and trousers. Over these I wore the simple tunic that Gerard de Villiers had left for me, with the cross of the Templars emblazoned upon it.

The Pinzón brothers rowed over to the *Santa María* in the gray light of early morning. The shallow sea was a beautiful light green, with large white patches where the bottom was sandy. When the sun was fully above the horizon, we boarded two launches, one for the captains and me and the Franciscan friar, the other for soldiers, their gleaming metal armor reflecting the bright sun. Above us, the mainsail of the *Santa María* hung limply with the Templar cross vividly visible in red.

The boats made their way through the rocks and approached the white sand of the beach. The sailors easily rowed through the slight shore break of the waves and ground into the sand. I carried with me the flag of Spain. We were all silent; the only sound came from the wind and the waves. Behind us, the ships slowly inched their way closer to the shore, but left off their sounding as the bottom shallowed rapidly and the many rocks became apparent.

I leapt from the bow so as to be the first on the new land. None of us had touched dry land for weeks, and the lack of movement under my feet made me feel unsteady and almost sick. I fell to my knees for a moment, an action I hoped my companions would interpret as a moment of piety. Quickly I used the flagpole to help me rise to my feet, planting it in the sand while declaiming proudly and loudly that this land and all its inhabitants would forever be "By the Grace of God under the reign of Their Catholic Majesties and Kingdoms of Spain."

The Franciscan priest came ashore, wading through the small waves with his cassock bunched around his bony knees and his cross high above his head. As I had, he fell to his knees. Perhaps his genuflection was more intentional than mine. He was followed directly by the rest of the sailors, and we gathered in a small group on the sand.

The priest wished to celebrate holy mass immediately as thanks to God for having brought us to this beach. The captains and I demurred, for we were much concerned about the source of the woodsmoke we had detected from sea. Looking around, we could not see easily over the small cliff of sand that the waves and tides had erected along the high water line. Clambering up through the soft sand, we could make out a lagoon filled with clear blue water, surrounded by low hillocks covered with scrub bushes and small trees. Scanning the shoreline to the north and south, we detected a low hill or bluff on the shore, protruding slightly out into the sea from the surrounding beach. It was from there that a plume of smoke arose.

"That fire does not come from a lightning strike, Admiral" said Martín Pinzón. "That is a sign of a village." He was clearly correct, and we could make out a small group of people coming along the shoreline toward us. The sailors were very excited, muttering among themselves that we were about to meet natives from the Indies, for that is where they believed we were. Would they be dressed in silks and gold? The stories from Marco Polo and John Mandeville described the inhabitants of the Indies sometimes as cultured pagans and sometimes as monkey creatures covered in hair. Which would these Indians be?

As the small band of men came closer, we discerned that, far from being clothed in silk and gold, they were barely clothed at all. One or two wore bead necklaces made from shells, and one man had a bird's feather tied into his long black hair. The other men—there were no women in the group—were naked except for a strip of cloth hiding their privates.

They approached us with some trepidation, for we were heavily clothed. Iron-armored cuirasses covered the chests of the common sailors, and the rest of us wore the clothing customary to our native climate (which, by the way, was far too warm for the sunny beach on which we stood). The priest wore the brown robe of his Franciscan Order, with the white rope knotted about his waist. He stepped forward with his staff surmounted by the Holy Cross and addressed the Indians in Latin. His failure to communicate was followed by a similar failure from the Cathayan interpreter who had sailed with us.

These gambits having quickly proved fruitless, we fell back on signs and gestures, which we combined with drawings in the sand. After much gesticulation and pointing in various directions, it became clear that these Indians (for so the crew called them, for lack of a better term) did not live on this barren island, but were here on a fishing expedition. They had come in dugout canoes like those I had seen in Africa. Their village was elsewhere. Martín Pinzón drew a circle in the sand and pointed down to the place where we stood and then made a querying gesture. In response, their leader pointed off to the south, indicating the direction of their home. He drew in the sand the shape of another island, and indicated through his drawings that there were many more islands lying to the south.

We spent only three days on this island, which I named San Salvador. Our stay gave the crews an opportunity to stretch their legs and find some fresh fruit. The Indians showed us a particular tree that yielded a delicious juicy small fruit they called "guava." It has a scent a bit like a lemon. When the fruit ripens, the skin becomes yellow and yields a sweet pulp.

We spent three days marking the island on our charts and collecting guava fruit. Then we weighed anchor and our little fleet sailed toward the southwest. Six of the Indians sailed with us as guides. Over the next few weeks, we were able to teach them rudimentary Spanish, and in our later encounters with Indians on other islands, they proved to be very useful interpreters.

The weather was difficult, with constant rain and poor visibility. We found ourselves in a bewildering sprawl of small islands, surrounded by water that ranged from wading-depth shallow to apparently bottomless. The water was so clear that we could often see the bottom, and even see fish and turtles swimming in the depths. Looking out over the gunwales of the ship, we saw that the sea varied from a beautiful green to an astonishing blue that reflected the sky. It was fortunate that the water was clear, for it allowed us to detect the many reefs and underwater pinnacles that would have torn out the bottom of the boats. Our lookouts were kept on high alert, and we were forced to continuously sound the bottom, for the water was deceptive in its depth. We had to heave to each night for fear of careening into a reef or sand bar. Fortunately, there were numerous cays and sheltered inlets that offered berths, providing us safety from the rough seas.

We wandered among these islands for some weeks. Guava fruit was abundant, but the only meat available came from birds, which were very wary and hard to catch, and occasional fish. There were no sources of fresh water other than captured rain, which we sluiced into barrels using our sails.

It was not long before the sailors used the guava to ferment a nasty sort of liquor. Finding crew members often attempting their duties in a drunken state, the officers searched the holds. Following the strong smell of guava mash, they secured the supplies of the liquor and doled it out in small quantities so that the working of the ships was not adversely affected. Truth to tell, the officers were also not unhappy to take a drink from time to time—sometimes to excess as well.

In some islands we found groups of Indians clothed similarly to the ones we had encountered on San Salvador. I visited their villages and entered their huts made of tree branches and covered in the leaves of palm trees. Interestingly, the palm-tree leaves, with their creased shape, made very efficient funnels to carry away the strong rains that pelted us intermittently. The Indians introduced me to their habit of inhaling the smoke from a plant that in their language sounds like the Spanish word *tabaco*. Those of us who tried it found that after an initial harshness that led to strong fits of coughing, we became used to it and found the effects to be relaxing and pleasurable. The Indians used the leaves as a poultice to cover small wounds, and also showed us how to use juice from the plant to repel the many annoying insects that frequently stung and bit us. I packed some barrels with these leaves, hoping to offer them to the court on my return to Spain.

At every encounter, I questioned the Indians closely for information about settlements of people from ships like ours, whom they referred to as "men from the sky." All inquiries elicited blank stares and incomprehension. A similar response came forward when they were asked about gold, which we saw on one or two of them, worn as small trinkets such as earrings. They made it clear that these had been obtained through trading with other tribes from a distant location. There was no gold to be mined on these island sand bars, for, in truth, they were not much more. The officers and crew members who had expected to gaze on roofs of gold encrusted with precious jewels were sorely disappointed. Still, we remained hopeful that we might be rewarded on the next landfall, or the one after that.

After ten days of sailing from one small island to another, we heard from the natives about two much larger islands, and this raised our hopes. Following their pointed fingers, we sailed southward, before the wind, and on Sunday, October 28, made landfall at a place the Indians called Cubanacan. There, a river flowed into the sea, open for our approach with no rocks or reefs to hinder us. This was clearly not just another large sandbar, like the islands we had been traversing, for it had substantial mountains rising inland. From the masthead of the *Santa María*, I could make out large forests stretching back from the shore. Was it indeed another, larger island, as the Indians had said? Or was it the continent depicted on my ancestor's map? It was hard to tell.

Ashore, the crews of our three ships found fruit and water in plenty.

The forests teemed with small, furry creatures that were easily brought down with our pikes and crossbows and provided meat. Everyone was much relieved, for although the homeward journey to Spain was still uncertain, there was now little doubt that we could survive in this abundant land. But, being who we were, once the satisfaction of our physical needs was assured, we naturally fell to quarreling.

"Quarreling" may be too strong a word for our disagreements. The three captains and I joined together to plan our way forward. Martín Pinzón favored further exploration of Cubanacan, to determine whether it was the mainland, as I hoped, or another large island. His brothers and Juan de la Cosa believed, after interrogating the natives closely, that this was an island, and that the source of their gold trinkets was to the west. They argued for sailing in that direction. I, too, was interested in finding the "mother of all gold," but I was even more intent on searching for the lost colony of the Knights Templar and their treasures, both sacred and profane.

After much disputation, we were finally able to agree on a common course of action. We had come to our present position from the north, so we agreed that Martín would lead the *Niña* and the *Pinta* to the northwest, as he fervently desired, thereby searching along the northern coast of Cubanacan. I would venture with Juan de la Cosa on the *Santa María* to the south and southeast. We would each take careful soundings and prepare charts of the coastline, and then the Pinzóns would return to a rendezvous on the southeast coast. We necessarily were to make detailed charts, and promised we would come together in thirty days to compare our findings and begin to load food and water for our voyage back to Spain.

And so, the next morning, the *Santa María* weighed anchor and stood offshore with the wind. We followed the coastline toward the southeast. After four days of sailing on this heading, I began to believe the coast we were following was that of a continent, not an island. But on the fifth day, after traveling about three hundred miles from our initial point, the coast turned sharply to the south. Sailing around the headland, the coast returned in the direction from which we had come. Either we had sailed along a huge peninsula that jutted into the sea from a continental land mass, or we were in the process of circumnavigating an island. My instinct told me that the latter was most likely the case.

After some discussion with Juan de la Cosa, we sailed the *Santa María* to the easternmost point and lay to there. Our crews went in hunting parties to explore the nearby land. There we enjoyed a lovely respite, awaiting the appearance of the *Niña* and the *Pinta*.

Once our little fleet was reassembled, we exchanged our reports, and I gave the Pinzóns' crews a few days to go ashore. They had sailed to land's end along the northern shore and, like us, found themselves turning the corner and returning in the direction of their origin. Martín Pinzón confirmed that Cubanacan was indeed an island, though very substantial in size.

We lay at anchor for a number of days. During our various explorations, we encountered groups of natives and gathered information about the interior of the island, using our usual methods of pointing and gesticulating, drawing in the sand, and helped by our Indian guides' improving ability to translate.

While in the forest collecting information from a local tribe, Martín Pinzón learned about a large Indian settlement lying in the interior. Without consulting me or any of the others, Martín, following a guide, took a group of men from the *Niña* in hopes that this would turn out to be a city such as had been described by Marco Polo. It turned out that the fabled city was merely a slightly larger encampment of natives, with no gold to be seen. After being pressed about gold, however, the Indians directed him to sail to the east. It was there, they said, that their legends told them gold was to be found in such large quantities that the local natives would dig it up on the beach and pound it into rods. The name of the island was given as "Babeque."

Returning to our anchorage, Martín assembled the crew of the *Pinta* and immediately sailed away in the dark of the night in search of this island. When I awoke to find them gone, I was much incensed, even more so once I learned from the Indians of his goal. This was obviously a ploy to obtain for himself alone the gold that, in justice, belonged to me, or at least to all the members of the expedition. Martín, in his greed and presumptuousness, had clearly decided that our explorations were not meeting the expectations of his family members, and he was determined to strike out on his own. It was nearly two months before we saw him again.

I was quite vexed at this betrayal and mutiny against my authority, but I dared not take too public a stand, as I still had to deal with his brothers and the crews that were loyal to him on the *Niña* and the *Santa María*. Accordingly, I put a good face on it and pretended that we had agreed to separate in order to widen our search. After my anger had cooled a bit, I began to see the advantage of being in full command, with no need to defer to Martín Pinzón or to seek his assent to my wishes. It occurred to me that I was now free to seek out the Templar colony, if it existed, and to acquire its treasure and the Holy Grail. There was no need to conceal my intentions or to go off on tangents in the search of what was more and more clearly nonexistent gold.

And so we continued in the direction of my initial bearing, heading south and east. We carefully explored the coast of Cubanacan, sending boats into the coves and up the various rivers that entered the ocean. We continued in this way until we reached land's end, where the coast turned sharply west again. We landed on the leeward side of this last promontory and awaited our planned rendezvous with the *Pinta*. While we waited, we hunted ashore, storing meat, fruit, and water for our return voyage to Spain. Finally, after two months, we were rejoined by a disappointed Martín Pinzón and the crew of the *Pinta*. We set sail due east, heading for home.

My hope was to pick up eventually the northeasterly winds we had encountered on our outward journey and be in position to begin our return voyage to Spain. Instead, within two days, after sailing only about thirty miles, our course was interrupted by the cry of "Land

Ho!" Land was sighted on the horizon about thirty miles to the east. We were apparently in the middle of a passageway between Cubanacan and a large land mass to its east. After some exploration, it appeared that we had landed at the northernmost arm of a great gulf that swept in an arc to the south, and then extended its lower arm to the west. The sea that lay between these arms was as large as the Bay of Cádiz.

The next day was the Feast of Saint Nicholas, December 6, so I named the place Puerto San Nicholas in honor of the saint. We rowed ashore and ground our launch onto the sand. Overlooking the beach was a bluff, which I climbed with my men to see the land beyond. Extending inland was a large flat expanse that reminded me of the lovely plains of Andalucía. On this hilltop, I planted once again the flag of Aragon and Castile, naming the land Hispaniola.

We explored inland over the course of the next few days. On the third day, we crested a hill and were surprised to find there a small group of naked men and women. My heart leapt. Both the men and women were much lighter-skinned than the natives we had encountered elsewhere. These people were tall, slender, and well-proportioned, in contrast to the somewhat squat, big-nosed, swarthy Indians on the more western islands. Indeed, two young women were so fair of skin and had such European features that I was certain we had finally met with descendants of the Templars. However, they gave no sign of such ancestry in their language or customs. The natives greeted us cheerfully with gifts of guavas and fish. In return, they received from us some trinkets.

A few days passed. Then, one morning, the Indians sent an angry delegation led by their chief and consisting of the families of the two beautiful girls. This group comprised almost every inhabitant of their village, and they came shouting and threatening, bearing arms— spears, bows and arrows, and clubs.

It quickly emerged that by revealing these women, Satan had introduced temptation into this Garden of Eden. Several sailors from the *Pinta*, having endured long abstinence at sea and throughout our voyages, and feeling rebellious against my commands for civility to the natives, snuck off in the night to the camp of the Indians. They were quite drunk on the liquor they had made from the guavas we had been given. Capturing the two young girls, they forced them away from their village and into the nearby forest. There they were repeatedly violated by members of the crew in turn, to such an extent that one of the girls died.

I did not learn of this until after we had repelled our attackers, for such I had deemed them to be, not understanding the reasons for their anger. I ordered the men to adopt a defensive posture with our backs to the water. Our protective armor easily withstood the blows from the primitive weapons, and their arrows bounced harmlessly from the cuirasses of the men. In our counterattack, our superior armaments of steel swords and pikes overwhelmed the Indian men and slew several of them. Those who survived fled back to the forest.

Much aroused by this little battle, our men were inclined to pursue—but I felt our heavy armor would be a hindrance in the dense forest and allow ambushes. So I ordered them into launches to make our way back to the ships anchored outside the reef.

Our return was perilous. The reef was a line of white, with the waves roaring on it so loudly that it was hard to hear orders. The tide was against us, ripping in through the narrow channel that broke the reef. Coral and rock rose on either side. A small error or a crabbed oar would throw the launch onto the barrier, where it was likely to capsize, throwing the men into the huge waves to be ground against the rocks.

We could not return to shore, where the hostile natives capered like devils on the beach, waving spears and shouting threats. So we rested on our oars in the calm lagoon. The hot sun beat on our heads, and the men tied bandanas soaked in sea water around their necks to stay cool. There we waited through the hours of daylight.

It was only in the dark of night that the tide turned, but in the darkness, the reef line appeared only as a white sheen on the ocean, and the channel of our escape was hard to discern. We cautiously rowed along the reef, seeking the channel. Suddenly, we knew we had found it; the bow of our launch swung to seaward as the ebbing tide created a strong outward flow. We shot through the channel to the sea and made our way to the anchored ships, which I ordered to raise sail and lay offshore. It was only then that I learned from the Indian translators the cause of the anger that had prompted the attack by the heretofore peaceable and friendly natives.

We learned a valuable lesson from this encounter. The Indians were no match for our superior arms. It would require only a small force to subdue the islanders and colonize these rich territories. The Indian population would provide a very suitable and sufficient labor force to clear the forest and plant such crops as were deemed suitable to the climate. Indeed, based on my experience in the Madeiras, the climate and soil would yield a bountiful harvest of sugar cane, and the local Indians could be pressed into service to work the cane fields.

Given the hostile nature of our treatment on this shore, I decided to quit this landing area and move the *Niña*, the *Pinta,* and the *Santa María* to a safer anchorage along the northern coast. The lovely winds from the northeast still blew strong offshore, but now they lay to our fore, not from aft. I found it necessary to beat into the wind by laying as close inshore as I could, taking advantage of the offshore breezes that blew only at night. With the shore on our starboard side, we cruised eastward along the northern coast of San Salvador. There were no good mooring locations for many miles. Surf broke high against the low cliffs, and there were multiple sand bars and reefs off shore, visible by the white breakers where they approached the surface. Worse still, we found ourselves against a lee shore, as the prevailing winds continued to come from the northeast, so that we had to constantly beat into the wind to avoid being driven by our leeway against the shore.

We sailed 170 miles before we detected a break in the reefs that was sufficient to guide our ships into sheltered waters. Christmastime was upon us, so I directed the ships' masters to find anchorage spots where we could land by launches to celebrate the birth of Jesus Christ.

On Christmas Eve, Master de la Cosa dropped the anchor of the *Santa María* on a lee shore with a sandy bottom. The *Niña* and the *Pinta* anchored a bit further offshore. Like the rest of the crew, Juan de la Cosa had been drinking the guava liquor in celebration of the Day of the Nativity. It was a calm night, and presumably this was the reason he left the bridge of the caravel in the control of Pedro de Salcedo, the ship's boy, a lad of only twelve. During the night the northeasterly wind rose and moved inshore almost imperceptibly. The resulting sea swell slowly drove the ship so that its anchors dragged in the sand. Before anyone realized something was amiss, the *Santa María* struck the nearby reef. I heard from my cabin young Pedro's outcry when the tiller ground on the reef. Leaping from my cot, I rushed onto the deck, the sharp angle of which made clear that we were no longer afloat.

Eventually, Juan de la Cosa emerged bleary-eyed onto the deck, only half-clothed. I ordered him to take our launch and row out to set an anchor to prevent the swell and tide from pushing us further onto the reef. I hoped by this to halt the sea's push onto the reef, and to be able to haul the *Santa María* off again using the launches. With some of the crew, the Master clambered over the thwart into the boat, and they rowed away.

At first I thought he meant to perform the task I had given him, but it soon became obvious that he and his crew members were fleeing to the safety of the *Niña*. That was so obvious that Martín Pinzón's brother Vicente, Master of the *Niña*, cursed him for a coward and refused to allow the occupants of the boat on board. Unable to find a path to land through the waves breaking on the reef, they were obliged to return to the *Santa María*. This was fortunate in that we once again had our launch. I cursed him for a fool and a coward. Despite my private concerns about the loyalty of the crew to the master, I ordered him and those with him in the launch to be arrested, and was pleased when the crew carried out that order without question. Now I was in sole command of the stricken *Santa María*. The ship was grinding most cruelly against the rocks of the reef, and each wave pushed her a little higher.

I hoped to lighten the caravel sufficiently to float her off the reef, and ordered the remaining crew who were not loyalists to de la Cosa to cut away the mast and dump our water overboard. Despite these measures, in the absence of a seaward anchor to restrain her, the rising tide pushed the *Santa María* further onto the reef and she began to founder. I could see the ship was lost, and that we had only a little time to save the crew and such of our stores that we could remove in time. By now daylight had arrived, and we could see well enough so the shallow-drafted launch could take our survivors to shore.

With the assistance of the leader of a nearby village of natives who had seen our distress, we were able to unload the whole of the stores of the *Santa María* before afternoon of Christmas Day. The headman of the village, a man named Guacanagari, provided canoes, and together we salvaged many of the timbers from the hull and deck of the foundering wreck. Despite some fears that the Indians would steal from us, an inventory revealed that not a single thing was missing. We piled up everything we had saved on the beach, and then sat in the sand, exhausted from our efforts. That evening, we watched as the caravel broke up and disappeared beneath the waves.

I looked around me at the men who crewed the *Santa María*. No one had been lost in the incident, and for this we thanked God. But now we were faced with a cruel reality. There was not enough room on the remaining two caravels to carry all the survivors. The ships' capacity was simply too limited to stow the food and water that would be needed for all three crews to make the voyage across the vast Ocean Sea to return to Spain.

The justice of our situation dictated that it was the officers and crew of the *Santa María* who should remain behind. There was some rumbling and whispering that that number should include me, but I quickly put that bit of mutiny to rest. I pointed out that I was the navigator, and I was the one with the map. Even Martín Pinzón agreed reluctantly that the return voyage to Spain would not be possible without my leadership. And so it was decided.

We built a sort of fort with the timbers we had salvaged from the *Santa María*, erecting a palisade with a moat on a small hill back from the beach. From these vertical spars we spread the canvas of her sails to provide a shelter against the elements. We dug underground storage areas to mitigate spoilage, and we filled them with enough food, water, and wine to last for a year. In addition, we left weapons with the men to provide resources for them to hunt. These included a few cannon from the *Santa María*. The local village of Indians proved friendly when they helped us salvage the materials from the foundered ship. We also left a launch for the purpose of fishing.

Many of the men remained voluntarily, seeing the opportunity to find the vast wealth of gold that they believed lay inland. This belief was encouraged by Guacanagari, who wore a necklace of shells with a few gold stones interspersed. When queried about their source, he waved vaguely inland, but that was enough.

The men who were to remain behind were commanded by Diego de Harana, my close friend from Córdoba. Among those we left on shore was also our priest, the Franciscan friar. He volunteered to remain behind, seeing this as an opportunity given by God to bring the Indians to Christianity. I hoped privately that his religious zeal would not turn them hostile, for though the natives' weaponry was primitive, they would have numerical superiority once the rest of us departed.

I assured the soon-to-be stranded mariners that I had carefully noted their position on the charts we had scrupulously prepared, and that we would return to their rescue as soon as we could get back to Spain and mount a new voyage. But truly, I saw little danger for them. The land was fertile, game was plentiful on land, and the ocean teemed with fish. The Indians were friendly and, indeed, helpful. The men could survive at least as comfortably as they might at home, while here they could hunt for the gold that was their objective. And we would return for them. The priest offered a mass before we weighed anchor, and we followed it with a feast for both the crews and the Indians.

On the fourth day of January, in the new year of Our Lord 1493, we weighed anchor and left the shore behind.

The antagonism toward me continued. Martín Pinzón blamed me for the sinking of the *Santa María*, and enlisted the loyal parts of his crew in support of the accusation. If he has survived on the *Pinta* in the same storm that now threatens to sink the *Niña* under me, I have no doubt there will be unpleasant and unfounded charges leveled at me before the court in Spain.

Fortunately, I have those on my side who will testify that the fault did not lie with me. Don Diego de Arena and Pedro Gutiérrez will vouch that I was blameless and, indeed, that my actions saved the crew and the ships' contents.

As I sit in my cabin aboard the *Niña*, riding the next onslaught of waves and wind, I thank God I had the foresight to demand special arrangements for the support of Beatriz and my two sons. Beatriz, being an orphan and, in any case, not coming from wealth, would have been in dire straits without my intervention with Queen Isabella before this voyage.

I can add nothing to my journal. I will now wrap it in waterproof oilskin and seal it into a cask. I will throw it overboard and watch it float away. If a reader should someday come upon it, it is my prayer that he or she will not think less of me for the human frailty I have revealed. I have endeavored to fulfill the mission that God has meant for me. I have found the lands depicted on my ancestor's map, though that holy cup and other Templar treasure have eluded me. If I survive, it is my firm intention to return to those shores where we left our little colony and continue my search for the holy relic that I am certain lies there somewhere, perhaps buried in the sand on some beach.

THE END

Epilogue

Columbus' diary and confession of sins ends at this point. Unantici-pated by him, though, he did not perish in the storm. The *Niña* survived the storm and made landfall at the island of Santa María, in the Azores. These islands are Portuguese territory, and the governor there arrested the Spanish landing party sent ashore by Columbus. Af-ter considerable wrangling over several days, the sailors were released, and Columbus again pointed the bow of the *Niña* at Cape St. Vincent and Palos. However, another fearsome storm arose and the ship was forced to land near Lisbon in Portugal. Several weeks went by as Co-lumbus dealt with the Portuguese officials, including King John, before he was able to set sail again for Palos. He finally arrived in Palos on March 15, 1493, to great celebration.

The *Pinta* also survived the great storm by beating northward be-yond its reach and ultimately arrived on Spain's northern coast via the Bay of Biscay. The Pinzóns were not aware that Columbus survived, however. They sent a message overland to Ferdinand and Isabella reporting their success, but the rulers declined to hear their report, wanting to hear instead from the leader of the expedition, Christopher Columbus. Martin Pinzón arrived in Palos on the same day as Colum-bus, but later that evening.

Columbus did not find the Holy Grail, but he found where it might be. With the blessing and approval of Ferdinand and Isabella, he re-turned with a fleet of seventeen ships and twelve hundred men. The *Niña* was part of the fleet, rechristened the *Santa Clara*. No Pinzóns accompanied the second voyage.

The little colony left behind after the first voyage was found de-stroyed. All the marooned were dead, killed by the Indians. The Span-iards were accused of enslaving the men and debauching the women, until the tribe rose up and slaughtered them. After increasing friction and growing ill will on both sides, Columbus led his men in a raid upon the Indians and killed thousands of them. Christopher Columbus, Explorer, was transformed into Christopher Columbus, Conquistador.

Over the course of the next years, multiple expeditions originated from Spain. It appears that there remained an undercurrent of search for the Templar treasure. Fabulous stories motivated searches for the Fountain of Youth, leading Ponce de León into Florida. Tales of a fabulous city of gold led to legends of El Dorado, leading Francisco Pizarro to search high in the Andes and Hernando Cortez to explore and conquer the Aztec civilization of Mexico.

But for Christopher Columbus, the Holy Grail and the treasure of the Knights Templar remained out of reach. He acquired all the titles and authority that he had demanded from King Ferdinand and Queen Isabella. But being granted authority and using it wisely are not the same thing. He descended into tyranny, and like many tyrants before him, was ultimately brought low by the failures of his own character. As with many who had sought the Holy Grail, it always lay beyond.

Christopher Columbus was not the Grail Knight.

Bibliography

About the Templars

Barber, Malcolm. *The Trial of the Templars*. Cambridge, United Kingdom: University Press, 1994.

Childress, David Hatcher. *Pirates and the Lost Templar Fleet: The Secret Naval War Between the Knights Templar and the Vatican*. Adventures Unlimited Press, 2003.

Huchet, Patrick. *The Knights Templar: from Glory to Tragedy*. Editions Ouest-France, undated.

Knight, Christopher, and Lomas, Robert. *The Second Messiah: Templars, the Turin Shroud and the Great Secret of Freemasonry*. Century Books, 1997

Laidler, Keith. *The Head of God: The Lost Treasure of the Templars*. London: Weidenfield and Nicolson, 1998.

Read, Piers Paul. *The Templars: The Dramatic History of the Knights Templar, the Most Powerful Military Order of the Crusades*. New York: St. Martin's Press, 1999.

Upton-Ward, J.M. (translator). *The Rule of the Templars: the French Text of the Rule of the Order of the Knights Templar*. Boydell Press, 1992.

About Christopher Columbus

Aleman, Gilbert S. *The Unknown Columbus*. Limited edition, 1993.
Brinkbaumer, Klaus and Hoges, Clemens. *The Voyage of the Vizcaina:*

The Mystery of Christopher Columbus's Last Ship. Translated from German by Annette Streck. Orland: Harcourt, Inc., 2004.

Columbus, Christopher and Magellan, Ferdinand. *To America and Around the World: The Logs of Christopher Columbus and Ferdinand Magellan*. Boston: Branden Publishing Co., 1990.

Dor-Ner, Zvi. *Columbus and the Age of Discovery*. Hammersmith London: Harper-Collins, 1991.

Dunn, Oliver and Kelley, Jr. James E. *The Diario of Christopher Columbus's First Voyage to America, 1492-1493*. Abstracted by Bartolome de las Casas with notes and a concordance of the Spanish University of Oklahoma Press, 1991.

Granzotto, Gianni. *Christopher Columbus*. Translated by Stephen Sartarelli. Norman and London: University of Oklahoma Press, 1987.

Landsdtrom, Bjorn. *Columbus: The Story of Don Cristóbal Colón, Admiral of the Ocean, and His Four Voyages to the Indies According to Contemporary Sources*. Macmillan, 1966.

Milton, Giles. *The Riddle and the Knight: In Search of Sir John Mandeville*. Sceptre, 1996.

Pastor, Xavier. *The Ships of Christopher Columbus*. London: Conway Maritime Press, Ltd., 1992.

"Where Did Columbus Discover America?" Supplement to the *National Geographic*. November, 1986. Page 566A, Vol 170, No 5.

Wilford, John Noble. *The Mysterious History of Columbus: An Explanation of the Man, the Myth, the Legacy*. New York: Alfred Knopf, 1991.

Woodward, Geoffrey. *Spain in the Reigns of Isabella and Ferdinand, 1474-1516*. Hodder and Stoughton, 1997.

On Sailing

Gardiner, Robert (editor). *Cogs, Caravels and Galleons: The Sailing Ship 1000-1650*. Brassey's, 1994.

Hapgood, Charles. *Maps of the Ancient Sea Kings: Evidence of Advanced Civilization in the Ice Age*. Adventures Unlimited Press, 1996.

Reid, George H. *The Quick and Easy Guide to Compass Correction*. Sheridan House, 1997.

Obregon, Mauricio. *Beyond the Edge of the Sea: Sailing with Jason and the Argonauts, Ulysses, the Vikings, and Other Explorers of the Ancient World*. New York: Modern Library, 2001.

Sobel, Dava. *Longitude: The True Story of a Lone Genius Who Solved the Greatest Scientific Problem of His Time*. London: Fourth Estate, 1995.

Toghill, Jeff. Celestial Navigation. New York: W.W. Norton, 1986.

Biblical Stuff

Avi-Yonah. *Pictorial Guide to the Model of Ancient Jerusalem at the Time of the Second Temple in the Grounds of the Israel Museum*. Herzlia, Israel: Holyland Tourism, 1992.

Bahat, Dan. *Carta's Historical Atlas of Jerusalem*. Jerusalem: Carta, undated.

Chilton, Bruce. *Mary Magdalene: A Biography*. Doubleday, 2005.

Cimok, Fatih. *Journeys of Paul: From Tarsus to the Ends of the Earth*. Istanbul: A Turizm Yayinlari, 2004.

Crossan, John Dominic. *The Birth of Christianity: Discovering What Happened in the Years Immediately after the Execution of Jesus*. HarperSanFrancisco, 1998.

Daniel-Rops, Henri. *Daily Life in Palestine at the Time of Christ.* Translated by Patrick O'Brian. Phoenix Press, 1969.

Feinberg-Vamosh, Miriam. *Daily Life at the Time of Jesus.* Israel: Palphot Marketing Ltd., undated.

Freud, Sigmund. *Moses and Monotheism.* Vintage Books, 1939.

Greek Bible Society. *The Apostle Paul in Greece.* 2008.

Hengel, Martin. *The Zealots: Investigations into the Jewish Freedom Movement in the Period from Herod I until 70 A.D.* Translated by David Smith. Edinburgh: T&T Clark, 1976.

Jockle, Clemens. *Encyclopedia of the Saints.* Konecky and Konecky, 2003.

Josephus. *The Jewish War.* Rev. ed. Translated by G.A. Williamson. Penguin Books, 1981.

Ludemann, Gerd. *Paul: The Founder of Christianity.* Amherst, NY: Prometheus Books, 2002.

Meyer, Marvin W. (editor). *The Nag Hammadi Scriptures: The Revised and Updated Translation of Sacred Gnostic Texts Complete in One Volume.* 2009.

National Geographic Society. *The Holy Land: Crossroads of Faith and Conflict.* Special Issue, 2010.

Osman, Colin. *Jerusalem: Caught in Time.* American University in Cairo Press, 1999.

Pagels, Elaine. *Beyond Belief: The Secret Gospel of Thomas.* New York: Random House, 2005.

"Paul's Conversion." Pamphlet, unattributed.

Quispel, Gilles. *The Secret Book of Revelation: the Last Book of the Bible.* McGraw Hill, 1979.

Stoyanov, Yuri. *The Other God: Dualist Religions from Antiquity to the Cathar Heresy*. Yale University Press, 2000.

Wroe, Ann. *Pontius Pilate*. Modern Library, 2001.

About the Crusades

Armstrong, Karen. *Holy War: The Crusades and Their Impact on Today's World*. Doubleday, 1991.

Bartlett, W.B. *God Wills It!: An Illustrated History of the Crusades*. Sutton Publishing, 1999.

Erlande-Brandenburg, Alain. *Cathedrals and Castles: Building in the Middle Ages*. Abrams Discoveries, 1995.

France, John. *Western Warfare in the Age of the Crusades, 1000–1300*. Ithaca: Cornell University Press, 1999.

Moore, R.I. *The Formation of a Persecuting Society*. Blackwell, 1990.

Mueller-Wiener, Wolfgang. *Castles of the Crusaders*. Translated by J. Michael Brownjohn. 1966.

Nicolle, David. *Crusader Knight, 1187–1344 AD*. Osprey Publishing, 1996.

Runciman, Steven. *A History of the Crusades*. 3 volumes. Cambridge: Cambridge University Press, 1997.

The Holy Grail

Day, David. *The Search for King Arthur*. De Agostini Editions, 1998.

Matthews, John. *The Mystic Grail: The Challenge of the Arthurian Quest*. Sterling Publishing, 1997.

About the Author

Martin Gregory Taschdjian has a long and successful career in business, government, and academia. His Ph.D. study of economics revealed to him how little we really know. He views history as the data source from which we draw our understanding of human affairs, and he is especially interested in early Christian and medieval European periods, for these so heavily influence our modern world. He has traveled the world working as an expert in legal and regulatory matters relevant to the telecommunications industry. He has written extensively in his professional life and taught for many years at the University of Colorado–Boulder and the University of Denver.

Martin lives in the foothills of Colorado, remains married to his first wife, enjoys his children and grandchildren, and frequently lashes the streams and rivers of Colorado with a fly line in hopes of catching a fish. He plays the guitar and sings the blues.

Made in the USA
Middletown, DE
27 May 2019